worldoflegends.com

A tale of two spinners

by
Nigel Osner

iUniverse, Inc.
New York   Bloomington

iUniverse books may be ordered through booksellers or by contacting:

iUniverse
1663 Liberty Drive
Bloomington, IN 47403
www.iuniverse.com
1-800-Authors (1-800-288-4677)

Because of the dynamic nature of the Internet, any Web addresses or
links contained in this book may have changed since publication and may
no longer be valid. The views expressed in this work are solely those of
the author and do not necessarily reflect the views of the publisher, and
the publisher hereby disclaims any responsibility for them.

ISBN: 978-1-4401-6320-3 (sc)
ISBN: 978-1-4401-6319-7 (ebook)

Printed in the United States of America

iUniverse rev. date: 08/21/2009

CHAPTER 1

The first sighting

THERE WERE ONCE two schoolboys. One was called Henry Prince. He was medium height, dark haired, and, until he changed to contact lenses, he wore glasses. He thought he looked a bit like Harry Potter. He sort of had the same first name. He had the same initials. But neither of his parents were wizards. He certainly wasn't. He whispered spells under his breath. He thought hard about making his least favourite teacher break out in warts. And one day she did have a remarkably unpleasant blister, but somehow he knew he could not take the credit. His spells failed. Yet he was quite convinced that magic did exist somewhere.

That was the link between him and the other boy, Rupert Stiltskin. Rupert was small, rather ugly really, with wayward teeth. Despite his odd appearance, he certainly attracted people to him, and he was funny and sharp and manipulative. He was interested in what made people tick. He was also very interested in magic, as Henry discovered one day.

It was after school. On the way home Henry decided to pop into a large local bookshop and as ever he was drawn at once to the section on fantasy. He was engrossed in a book called 'The Reality of Magic', when a voice said:

"Don't waste your time with that. It's rubbish."

Henry turned to see Rupert leaning against the science fiction section and holding a novel with the picture of a vast space ship on its front cover.

"So's science fiction," he said by way of retaliation.

"Yeah, but it's fun. Magic isn't rubbish though. I didn't mean that. Just that book."

"You've read it?"

"I've read most of the books in the section. And most of them are crud. They just don't get what magic's about."

"What is it about?"

"It's actually about what that book is trying to say, but doesn't know how to say it."

"You believe magic is real?" said Henry, amazed, as it was unusual to find many eleven year old boys prepared to be quite so definite on the subject.

"O yes," said Rupert with a warm and confidential smile, as though he had just discovered a soul mate in Henry. Of course, that is exactly what Henry thought he had found in Rupert.

After that the two boys went around together for a while and spent a lot of time talking about magic and what it might be and where it might be found. They saw and read everything on the subject. However, although they were both firm believers, they did not see things identically. Henry took the concept of magic being real quite literally. He felt that it was there somewhere but he had no idea how to find it. His lack of success in tracking it down began to get to him, especially as other interests started to take over. Rupert, on the other hand, used to say there was no use looking for it in this world, it was somewhere else, and it was findable. He was quite positive about its existence.

"How are you so certain," demanded Henry, "when there's no proof?"

"Faith," smiled Rupert.

"That makes it sound like a religion."

"That's exactly right," replied Rupert.

The months went by and Henry found that his interest in magic had faded into a sentimental affection and a vague longing. Life was beginning to get real and he had to get on with it. Rupert was unchanging in his conviction. He would talk about it a great deal, to anyone and everyone. So strong was Rupert's personality that nobody laughed at him, certainly to his face. It was simply a boy being weird. A boy who was popular because of his quick wits and ability to make teachers seem small and stupid without getting himself into trouble.

More time passed. Henry was less friendly with Rupert, but was still rather in awe of him. It was October 31 and a very atmospheric Halloween was promised. It was windy and stormy. Henry wished that he still believed in magic, because this was certainly a good night for witches. He was on his way home when Rupert came over to him. Rupert was rather excited, but then of course he had just managed to rid the school of one of its most unpopular masters. It was done quite brilliantly. A word here and there, a clever nuance in the school magazine, nothing dishonest but not very nice all the same. And on that particular day the master had resigned.

"Congratulations," said Henry.

"O yes, that was so good." Rupert grinned. "It's very easy to manipulate people, you know. The trick is to make them think they always thought what you're saying."

"I know that," said Henry

"Sure, but it's one thing knowing etc etc. Anyway, never mind about that. I've got something much more interesting to do. And I want you to see it."

"What?"

"You've always wanted proof that magic exists. I'm going to give it to you."

"O right, it's Halloween and all the evil creatures are stirring abroad. I'm trembling!"

"Don't be a prat. Haven't you been listening to me for the last two years? Nothing is stirring. But this is a special night. There's a link."

"To what?"

"To the world where magic exists."

"Right," sighed Henry. He finally realised he had started to grow up. But Rupert was determined and Rupert was not an easy person to refuse. He never put any pressure on you, but there was a sort of power there. Also, Henry was beginning to feel that Rupert, if he ceased being a friend, could be rather dangerous. So they agreed to meet later. Shortly before midnight. Naturally.

Shortly before midnight is not an easy time to meet anyone when you are barely thirteen, as the idea is that you are at home in bed. May be reading with a torch. Possibly reading something unsuitable too. All that is within normal expectations and parents deal with it. But whatever goes on is supposed to be home entertainment. Henry had to get out and by nature he was a very law abiding boy. He remembered this as soon as he had left Rupert and sensed it more strongly as the evening progressed. Furthermore the weather was cold and rainy, whereas home was warm and dry.

He went up to bed. His parents, friendly, untroublesome, trusting, also went up to bed. Henry felt bad that he was about to let them down. Nevertheless, at quarter past eleven he pushed up his window and looked outside. Not good. Trees were thrashing about all over the place and a soggy leaf splodged onto his face. He ripped it off, shuddering, because he thought it was a bat. Then he just felt stupid. A pity, because if it had not been for that leaf, he would have stayed at home. Instead, he decided he was behaving like a wimp. So he climbed out and easily scrambled down the wisteria attached to the side of the house. He glanced up. No lights had come on. He set off.

As he jogged down the street, he began to feel rather pleased with himself. He had done something moderately rebellious and he was a teenager after all. He was warm enough inside several layers and a hood. It wasn't raining that hard. Altogether this was the right thing to do. So he was fairly relaxed as he went past the dark churchyard, although he did speed up a little bit. However, there were still people about and cars drove by. He reached the side turning which led to Rupert's house. This was, it had to be admitted, rather a dark road, but that was partly because one lamp had gone out. He arrived at Rupert's gate. It then occurred to him he had never arranged with Rupert what was to happen at this point. It was far too late to go up to the front door, ring the bell and announce that he had come to see Rupert.

A hand touched his shoulder.

"I've never seen anyone jump like that," said Rupert with a satisfied smile.

"That's stupid, isn't it, to come up behind me?" said Henry.

"More funny really. Come on."

"What, inside?"

"Like my parents are going to want to see you at this time of night. 'O hi there, I just dropped round for a cup of cocoa.' No not inside. Next door."

"Why, are they expecting us?"

"O Henry, don't make me regret asking you. Nobody's expecting us. The place is empty."

Rupert led Henry to the next door house, which was in complete darkness, and produced some keys. Apparently his parents were keeping an eye on the property while the owner was away. The boys went inside. It was a big Victorian house, with a long cold hall and an unwelcoming atmosphere. Rupert switched on a torch, which he pointed downwards, and led Henry up two flights of stairs to the top of the house. Even in the dim light Henry could see how neglected everything was, with piles of books and newspapers, and threadbare carpets. At the top it was even worse. Rupert took him into a room, drew the curtains and switched on a lamp. On one side was an ironing board and endless piles of clothes which had been washed, ironed and abandoned. On the other was a bed, some old chairs and a big carved wardrobe with a full size mirror in the centre between two doors. Above a dead radiator was a sooty black mark which reached up to the cracked ceiling. Most of all the room was freezing.

"It's horrible in here," said Henry.

"Yes, but it's private. And there's a fire. I brought one from home."

Rupert switched on a little fan heater and pulled out a thermos flask.

"I always believe in a bit of comfort."

"What happens if we get caught?" asked Henry nervously, thinking of the very large number of rules he must be breaking.

"We won't be. Anyway, the owner said I could use this place if I ever wanted to get away somewhere."

"Did they mean in the middle of the night?"

"O give it a rest."

The room, or their bit of it, warmed up quickly and the soup helped too, so Henry decided to cheer up. Rupert checked his watch. Quarter to twelve. He pulled a book out of his jacket and some candles.

"Some sort of incantation?" Henry asked warily.

"Exactly right," said Rupert.

"For spirits, for ghosts?"

"You just never listen. There are no spirits. There are no ghosts. But there is a parallel reality. Actually, I've now learned that it's really a parallel unreality. It's the world of fable. Of legend. Of magic. It all goes on there and I want to connect with it."

"And tonight is a good night because it's Halloween."

"Yeah. That's all true. This is a very good night to do it. The best."

Rupert got out some sort of coloured powder and

made a circle. Then he lit the candles and put them at equal points round the circle.

"You're not thinking of sacrificing a chicken?" asked Henry, who was beginning to find this rather funny.

"No," replied Rupert seriously, concentrating on what he was doing, "It doesn't say I have to."

"Would you, if you had to?"

"Of course."

Henry could see the earnest look in Rupert's eyes and decided that the boy he now thought of his former friend was seriously loopy. After tonight he would keep as much distance from him as possible.

"Right," said Rupert, "it's five minutes to midnight. Stand behind me and look into the mirror."

"Why?"

"Because that is the way into the other world."

"Are you sure we aren't better off walking into the wardrobe? There seem to be lots of coats there."

"Funny man," said Rupert. "Just look will you."

Rupert stood in the middle of the circle and opened his book. Henry stood outside and stared into the mirror. He watched Rupert turn the pages and begin to read.

" 'From the world where nothing is understood to the world where nothing is understandable, greeting. On this special night, when the force of reality is weak and the force of unreality is strong, let the barrier break and the two worlds merge. Let fact and fable combine, for truly there is no fact unless people tell the story of it and there is no story when all believe the fact of it.' " And so on.

"A mirror," thought Henry. "That's such a cliché.

It's always a mirror. And all these words. It's a load of rubbish. Rupert's an idiot. What am I doing here!"

Rupert finished.

"It's a minute to midnight," he whispered.

"Don't you think —"

"Keep quiet. And keep looking into the mirror."

So Henry kept quiet and kept looking. For a few seconds there was nothing. Then Rupert mouthed "midnight" and the house was attacked by a violent gust of wind. The windows rattled and the electricity flickered. Rupert gripped the book with excitement. Despite himself, Henry stared into the mirror. There seemed to be a cloud forming – but it was only a patch where the silver had discoloured. Time passed by and nothing happened. There was no swirling mist parting to reveal a   glimpse into another world, no sonorous voice asking what they wanted or even, thought Henry, offering to say who was the fairest of them all. Definitely not Rupert, plain at the best of times and now scowling with disbelief.

"This doesn't make sense," he muttered.

"That is very true," Henry agreed. "Don't you think —"

Fear shut him up. There was now a third figure in the mirror, not coming through it though, but reflected in it, like they were. He was standing behind them. Neither of them turned round. They inspected the reflection. It was a small man with a knobbly head, as though it had been made roughly with clay but never smoothed out. His ears and nose in particular needed considerable attention, and all three were extremely hairy and rather gross. He was wearing a dirty robe and a red pointed hat.

His eyes were sharp and – that was it, very like Rupert's. In fact, Henry realised, for all that this man was a lot older and a great deal uglier, he resembled an unpleasant adult version of Rupert.

If Rupert recognised this, he was untroubled by it. "Yes!" he said triumphantly.

"Yes what?" enquired the little man smiling a Rupert type smile.

Both boys turned round.

"Yes I knew it would work," said Rupert.

"O did you indeed!" said the man. His voice was at odds with the rest of him. It was melodious, reassuring, friendly. If only it were unnecessary to look at him.

"Well you're here," said Rupert, sounding very much like a younger version of the man.

"I certainly am, although I don't know where. Maybe I had too much to drink at supper." He looked round him. "It doesn't look too good though. I expect you'd like me to get you out."

"Out of what?" asked Rupert, puzzled.

"Out of this castle or prison cell. Whatever it is, it's not a very healthy place for two young boys."

"I'll give you that," agreed Rupert.

"Of course, there'll be a price," smiled the little man. "But do say, how did I get here? Did you summon me in some way? Did I respond to your deep feelings of despair and arrive as a sort of reflex action? I'll have to watch that."

"I brought you here," said Rupert.

The little man squinted at him. "With that book?"

"Yes."

"It must belong to a sorcerer. It's too dangerous for

a boy your age. May be I'd better take it," and quick as a flash he was at Rupert's side and a dirty hand with cracked nails was grasping at the book.

"Oh, no," said Rupert, throwing the book at Henry, who caught it, much to his surprise.

"Well, unless you give it to me, I won't help you."

"We don't need your help to get out," said Rupert.

"Doesn't look like that to me."

"Well we don't."

"How about some gold then? Most people are desperate for a bit of gold."

"Who are you?" asked Rupert, trying not to show how excited he was.

"Oh, I can't tell you that," exclaimed the little man in mock horror, twisting a tuft of hair in his ear and winking at Henry. "Horrible habit isn't it!"

"Why can't you?"

"Because," said the little man, "it's for me to know and you to find out."

"Look," said Rupert, "it's quite safe to tell us here. We're not in your world."

"Are you truly boys?" asked the little man suspiciously. "Or are you goblins or something of that sort. If so, you really ought to know I shouldn't be messed about with."

"Of course we're boys. I'm Rupert."

"I'm Henry," said Henry.

"Are you sure you don't want any gold? I know you're young, but you're old enough to know what gold can do for you. Everyone wants gold."

"A bit wouldn't do any harm I suppose," said Rupert.

"Well, there you are," beamed the little man. "Just

what I would have said at your age. Actually, you rather remind me of what I was like at your age. Now, give me that book and I'll see what I can do."

"I think we need to see the gold first," said Henry, who was developing a deep dislike for this musty smelling, nasty looking stranger.

"That's very reasonable," agreed the little man. "You're brighter than you look, Harry."

"It's not Harry." said Henry.

"Never mind," said the little man, edging nearer to Henry. "I'm probably still confused from getting here without meaning to."

"It's Henry. Henry Prince."

"Prince Henry!" laughed the little man derisively. "Oh, I don't think so."

"I didn't say Prince Henry. I said Henry Prince. It's not the same."

"No, it can't be. You're such a poor specimen."

"You can hardly talk," cried Henry, who was getting very angry.

"No," agreed the little man, "But I can nip." And so saying, he twisted the skin on one of Henry's arms, causing him to drop the book. Quick as a cormorant, the little man darted down and picked it up.

"Give it back," demanded Rupert.

"Why?"

"Well for a start, you haven't done anything for it."

"That is true," admitted the little man. "And a bargain is a bargain."

"This is going to be good!" said Henry, who found himself getting increasingly hostile.

"But not until I know where I am and how I got here. I don't like riddles – unless I set them of course."

"You're in another world and you came here through the mirror," replied Rupert.

"Through the mirror! I don't think so." Suddenly the little man jerked. "I've got to go back. I'm being sent back."

"No wait," said Rupert.

"May be another day," said the little man, clutching the book tightly to him. "I'll come back and rescue you, provided I can find you again. And provided you aren't nasty little apprentice wizards."

"No!" shouted Rupert, "I've got so much to ask you? You can't go yet."

"I think I can," replied the little man amiably. "O, sorry not to have come in by the mirror by the way. But how am I supposed to for goodness sake? It's a solid object."

"Yes but —" protested Rupert.

"I'm off," interrupted the little man, wobbling a facial bump at Henry. "Prince Henry!"

And with that, he gently vanished, exactly like the Cheshire Cat. Most of him faded away quickly, but his smile remained for a lot longer. That faded in the end, though not before the mouth repeated in a mocking tone, "Prince Henry!" But the book stayed behind, never fading at all, but at the last minute, just before the little man disappeared, dropping to the floor with a loud bang.

Henry stopped shivering and said, "A ghost."

"No, said Rupert, who was puzzled, "but you did spook him though."

"Where did he come from? How did he disappear like that?"

"He went back through the boundary."

"The boundary to what?"

"Henry, you never listen do you? To the other world, the world with magic."

"I —" Henry began, then stopped, because he had no idea what to say. If the visitor were not a ghost, then unless – "Hold on, was that a hologram? It was, wasn't it? How did you make it work?"

"No it wasn't," replied Rupert indignantly.

Henry hoped it was a hologram. That would be a lot easier to deal with. He could see Rupert setting up something like that to play a game with him.

"Prince Henry," said Rupert thoughtfully. "Who's that I wonder?"

"No one. He was just being unpleasant."

"No. I think for a moment he thought you were claiming to be someone else."

"That's just stupid," said Henry. "Anyway, it's time I went."

"You can go. There'll be nothing else to see now."

"Aren't you coming too?" Henry was doing his best to adopt a sceptical attitude, but that might not last all the way down two flights of dark creaking steps in a strange crumbling house.

"No, I want to think about what happened and what went wrong. I don't think you helped. You didn't show him any respect." He gave Henry a beady look and Henry knew that the friendship was over on both sides. Rupert also gave Henry the torch, which was a kind parting gesture. Henry made his way carefully downstairs and, try as he might, half expected that repulsive little man to reappear, with a knife may be, or some unpleasant associates. He crept along the hall with a growing belief in other worlds, telling himself that in ten minutes he would be back in his own room. He reached the front door and stretched out to open it. Then he gasped and prepared himself for a confrontation with something evil. The door was opening.

The hall light went on and Henry discovered the consequences of breaking rules, for the owner of the house was not pleased to see him.

CHAPTER 2

worldoflegends.com

THE YEARS WENT by. Henry grew up, mostly. He stopped seeing Rupert from that Halloween. He was very disturbed by the little man, but was unable to get anyone to believe him. His parents decided he had been drinking, or worse, and made his life difficult for a long time. They suggested he threw away all his books about magic and Henry entirely agreed.

As that night slipped further into the past, Henry let himself rationalise what had happened. It probably was a hologram. If not, then it was the overwrought imaginations of two boys. He put the memory aside. He had little time now for childhood fantasy because his life was bound up with rules. He decided to become a law student, so studied hard through school and university. He began to learn more and more rules, which might seem fantastic on occasions, especially when they were old or badly constructed, but were firmly based in fact. They could be overturned or sidestepped or not applied, but they did not fade away, leaving little bits of themselves in mid air. Well, only if you were a very clever lawyer.

He took his law finals and was waiting for what everyone knew would be a first class degree. It was the beginning of June and Henry had to decide what to do for the summer. He should of course be travelling or going on holiday, but Henry did not do that sort of thing. He felt obliged to study, much to the despair of his father, who now longed for a bit of rebellion.

"You know," said his father, "I was so out of control at your age." He raised his eyebrows. "It's amazing when I think back. Did I ever tell you about my trip to Marrakesh?"

"Fifty three," said Henry.

"Fifty three what?"

"Story fifty three. I'm giving them all numbers."

His father adopted another, more aggressive, approach.

"You know you don't get anywhere in life without drive."

"I know. You keep telling me that."

"Life's a rat race. You've got to go for what you want."

"I am going for what I want. I want to be a lawyer."

His father gave up and Henry went to his bedroom, switched on his computer and started to look up some recent law reports, which was his idea of a pleasant afternoon.

After an hour or so a little box appeared on one side of the screen. He got rid of it without thinking. However, when he clicked on the next law report, it appeared again. He got rid of it again. It appeared once more when he clicked on a further report. What were the Law Reports doing allowing someone to advertise on their site? May be it was just an error. He removed it for the third time. He went out into the garden for some fresh air and decided that he ought to spend a little less time in his room despite his fascination with the law. He then went back up to his room.

The box had appeared again on its own. This irritated Henry, who disliked anything which broke the rules. This time he paid more attention to what it said:

ATTENTION STUDENTS
WISHING FOR A
SUMMER ADVENTURE

Are you looking for fantasy and magic during your long summer break?

Click on www.worldoflegends.com

Enter a different realm

What a stupid advertisement, thought Henry and ignored it. It came back again five more times, and he grew increasingly irritated with it.

When Henry woke up the following day he decided that he would have the morning off and go for a walk. He was therefore very disappointed when it started to rain. He turned on his computer with less enthusiasm than normal. He perked up a little when he realised it had been a long time since he had checked some European case law, and entered a site. He was reading through the first case when yesterday's advertisement suddenly appeared again. He disposed of it. It returned ten minutes later. This time Henry left it. If it was going to keep coming back, he would simply ignore it. But somehow he could not ignore it. Today it had little lights which flashed round its border. Henry gave in and clicked on the name of the site.

He laughed scornfully to himself. He should have guessed. World of Legends was only a theme park looking for students to work there for the summer. Still, because he was, well not bored of course, but lacking his usual concentration, he found himself scrolling through the site. It promised a place of magic and imagination, but delivered rides through Fairyland, animatronic trolls and four shows a day by 'world renowned magicians'. O yes, there was also a dragon breathing real flames.

It was a waste of his time, but somehow Henry found himself reading through it all. It had a story of the week. Henry read it.

Louring over several small kingdoms were some extremely high and mean looking mountains. They had unpleasing jagged tops and were the sort of place nobody in their right mind would ever want to visit. So nobody ever did. Deep in their heart was a huge set of caves and deep inside them lived a large dragon. Being ancient and legendary, the dragon spent a great deal of time asleep. But every so often he would wake up and fly off somewhere for a meal, fulfilling a double need of keeping both himself and his legend alive. On occasions, by special arrangement with some nearby King or wizard, he would fulfil a contract killing and polish off an irritating threat. His price was always the same, a substantial amount of gold and jewels. He was a traditionalist in these matters.

The dragon awoke, for tonight he was on one of these special errands. A young knight was gaining a reputation for noble deeds which made a cruel local King feel vulnerable. This matter had now come to a head and the knight had been tricked into challenging the dragon.

It was a cold night with a full moon, which meant there were werewolves about. The more stupid among them would fancy their chances with the dragon, but never survived to try again. Nobody else, nothing else, usually had the power to kill a werewolf, so as the dragon swooped down from his cave, he was a little surprised to see a beheaded werewolf lying on the path along which the knight must have travelled. But there you were. These things happened sometimes.

In an open space half way down the mountain the young knight was waiting. He was wearing full armour – silver noted the dragon without approval, as silver tarnished – and was standing still, showing no sign of fear. Impertinent little creep. As the dragon flew down to land, he blew out an impressive burst of flame, which unintentionally, but most satisfactorily, incinerated the knight's horse.

"Foul creature from the dawn of time," stated the knight, "you will pay for that."

"Yes," said the dragon, "that's all very well, but I can do the same to you with minimum effort."

"I dare you to try," returned the knight, without moving a millimetre.

"No," said the dragon, "I don't like burned food. But I could warm you up on a low heat until you pass out. Then I'll eat you."

"You have it all wrong. I will kill you and then the whole town will eat you, though I doubt you will taste very palatable"

"Be that as it may, you will not be getting the chance to find out."

So saying, the dragon blew a gentle flame and was rather startled when it circled round the knight and started to come back to him. He was forced to move his head out of the way.

"Surrender," demanded the knight.

"I don't think so," said the dragon. "One little magic trick anyone can learn at school is hardly going to make me tremble. Actually, I'm not even sure I can tremble."

"Be warned, ancient nightmare, the dawn approaches and we will awaken soon from our thrall to legendary evil."

"'from our' what?" asked the dragon who had grown a little deaf over the last three centuries.

"From our slavery to the likes of you," answered the knight and, almost before the dragon was aware, he had leaped across, stabbing at the scales in the dragon's neck. No wound resulted, the scales were too thick, but the dragon was angry and alarmed. Nobody had ever done this to him before. He roared and sent a vast spurt of flame at the knight who jumped out of the way. Nobody had managed to do this before either. What was going on?

"Yield," demanded the knight. The moon shone brightly on his silver armour and the dragon had an unfamiliar sensation. For the moment he was unable to identify it.

"We've already been there," said the dragon, "and the answer is still no."

"In that case," replied the knight, "die!"

Once again the knight moved almost too quickly for the dragon to see and was perched on his neck, aiming his sword at a fierce red eye. But of course, when all is said and done, a young knight is no match for an experienced dragon, and moments later the knight lay dead on the ground, smashed to pieces inside his battered silver armour.

Five minutes after that the dragon was back inside his cave. He left the body and armour where it lay. He wanted nothing to do with it. Something was definitely wrong about what had happened. The dragon had had awkward moments in the past, obviously, but ordinary human beings, however brave and well trained, should not be able to put his life at risk. He was supposed to play with them until he was bored, then dispose of them without effort. Those were the rules of the world he knew. He now identified the unfamiliar sensation. It was fear.

It was an odd story, thought Henry, remembering all the stories he had read as a boy. The dragon should have been killed, that would have been more normal. Alternatively the dragon could have won but without feeling fear in that way. Instead there should have been a moral aimed at the foolhardiness of youth. The following day the box appeared yet again and the Henry read the story once more. For some reason he could not explain, he printed it.

The day after that was Monday and the World of Legends proudly announced a new feature. They had a splendid model of the wicked Queen in the story of Snow White. Everyone should come along and see her talking to the magic mirror. The web site also had a new story. Henry read it.

"The thing is," said the Queen, staring into the mirror, "I know I am not the fairest of them all any more. I look faded."

"Rubbish," replied the mirror, "to me you are a peach."

"Don't get fresh," said the Queen sharply. "You're good. But you're not that good. Make me angry and I'll have you smashed."

"Please yourself," answered the mirror. "But remember I'm a magic mirror. Harm me and you'll be cursed for a hundred years."

"With this complexion I think have been."

"Your Majesty," the mirror began again in a more conciliatory tone, "you are a fine figure of a woman."

"*That isn't the same as being the fairest of them all. It sounds good, but it isn't the same*"

"*You know I always speak the truth.*"

"*Well, tell me then. Am I the fairest?*"

"*You are undoubtedly the fairest Queen in the world.*"

"*That doesn't answer my question. Stop being clever —*"

"*'Caring' I would have said.*"

"*Whatever. Just tell me.*"

"*Well your Majesty,*" said the mirror with a sigh, "*you are looking a little wan. I'm sure it's just a temporary phase.*"

"*I don't think so.*" The Queen inspected her reflection. "*I really don't think so. Every day I'm looking older and less beautiful.*"

"*Beauty has nothing to do with being young,*" observed the mirror. "*It comes from within.*"

"*In that case I have no chance at all. There's little that's beautiful inside me. I'm bad. That's my whole purpose.*"

"*Look your Majesty,*" said the mirror, "*I think you're taking this too hard. You just need a change of image. I'm seeing pale blue silk, ermine collar and cuffs, softer lips —*"

"*Don't be ridiculous,*" snapped the Queen. "*I don't do pastel shades. It's black or scarlet. That's it.*"

"*I was only —*"

"*My image has nothing to do with this. It's a power thing. Each day something is leaving me. I can feel it. And out in the forest that syrupy little Snow White is growing stronger."*

"Now I understand," said the mirror. "You're jealous of her youth."

The Queen gave the mirror a glare which would have cracked an object with less magic in it. "Of course I'm jealous of her youth, but that isn't the point. What I'm telling you is that there's something protecting her. I'm not sure I'll be able to kill her."

"O that is a blow!" said the mirror.

"You just don't get it do you," said the Queen. "It's affecting all of us. Tell me again what you can reflect."

"The whole world your Majesty."

"Try it. Show me a scene from the other side of the world."

The surface of the mirror went milky, then stayed that way. "O my goodness, I can see for miles but I can't see that."

"Exactly," said the Queen, then watched with surprise as the image of an ugly young man appeared in the mirror. "What is that!"

"I don't know," answered the mirror. "But I'm getting a very bad feeling about it."

This was another most unusual tale with a very abrupt ending. What was the point of it? Why suggest that things were going awry in the world of legends? It would completely confuse any child who was reading it. It was confusing him. The story was illustrated, as the previous one had been, and the picture was of that final moment - the ugly boy's face in the mirror. It looked rather familiar in a funny sort of way but Henry had no idea who it was. He printed it and turned off his computer. He was no longer in the mood for law. It had stopped raining so he went for a walk.

The streets were quiet as most people were at work or school. It had become extremely hot. This was the wrong time of day for a walk. He would have done better to wait until the evening. But now he had started, he had no wish to go back home. Very slowly he wandered down the road, keeping to the shade where he could. Somewhere, up until now a willing captive of the laws of England and Wales, his soul was beginning to think it needed time off for good behaviour. Or may be bad behaviour. But definitely time off. This hint of rebellion reached Henry's brain and was quickly suppressed.

Henry meandered onwards. He had set off with no particular goal, but he knew where he was heading. Rupert's road. Yet Rupert was hardly likely to be there, and even if he were, Henry surely had no wish to see him again. May be not, but Henry mooched along until he got to Rupert's street. He stopped for a bit, turned round, turned back again and slowly approached Rupert's house, a dazzling white in the student afternoon sunshine.

"Hi there," said Rupert, appearing in the gateway.

"Hello," said Henry. "That's a surprise."

"Is it?" asked Rupert. He was even uglier than before, but as if to make up for that, his voice was developing so beautifully that any passing actor would have turned green with envy.

"Of course it is," protested Henry.

"Well I was expecting you." He smiled and Henry remembered what a powerful personality Rupert was.

"What are you doing nowadays?" asked Henry, although he really didn't care that much.

"Well, I'm waiting for my results. In the mean time I've got an excellent summer job. It's because I'm so clever you remember! I've been offered three months in the press office at the Treasury. I'm going to be a sort of trainee spin doctor for the Chancellor of the Exchequer."

"I wouldn't have thought you needed much training."

"Of course I don't," said Rupert, "but I could do with the opportunity to put my skills into practice."

"They can't be letting you do anything important."

"Can't they? What are you doing?"

"I'm catching up on European case law."

Even as he said it, Henry knew he should have lied! But Rupert made no comment. None was necessary. Instead he asked, "So what do you make of worldoflegends.com ?"

"What is there to make? It's a site for a theme park." Henry stopped. "How did you know?"

"Because that's why you're here."

That was true, but Henry was not going to admit this. "It's just an irritating advertisement."

"Specifically aimed at students. Who would go to all that trouble just to get a few student helpers? And don't you think their website is weird?"

"I haven't —"

"Of course you have. And seen those stories."

"Well yes, they did strike me as odd."

"That's exactly right," said Rupert. "It's all very odd."

"You'll be telling me next there isn't a World of Legends."

"O there is, I checked. I thought I might try a different sort of summer job."

"What?" Henry was genuinely startled. "Give up your brilliant opportunity in order to work in a theme park."

"Yes, that's all it was. I didn't get any special feeling about it."

"What exactly were you looking for?"

"A sign."

Henry shook his head. "The Treasury should give all the fantasy you need."

"Come inside," said Rupert. "I want to show you something."

They went up to Rupert's room. It was full of books. Smart books, read once only, on politics and public relations. And grubby books, read many times, on magic and fable. Rupert's computer was on. Henry looked at the screen and was startled because the screen saver had a lot of fairies flying across it. Rupert hit the mouse and there was www.worldoflegends.com .

"Have you looked at the links?" he asked Henry.

"I'm not that sad," Henry replied.

"Well I am," said Rupert, bringing them up. "Mostly they are to other theme parks in the same group, or to toy shops etc, but there is one I can't get into."

Henry decided it was time to leave. "That's not uncommon is it, a dead link or one to a club."

"It's not dead and you can join a club. This one is protected by a password."

"So isn't that —"

"Look," Rupert interrupted. "Don't you think that's unusual?" The recalcitrant site was www.parallelreality. universe .

"When did you see a name with universe at the end?"

Rupert tried to get into it. On the screen came this sign.

Find the password then enter a parallel reality
where magic and fable truly exist

PASSWORD:

"There is nothing to say how to get a password," said Rup0ert.

"So the link is defective," said Henry. Get a life Rupert!

"No, I don't think it is. I think I'm supposed to work it out."

Henry stared at his former friend. "You in particular?"

"Of course, it's me they want. But there'll be others. I've got to get in first." Rupert looked anguished, but then smiled sweetly. "You think I'm crazy. How can you doubt your own eyes?"

Henry was going to agree, but could not. Rupert had turned on him the full strength of his personality, a mixture of charm, self-belief and a hint of cruelty. "I – don't really understand."

"Ah well," said Rupert, "I've never been able to convince you. Anyway, I'll keep working on the password. You can try too."

"So what happens if I find it before you? I thought —"

"It doesn't matter if you find it." That was almost said with contempt, but then Rupert smiled again. "Because you'll let me know."

Henry turned to leave.

"I get it," said Rupert, "you didn't recognise me did you?"

"When?"

Rupert clicked on the story about the queen and the magic mirror and scrolled down to the illustration. Henry looked at the face in the mirror in the illustration. It was Rupert's.

CHAPTER 3

parallelreality.universe

A COUPLE OF days went by. The weather was sunny and mid June was at its most enticing. Yet this Henry could almost resist. What took him away from the law was the web site. The advertisement kept turning up. It made him restless and he found himself furtively reading fantasy novels in bookshops, glancing up anxiously in case anybody he knew spotted him – unlikely as it happened since he hardly knew anybody. He was a solitary type. Most of all, though, he became obsessed by www.parallelreality. universe. He was determined to find that password. Not because he wanted to get into it, like immature Rupert, but because of the intellectual challenge. He was sure that was the only reason.

He was forced to contact Rupert, to see if he had got in yet. Rupert had not and Henry could tell he was most upset about it. But then Rupert still believed in his parallel magic world.

On 17 June Henry was woken up by a phone call from Rupert who sounded very excited.

"You've worked it out?" asked Henry, disappointed.

"Listen to the news. Meet me this evening."

Henry turned on the radio. The first item was about the Chancellor of the Exchequer, an individual who spent quite a lot of his time wondering how he could take over as Prime Minister. He seemed to have had rather an eventful time yesterday evening. He was being driven to an event in a London suburb, when his ministerial car was almost forced off the road by a speeding security van. Suspicions aroused, he asked his driver to give chase, which they did, and were shot at for their impertinence. A bullet smashed through a headlamp, happily missing both the occupants of the car and the petrol tank. At this point the driver apparently suffered severe chest pains – a heart attack through stress seemed the obvious cause - so the Chancellor of the Exchequer took over the driving and whisked the driver off to hospital. Latest reports, incidentally, indicated that the driver had only suffered a panic attack. Anyway, having left his driver at the hospital, the Chancellor decided to drive himself to the engagement, as he had no wish to let anyone down. Quite unexpectedly, as he was continuing his journey, he came across the security van once more, now parked outside a house. Sensibly, he then called the police on his mobile phone and they turned up *within minutes*. But after all, it was the Chancellor of the Exchequer who had called them. They surrounded the house and were able to arrest a gang of robbers who had just stolen £10,000,000 belonging to an English billionaire. "Well," quipped the Chancellor, "several million of that belonged to the Treasury as tax. I couldn't let them get away with it!"

It was an unexpected side of the Chancellor, who had

struck people until then as rather a dour and cautious individual. However, one or two old college friends gave interviews on the radio and television. Apparently they had seen that side of him before. Two recalled an incident when the Chancellor, then a twenty year old student, had gone to the help of a young Asian man being attacked in the street by a gang of thugs. It was not something the Chancellor liked to talk about himself, his friends explained. Obviously this was why no one had heard of the incident until now.

Brave, modest and responsible, these were unusual qualities for a politician, and a quick opinion poll had indicated how much they were appreciated.

That evening Henry went round to Rupert's house. He really wished he had been strong enough not to go.

"So, what a story!" said Rupert, grinning a scary grin.

"A lucky break," said Henry. "You've been pushing it for all its worth have you?"

"I tell you what it's worth. Its weight in gold, that's what it's worth."

"Which is —?"

"And it was hardly a lucky break. Even you, little Henry, can't be that naïve. It was a careful plan. And it was my plan."

Little, thought Henry, he was almost half a metre taller. "You mean you set up the robbery!"

"Of course not, but we knew it was going to happen?"

"How could you?" asked Henry.

"The police have information."

"Why would they give it to the Chancellor of the Exchequer?"

"They didn't as such. They gave it to us."

"Why —"

"No more questions, I'm afraid. Or at any rate no more answers on that one. But let me answer another sort of question. You know, the one you asked me this morning." Rupert beamed complacently. Even when smiling, he was still extremely ugly.

"The link," said Henry, irritated beyond measure that Rupert must have worked it out.

"The link indeed," said Rupert. "I have got into the site." He tapped on his mouse and the screensaver on his computer screen disappeared. On the screen was a big sign saying:

www.parallelreality.universe
welcome to the world of legends

"How did you work it out?" asked Henry.

"It was a riddle," answered Rupert, "and that's all I'm saying at the moment."

"You aren't saying very much then, are you, about anything?"

"I think I am actually," said Rupert amiably, "At any rate more than you think. But certainly not as much as I could." He patted Henry on the arm. "Never mind about all that. I'm going to show you the site, Henry, the real world of legends."

Rupert clicked on "welcome" and the screen went swirly, like a mist.

"Neat effect," observed Henry who was extremely

out of sorts. He felt that Rupert was his superior in every way - intelligence, self confidence, achievement. Well, not looks of course. Henry was not a vain individual, but he knew he was a great deal better looking than Rupert. Who wouldn't be? That bumpy nose, those pointy ears and jagged teeth, and some unpleasant red spots gave Rupert quite a disturbing appearance. Yet when he spoke, and when he wanted to make an impression, he could be so charming that you almost forgot how ugly he was. Just at the moment though, he was not in a charming mood, he was in a triumphant one.

The mists cleared and there was a map of a different world. The place names were all rather fanciful, like 'mines of the dwarves' and 'palace of the fairy King'. Henry sighed inwardly. He was suddenly over his irritation and started to think again what an immature idiot Rupert was, for all his great intelligence.

"So where would you like to visit?" enquired Rupert.

"Cinderella's ball," said Henry, making something up.

"No Henry," said Rupert. "That's an event, not a place. Choose something from the map. Don't make it up."

"All right," said Henry, who was going right back to his irritable state. "Try 'lair of the mountain dragon'."

Rupert clicked on the words and the screen went misty again. When the mists cleared, the screen was gloomy and unclear.

"Most impressive," sneered Henry.

"We're inside a cave deep in the mountains. Just be patient and look."

Henry looked. He could see a huge dark shape. It was breathing. And that was that.

"Isn't this rather —" he began, then stopped. The huge dark shape moved. Then it went back to breathing again.

"As I was saying," Henry began once more. Then he stopped once more. The dark shape not only moved, it let out a small roar and Henry could see a pair of nostrils and some wispy smoke coming from them. "That's a bit better," he said, "although hardly worth —"

The shape hurled itself to its feet and gave a mighty roar. Flames poured from its nostrils and lit up the inside of the cavern. They sparkled off a great pile of gold and revealed a dragon with red, angry eyes.

"Now that's quite good, I grant you," said Henry, "and I haven't seen anything quite as —"

The dragon glared at him through the screen. "Whatever you are, wherever you are," said the dragon, "prepare to be eaten."

"It's fun," said Henry, "for children. So what's the point of making it so difficult to enter?"

"Show yourself," demanded the dragon. He was now breathing little flames, as if to keep himself going, so the cavern still had some light in it. "Being invisible won't save you. I have magic too."

"It's a lengthy clip," said Henry. "Usually they're less than a minute."

"Talking of less than a minute," remarked the dragon, "that's about how long you've got to live." He expelled the most almighty burst of fire which must have scorched every wall in the cavern.

Despite himself, Henry moved backwards. "It's

interactive," he cried. "This isn't a website, is it, it's a game."

"This is no game," answered the dragon. "This is a fight to the death. What are you? I thought you were another over confident knight, but you seem less aggressive than most of them. You're young. You must be an apprentice wizard. Haven't they warned you not to tangle with dragons?"

"Interactive with voice recognition," said Henry. "It's very good. Though not really my kind of thing."

"Of course not," said Rupert in a rather patronising voice.

"Two of you," said the dragon and Henry thought he heard the slightest hint of anxiety in the dragon's voice. "The more the merrier!" No, there wasn't any anxiety there.

"All right," said Henry, "I'm hooked. Let's visit somewhere else."

"There's the map," said Rupert, "choose."

"How about 'The magic mirror'?"

"Don't bother with that," said Rupert. "I've tried it and it's not worth the effort."

"I don't know – 'The maiden in the turret'? Or is that in the dead of night too?"

"Probably. But I expect there'll be a few candles."

"I can see you," observed the dragon in a tone of pleasant surprise. "Now we're cooking. Prepare to become cinders."

"Complicated." said Henry. "I thought you said Cinderella was just a story!"

Rupert shook his head and touched the mouse. But

even as he did, the screen turned brilliant orange before the mist came back again.

"I've had a thought," said Henry brightly. "Isn't 'The maiden in the turret' a bit specific? Like Cinderella's ball?"

"It does seem so," replied Rupert, "but no doubt there's always a maiden in a turret somewhere. It's an occupational hazard of maidens in legend."

Sadly, thought Henry, that made its own sense.

The mist cleared and the screen showed a fairly bare stone room with a narrow window. As it was dark outside, it was not possible to assess how high up the room was. The room was reasonably lit with several candles. Sitting at a spinning wheel was one of the most beautiful girls Henry had ever seen. At any rate she was beautiful in profile and he took it on trust that the other profile was broadly similar. She had long golden hair and a slender neck. If only she were real. She could almost be. Though if she were, Henry was not too sure what he'd do about it.

She was muttering angrily to herself. "Spin straw into gold. I mean who in their right mind would think any human being could do that."

Rupert moved away from the screen and whispered to Henry, "Say hello."

"I can't," whispered Henry back.

"Come on, it's only a computer image!"

"Hello," said Henry.

"Is that you again?" asked the girl. She went to the window and looked out. Then she looked round the room. The other profile must obviously be just as good because the whole face was perfection.

"It is me," replied Henry, "but not again."

"You certainly don't sound the same. Where are you? What are you?"

"Funnily enough, I was asked the same question a few moments ago."

"Not by me," said the girl. "What sort of creature is it this time? More to the point, can you spin straw into gold? And what do you want for it?"

"No," answered Henry, "that's not one of my skills."

"Well can you make gold some other way? Spinning isn't the important part. It's the gold."

In order to keep this conversation going a bit longer, Henry asked, "Why do you need it?"

"As I'm sure you know," she replied, "my father is being held prisoner by the King and if I don't produce the gold by morning, he'll be executed. Although first he'll be hung drawn and quartered. Except before that he'll be placed in the iron maiden and be spiked."

"That seems – very thorough."

"O, I can see your face now. And your neck and shoulders. Where's the rest of you? Are you going to turn into a Prince and save me?"

"Well," said Henry, "I'm sort of a Prince. My name is Henry - Prince."

"Prince Henry," said the girl, "you must make the rest of you appear and rescue me. After that, rescue my father and imprison the King. Then we can live happily ever after."

"That seems fairly straightforward."

From beside him Rupert laughed. "There you are Henry, that's your life sorted."

The girl started. "So you are there again. Is Prince Henry simply a trick?"

"Who's to say?" replied Rupert.

"Please," begged the girl, "you must help me. I'll find some way to repay you."

"I'd like to help you," said Rupert, "but I'm not quite ready."

"You did yesterday," said the girl.

"Did I? Take a closer look." He moved in front of the screen. No, what he actually did, Henry realised, was to move in front of a webcam.

"O," cried the girl, "you seem a lot younger."

"So you've played this particular game before," said Henry.

"No," said Rupert. "And that's enough now."

"But," protested Henry, "aren't we going to help?"

"You can do that," replied Rupert, "once you've found the password." He clicked on the screen and came out of the site altogether. "So what do you make of it?"

"As I said —" Henry was sensing a slight loss of dignity on his part and decided a calmer approach was required, "it's an impressive site, which is really more like a game."

"Yes. Tell me though, why did that girl think she knew me."

"Because you had actually been there before."

"So why did she say I seemed a lot younger?"

"I don't know. Part of the game."

"All right, well answer me this then. Why was it my face in the magic mirror? Before I'd got into the site."

"Just a coincidence," answered Henry. "It looked like you, that's all." What other explanation could there be?

CHAPTER 4

Like monkeys and Shakespeare

ANOTHER DAY WENT by. Henry spent most of it sitting at his computer, trying to work out how to get into www.parallelreality.universe and why it was so difficult. This left him little time to think about what he had seen there and how it worked. He was not an expert on web sites or computer games, but this one did seem unusually high-level and presumably must cost something to join. But that was the least of his problems.

The weather was even hotter and his parents did their best to encourage him outside. He simply muttered about his work and remained in his room. He did have the odd break and watched the lunch time news. There was an interview with the Chancellor of the Exchequer, rather a jokey one, and the interviewer quite forgot to press the minister about a fall in share prices. Instead the interviewer went so far as to suggest that "with a few more escapades like the evening before last" the Chancellor might be able to bring taxes down "by single-handedly topping up the nation's finances." The Chancellor laughed and said that he merely sought to do his best for the country he was proud to serve. Behind the Chancellor were some of his officials, including, right at the back, a small young man with an ugly face and a charming smile. Rupert.

"That looked like your friend Rupert," observed his mother, "How well he seems to be doing."

"What have I done," Henry asked himself, "to deserve this?"

Henry returned to his computer screen. He decided to make some sort of attempt to read more cases. He managed a few pages before realising that the little box referring to the World of Legends was no longer appearing. Perhaps no more students were required or the advertiser had paid for a certain number of days and they had run out. May be, but Henry felt it was a lot less simple. He turned his attention back to the main World of Legends site to see if any explanation appeared. He discovered a new story. It had arrived less than a week after the last one, and this annoyed him. How could a story be a 'story of the week' if it lasted for only a day or two? He disliked sloppy definitions.

He read the story:

> *Everyone remembers the tale of the Swan Lords and their curse. At any rate they remember one version or another of the tale. The exact number of the Swan Lords is a bit of a moot point. Everyone rejoices when the curse is lifted from them. Pedants*

might quibble in the case of the youngest brother, but he was almost curse free, apart from that one bit of his body. Besides, there was every chance that bit could be restored if the right witch or wizard came along.

Everyone assumes their tale ends when the curse was removed. But that was only the first episode. They went on to play a part in a much greater story. The reason nobody remembers this is because the story was about someone much more famous.

A few months after they were restored, the ten eldest brothers sat at their lunch in the large hall of their manor house. Regrettably they were not enjoying their meal of sedge, pondweeds, bulrush, water milfoil, widgeongrass and pond lily. It was not the menu that was upsetting them – they had developed a liking for marsh plants during the period of their curse - it was the argument about their youngest brother, who was missing.

"I said we shouldn't have sent him," said one.

"You were happy enough not to go yourself," said another.

"That might be so, but we always take advantage of him."

"What I don't understand —" began a third.

"But you know his soulful expression when he doesn't get his way."

"— What I don't understand is why we've heard nothing at all."

"That's my view too," said the eldest brother. The others subsided. "If Gervase had been captured

or killed we would have heard by now. There would have been a legend."

"The same if he had been the victor in a famous battle," added someone else.

The eldest smiled fondly. "Gervase! That is rather unlikely, but he might have met up with the great hero and assisted, in so far as he could, in some prodigious struggle. Or even a skirmish. But we should have learned about that too. It is a mystery indeed."

"An even bigger mystery," said one of them, "is where the hero sprung from. Who'd heard of him until recently? Now he is celebrated as one of the mightiest heroes ever."

"But what has he done to earn his reputation?" asked the brother who had spoken first.

"It is curious," agreed the eldest. "I have to admit that nobody has been able to tell me anything about Prince Henry. Yet we all believe he is a great hero and needs our support."

"Gervase was so excited at the thought of meeting him. And so proud that we let him represent the family."

"We must go out again and search for Gervase," said the eldest. "Now I wish we could still fly. Just think of the countryside we could cover."

The others looked shocked.

"You want us cursed again?" cried one of them.

"No of course not," said the eldest. "All I meant was being swans had some advantages. For *a time like this. When all is definitely not right. I can feel it."*

So could the others. The general view was that their world was somehow unsettled. Yet, in the same way that none could explain what made Prince Henry a hero, none could say what was bothering them. This might have been because these brothers were, undeniably, fairly unsophisticated military types who had difficulty expressing themselves. Yet there was more to it than that. With a deep feeling of unease, the brothers threw their lunch into a pond – where it would keep until later - and set off to find their youngest brother.

As ever the story ended unsatisfactorily. And how to explain the reference to Prince Henry? It could have been a coincidence. Or had Rupert found some way or someone to tamper with his computer. Henry logged out.

He took the afternoon off and moped about. He had an argument with his father at dinner, watched a lot of television, then went up to his room after midnight. He logged into the computer. He called up www.worldoflegends.com. He tried all the things he had tried in the past, including the search engines, and once again failed to get into www.parallelreality.universe. It made him very tired and even angrier. He began to wonder if the site really existed. What proof was there that Rupert had indeed found the password and entered the site? Perhaps it was simply a computer game after all.

Suddenly Henry lost his temper. He clicked on any number of different icons. Things came up, things disappeared. He was on the internet. He was out again. He opened one browser window. He opened another. He opened a third. He shut one. It was all aimless, but finally he saw he was back at www.worldoflegends.com. He clicked on 'Links'. He clicked on www.parallelreality. universe. He was expecting yet again to see on the screen:

Find the password then enter a parallel reality
where magic and fable truly exist

PASSWORD:

But he didn't. He saw one word only. **ENTER.** He clicked - and suddenly he was in!

www.parallelreality.universe
welcome to the world of legends

But how? He had no idea what he had done. Never mind. He would try to work that out later. For the moment he wanted to have another look round the map. He would begin with 'The maiden in the turret'. There she was, sitting at her spinning wheel, with long golden hair and a slender neck. He heard her sigh. Should he speak? Yes he should.

"Hello," he said.

She did not reply.

"Hello," he repeated, but in a louder voice.

She did not reply. How could she? He had no webcam or any way to make her see or hear him. How stupid of him to forget that.

She sighed once more. "What is it with Princes nowadays? Don't they rescue maidens any more? I've been here for – o I don't know – and so far I've only seen one Prince for less than a minute. And not even the whole of him at that. Just his head and shoulders."

She must mean him, thought Henry. "This is so unfair. I'm here now."

"And he looked quite promising too."

Promising! In what sense exactly?

"Mind you, what sort of Prince shows you his head and shoulders then vanishes!" She shook her head, sighed yet again and fell silent.

This was unbearable and Henry had to go somewhere else. He clicked the mouse, the screen went misty and then the map came back. He supposed he should check out the dragon. He did, but this time the dragon remained asleep. He had another look at the map. There was 'The magic mirror', which Rupert had told him was not worth the effort. Why should he trust Rupert though? He would check it out.

The mist cleared. There was simply an empty room, with silk covered walls and tall windows with heavy brocade curtains. The furniture was carved ebony, upholstered in deep red velvet. In fact every item in the room was either red or black, except for a round mirror on the wall facing the screen. That had an ornate gold frame and a glass which must never be cleaned as it was cloudy and reflected nothing. The room glowed a deep amethyst in the flames from two huge scarlet lanterns and many thick black candles.

Perhaps Rupert was correct. It was an eerie and powerful room, but nothing was going on there —

Except the surface of the mirror was becoming clearer and a vague impression of the room was showing in it.

"All right, who's there?" enquired a lightish voice.

There must be a person in the room, but not showing on the screen. What was the point of that, or perhaps it was simply a way to build up suspense.

"I can tell someone's looking at me," said the voice, "so don't mess me about." The owner of the voice remained concealed. Come on, Henry didn't have all night.

"Let's get one or two things straight," said the voice, with a slightly peevish tone. "You may be invisible, but if you'd given this a moment's thought you would realise that doesn't matter. I can always sense when someone's watching. That's the way I'm made."

This was all a bit disappointing in Henry's opinion. It was a pretty obvious bit of script and reinforced the evidence of this being no more than a game. It was exactly the same as a talking model in a theme park.

"I'm sensing a lot of negative energy," said the voice. "Doubt, suspicion — Well go away then. No one asked you here."

Of course, Henry was being really slow. It was the mirror talking.

"You do know I'll work out where you are eventually, don't you?" said the mirror. "And then I'll have to tell her. She won't like you nosing around in here – which is a BIG understatement. There'll be trouble!"

"Oh, I'm so scared," said Henry to the screen.

"You should be," answered the mirror. "She's a wicked woman."

Hold on, how did the mirror answer him? Perhaps a lucky bit of programming?

"Wicked is she! Like what, a wicked stepmother?"

"Not 'like'" said the mirror. "She *is* a wicked stepmother."

That was more than luck. What was going on?

"And when she finds you," added the mirror, "it'll be the spiked barrel."

"Not the spiked barrel!"

Henry stared curiously at the screen. The mirror was losing its clarity and going milky again.

"I'm beginning to see you," said the mirror sounding rather excited. "And you're not in the room at all."

"O what a surprise."

"You're not even from this world!"

"That's right, I'm an alien!"

"Goodness me," said the mirror. "That's a mistake."

"What's a mistake?"

"That yellow shirt. It's not your colour at all."

"Hell," cried Henry in exasperation, "you're simply a chip and I don't know why I'm even having this conversation."

"I told you I'd find you," said the mirror. "Here you are."

The milkiness disappeared and Henry saw himself in the mirror. It was not his reflection. It was a still image, but it was definitely him.

"How did you do that?"

"Magic," replied the mirror in a matter of fact tone. "That's my job."

Henry heard a woman's voice from outside the room. She sounded both powerful and angry.

"The Queen," said the mirror.

"I'd like to see her"

"She'll not be in. She's off to do some unspeakable deed."

"What's upset her?"

"She's feeling insecure."

"Why's that?"

"That's enough questions," said the mirror. "Until I'm sure about you."

"O mirror, mirror, you know I love you!"

"Hysterical," said the mirror. "If I laugh any more I'll crack myself."

"At least you can tell me one thing," said Henry. "Am I the fairest of them all?"

"Hardly," replied the mirror and refused to speak again.

The angry woman's voice could no longer be heard and there was no point hanging about. Henry went back to the map. Whatever was going on, he did not like it. He would have to apologise to Rupert and see if his former friend had anything to do with this. He should go to bed, try to sleep. He must be missing something obvious. He was simply too exhausted to work it out. He thought about the blonde girl with the slender neck. He would have one last look before he gave up. He returned to the 'The maiden in the turret'.

She was still there, but was dozing, her face full onto the screen. She truly was the loveliest thing he had ever seen. So to make everything worse, he fancied a computer image.

There was a noise from outside and a figure appeared at the window. For a moment Henry experienced a pang of jealousy. Was this a real Prince come to rescue her? However, if this were a fairytale prince, it was a very small one. May be it was a very young one. It was impossible to say because the head of the intruder was concealed by a large hood. He climbed through the window with a certain amount of puffing and muttering then stood beside the sleeping girl. He reached out a grubby hand to the golden hair, and touched it lightly. Did the hair lose some of its lustre? Then he pushed back the hood and Henry swore. It was the strange little man he had last seen on Halloween all those years ago.

He actually felt quite sick for a moment. It was the sight of that knobbly head, with its hairy nose and ears, leering at that beautiful girl. The little man was wearing the same dirty robe. His red pointed hat had been squashed under the hood. And of course, now that Rupert was that much older, the resemblance between the two of them was even more noticeable.

"Well my pet," said the little man to the girl, "you didn't even stay awake for me." His voice was just as melodious and reassuring as before. The only thing was, he now sounded almost the same as Rupert.

The girl woke up with a start and saw him. She failed to hide a split second look of revulsion. "I've been hoping you'd come back," she said. "I have to spin more gold."

"Indeed you do," beamed the little man. "And I'm here to help."

"It's very kind of you."

"No it isn't," replied the little man. "There'll be a charge. I never work for nothing."

"We're very poor."

"I don't want your money."

"In that case —"

"Leave it for now. We'll sort out a price." He grinned. "There's always something I need."

"Anything," she replied.

" 'Anything'," he repeated. "One of my favourite words."

That is an evil creature, thought Henry. Surely she can see that. "Don't trust him," he called out, but neither heard him. How could they? There was no web cam, no magic mirror.

"Please start," she implored. "It will soon be light and if I don't have the gold they'll kill my father."

"Well I shan't let them," said the little man. "Let me sit down and I'll get spinning."

The girl stood up and moved out of the way.

"It occurs to me," said the little man, getting hold of a bundle of straw, "that you're causing a lot of trouble for yourself."

"How?" asked the girl.

"Well what sort of reputation do you think you're building up? Someone who can spin straw into gold. Once you've delivered something like this, they'll be looking for magic tricks all your life. They won't let you get away with saying it was just a phase you went through, or telling them to be grateful for what you did in the past."

"No, It'll be fine. This is just a test because my father has a big mouth. I'm only supposed to do this three times."

"That won't satisfy the King."

"He promised he'd free us after the third time. We can go home after tomorrow night."

"But for how long?" The little man shook his head. "A single afternoon would be enough to keep his promise."

A stream of gold coins was pouring out of the spinning wheel and chinking onto the stone floor of the turret. The sky in the window was a lighter blue and a single bird decided to begin the dawn chorus.

"I have to believe the King," said the girl. "But even if he's lying, I still have to give him the gold."

"As to that," said the little man smugly, "you have nothing to worry about."

They both fell silent. The sky grew brighter, more birds started singing and the coins kept crashing to the floor. Henry watched the flow, mesmerised. Because he was so tired and it was so nearly dawn, he fell asleep. When he woke up it was nearly nine, the screen was blank and he had no idea how to get back into the site.

CHAPTER 5

Midsummer's eve

HENRY NEEDED TO discuss what had happened and there was only one person he could discuss it with. He phoned Rupert on his mobile and arranged to meet him that evening. He spent a fruitless hour trying to work out how he had got into www.parallelreality.universe, gave up and sat in the garden. His mother felt this was a slight improvement on normal, as at least he was out in the air. His father had various thoughts about his son's lacklustre attitude to life, but managed to keep them to himself.

At lunchtime he watched the news. There was an interview with the senior political commentator at the BBC. An opinion poll that morning had suggested the Chancellor of the Exchequer would be a more popular Prime Minister than the present Prime Minister. When asked to comment, the Chancellor had indicated that the thought of becoming Prime Minister was the last thing on his mind. He had an important job to do and this was enough for him. If and when the present Prime Minister chose to stand down – and that would not be for a very long time – he would consider his options. It was therefore obvious to all, in the view of the commentator, that the Chancellor was bursting to take over at number 10.

"Ambition," said Henry's father, "is a quality I admire. Above everything."

"I'm ambitious," said Henry, "I intend to become a Judge."

"That's all very fine," observed his father, "but how many Judges are leaders of men?"

"I want to become Lord Chief Justice," said Henry. Well, he supposed he did. "He's a leader of men."

"To be a leader of men," said his father, "you have to show leadership."

"That would seem fairly logical," said Henry.

"And show drive."

Henry left the room.

In the afternoon he went out to buy a webcam and set it up. In the unlikely event of his ever getting back into the site, at least he could communicate with whoever, whatever was there.

At eight-o-clock he went over to Rupert's, but he was still not back, although due shortly. Henry decided to wait in the front garden. It was warm, with late bees cruising around. There was a rustic bench just outside the door, so Henry sat down there. Unlike his own front garden, where any attempt to grow wild had been ruthlessly crushed by his father's oppressive gardening, this one had been allowed a bit of self expression. Plants had been left to self-seed, and the beds were chock a block with old English flowers. It was very pretty and very traditional.

Next door the big Victorian house was its usual unfriendly presence. Even on a muggy evening it managed to look cold. For a moment Henry thought he saw a face in a window, but was distracted by the arrival of a Daimler in the street outside. There were three passengers and a driver. The front seat passenger was Rupert. The nearside passenger in the back had a strangely familiar look. Rupert got out.

"Hello Henry," he said, at his cockiest. He addressed the other passenger. "Chancellor, this is my very old friend Henry Prince."

The Chancellor of the Exchequer politely lowered the window. "Good evening," he said.

A few days before Henry might have been slightly nervous at meeting so significant an individual. Now, unless the Chancellor proposed to breathe fire or put him in a spiked barrel, what was there to be nervous about?

"Good evening," said Henry, walking towards the gate.

"So, are you interested in public relations too?" enquired the Chancellor, with the show of interest necessary when meeting an impressionable young voter.

"I don't have Rupert's flair," replied Henry. "I'm going to be a lawyer."

"Very prudent," said the Chancellor. "No doubt you want to become a rich city solicitor."

"No," said Henry, "the Lord Chief Justice."

"Good luck to you," said the Chancellor and turned away. "We'd better get on," he said to the driver.

"Knock'em dead Chancellor," exhorted Rupert. "You'll be brilliant."

"Let's hope they like your joke," smiled the Chancellor.

"They'll love it," said Rupert. "I promise you."

The Chancellor laughed and rolled up the window. The car drove off.

"How come he gave you a lift?" asked Henry before he could stop himself.

"I discovered he was going this way. I managed to let him know I lived en route. And he's very pleased with me at the moment."

"That makes two of you," said Henry. "I've got something to tell you."

Henry watched Rupert's expression - rapt attention and a little hint of irritation that Henry had managed to enter the site.

"So," said Rupert, "do you now accept the truth of all that I've been telling you over the last few years?"

"How do I know it wasn't a dream or some sort of delusion?"

"But Henry, you don't think it was."

"Who was that ugly little man?"

"The one who looked like me!"

"Sorry," said Henry, "It was only a superficial —"

"No it wasn't superficial at all. I've seen him there."

"Who is he?"

Rupert stretched back on the bench, as the two of them were still in the front garden. The bees had all gone away. The sunset turned Rupert's face a devilish red. Presumably Henry's face was red too, but he guessed it would not seem devilish.

"Come on," said Rupert, "you know who it is."

"Rumpelstiltskin?"

"That's exactly right."

"This is some sort of game isn't it? You've managed to do something to my computer?"

Rupert grinned. It was not a pretty sight. If he had been an ordinary devil before, he now resembled one of the worst, Beelzebub perhaps

"Even if I had, how does that explain the fact we saw Rumpelstiltskin on Halloween when we were both thirteen?"

"How can it be Rumpelstiltskin? He's in a fairy story."

"It's time I went inside," said Rupert.

"I have to admit," said Henry, "I would like to get into that site again."

Rupert laughed. "I expect you do Henry. Find it for yourself. I don't want you here any more. Not this evening. Especially not this evening."

"What's so special about it?"

"Work it out for yourself."

"Where's all the charm gone?" asked Henry.

"I save it for when I need it. And it's not as if you like me."

"That's not —"

"Goodbye Henry. I'll see you later."

Henry left the garden. He was angry with Rupert, for being superior and in control, and angry with himself, for being sneery and jealous. Henry admitted he was not a very nice individual and that was unfair, because he really wanted to be. Yet he had cause to be annoyed with Rupert, who could have told him the password and been a lot more forthcoming.

Henry glanced at the next house, where he and

Rupert had seen, or not seen, that strange little man so many years ago. It had a neglected, disturbing look, with dark windows which would seem grimy even if they were cleaned. Two hefty pillars stood either side of an opening in the high wall which protected the house from the street – or the street from the house. Through the opening was a gravel drive, a lot of feral bushes and the corpse of an old car, rusting away, covered by ivy and bird droppings.

Who lived there? Who had found Henry by the front door on that Halloween night? Henry was unable to remember. He wondered if Rupert had ever been allowed back?

Henry wasn't ready to go home. He started to walk up the hill towards Hampstead Heath and kept on going until he reached the White Stone Pond. Then he set off towards Parliament Hill Fields. It was a quarter to nine, so still light, but no longer hot, just pleasantly warm. The trees were all an enthusiastic green and the pollen count was lethal. A perfect summer evening.

Henry sat on a bench under a tree in an open field which sloped down to the first pond. He brooded. He envied the mellow walkers and their happy dogs. Things were working out for them – and for Rupert – but not for him. Life was a puzzle, Rupert was a puzzle, the website was a puzzle – he had no idea what to do about any of it. He sat and drifted off until eventually the peaceful evening got through to his discontented little soul. He was sad but he was calm. The night breezed in and the walkers took their dogs home, but Henry stayed where he was. It was after ten when he came to himself and wondered if he could find his way back.

He stood up. Well, it wasn't even dark and he had a reasonable idea of the direction he had to take, which would be straightforward once he found the main pathway back to Hampstead village. There were people about somewhere, although he was unable to see all of them. He could hear music down by the pond and laughter somewhere else. He set off fairly briskly, but as he moved across the grass, he noticed someone coming towards him. Why not? People were entitled to enjoy such a beautiful night.

It was a young man wearing – fancy dress surely? He was in the sort of outfit people wore in the fourteenth century, a tunic with flowing sleeves, tight leggings and pointy shoes. His hair was long with a fringe. May be that was a wig.

"Excuse me," said the young man, "can you help me? I seem to be lost."

Obviously on his way to a party.

"I don't really know this area very well myself," said Henry. "Where are you looking for?"

"It's not where," replied the young man, "It's who."

"I'm not likely to know who," said Henry.

"You might if I told you."

"I might I suppose, but it seems improbable."

"People say that," observed the young man, "but quite often they do know. Mind you, even if they do, they're far too fond of answering questions in riddles. You aren't going to do that are you?"

"No," said Henry, who felt this conversation was getting out of control.

"Good," said the young man. "I'm not the brightest

in my family. I'm the youngest, of course, which is why I get sent on lots of errands or quests or whatever."

"I'm an only child," explained Henry, rather surprised that he was volunteering this information

"Hey," said the young man. "That must be great. Not that I would be without my brothers, but a bit of time away from them would be brilliant."

"How many brothers do you have?" asked Henry. Why? He didn't care.

"Ten! And one sister."

"That is a lot."

"You're telling me!" The young man looked round. "I know I said I didn't want to know where I was, but I do. I've never seen any countryside like this. And yet I wasn't in it five minutes ago."

"Hampstead Heath can be a bit confusing."

"Hampstead Heath?" The young man shook his head and clutched at it. "This is weird."

Henry stared. Yes, that was weird. The young man's sleeves were rather long and had hidden his hands before. When he clutched his head, it was apparent there was only one hand. Where the other should be was the tip of a sizeable white wing.

"Something wrong?" asked the young man.

"Mm, no, of course not." Henry was very sensitive to others' disabilities. Even so – "I'm sorry, it was rude of me, I was a bit startled that's all."

The young man saw where Henry was looking and seemed startled himself. "I don't blame you. That's very rum. It shouldn't be like that."

"It's not a question of 'shouldn't'," said Henry. "It's

how you are and I ought to have accepted it without
—"

"Absolutely not," returned the young man. "This isn't right at all."

"Well, I wouldn't —"

"The sun's gone down and it should have reverted."

Sun gone down. That normally affected only vampires, surely? Henry pulled himself together. "Reverted?"

"You know, to an arm."

"If you could just explain a bit more."

"Oh." The young man appeared surprised. "I thought everyone round here knew. Ah, but then may be I'm not round here any more. All right, look, you're obviously puzzled."

"That's certainly right."

"The thing is, my brothers and I were cursed by a witch."

"Ye-es," said Henry, who was getting a little uneasy.

"Yes. It meant we were only human at night but turned into swans during the day. You can see how awkward that was."

"O yes. I can see that would be awkward."

"But my sister decided to knit us all special shirts. She had to complete them by a certain time and then when we put them on, we would become human again."

"That does vaguely ring a bell," said Henry, mainly to himself.

"Unfortunately, although she's a great girl and all that, she's not a quick knitter. When she reached her deadline, she hadn't quite finished. There was a sleeve missing off my shirt. That means my arm still turns into a wing during daylight hours."

"Grimm," muttered Henry.

"It certainly is," agreed the young man. "But at least it's back to normal once the sun goes down. Except of course it isn't tonight. That's very disturbing." He looked forlornly at the wing.

"I have to get home," said Henry.

"Yes of course, sorry to hold you up. But can I just ask you about the person I'm searching for."

"Okay."

"It'll be such an honour to meet him. He's got a brilliant reputation. I had no idea he was so near us. Assuming I'm still where I'm supposed to be that is."

"I don't know anyone with a brilliant reputation," said Henry.

"That's a pity. Anyway I'll tell you his name. You're bound to have heard of him. It's Prince Henry."

"Prince Henry?"

"Yes."

"That's – odd. My name's Henry Prince."

"Henry Prince!" cried the young man, and bowed deeply. "Then it's you. Though why do you put your title last? Is it a foreign custom?"

"No," said Henry and left it at that. He was getting increasingly bothered. Not by the young man who seemed dim but decent – and not mad, unless that wing was false. It was the whole situation, which had a similar resonance to the scenes on the website.

"Your Highness," said the young man, "I am Gervase and I have been sent to warn you to be on your guard."

"Against what?"

"Lurking danger of course."

"That's not very specific is it?"

"Well – I think they thought you'd know. Especially with it being a bit odd at the moment."

That was certainly true. Henry was about to press Gervase on this, when he became aware that a lot of people were moving in their direction although were still a fair way off. It was that much darker now, so it was difficult to see what they were like, but Gervase reacted strongly at their appearance.

"This is an honour," he cried, "to be at your side while you put these evil-doers to the sword."

Perhaps Gervase *was* mad. "What are you talking about?" asked Henry, but he was getting a bad feeling about this group, who were moving in a very stealthy manner.

"Your Highness, these are the phouka and they are hunting us."

"Well, whatever they are, I don't have a sword," said Henry, half irritably and half frightened.

"So you don't —- What about an axe?"

"Does it look like I've got an axe?"

"Right, then we should run off and hide, perfectly in order in the circumstances."

"What —"

"It won't be held against you. Affect your legend and so on. These boys are dangerous and you need to be armed – unless you have some special strength that is."

"No I don't."

"Or magic powers? They'd come in useful."

"No."

"In that case —" said Gervase and ran off towards the trees. Henry ran off too, but could not resist turning his head. The group were racing after him, but seemed to be on all fours. Even so, they were catching up fast.

"Wolves," shouted Gervase.

"What?"

"Wolves," repeated Gervase and rushed into the trees.

"Where are we going?" gasped Henry.

"Wherever you lead, your Highness."

Where could he lead? Why was he rushing? What was he rushing from? This was all a mistake. Then he heard a howl and he simply stopped. Gervase stopped too and stared at him expectantly. In the remains of the light Henry could see the trust in his eyes. He saw lots of other eyes too, all yellow, as a pack of wolves surrounded them. How could this be happening? One of the wolves rushed towards him and leaped. Henry could do nothing. The wolf knocked him backwards, and Henry smelt fetid breath, winced as sharp teeth pressed into his neck —

"That's enough of that," said a familiar voice.

The wolf stopped his bite, but left his teeth where they were, which was in the very act of breaking through Henry's skin.

"That's a bit over eager isn't it?" suggested the voice. "Was that really part of your instructions?"

Henry could see the wolf's eyes glaring at the person speaking. Rupert.

"Who asked you to kill him?"

The wolf removed his teeth from Henry's throat, as he needed his mouth to speak. "That goes with being a wolf. Wolves kill."

"Yes but only for food."

"And your point is —"

"You're not going to eat him."

"Why do you assume that?

"Because you're not really a wolf."

"Well I am tonight."

"Indeed," said Rupert, "but tomorrow you won't be and you'll have dreadful indigestion."

"Granted," agreed the wolf, "but I could tear him limb from limb."

"I repeat," said Rupert, "who asked you to kill him?"

"It was sort of implied," replied the wolf.

Henry, still lying on the ground, felt terrified. These creatures might not really be wolves but they were doing a very good job of looking like they were. A trickle of blood slowly ran down his neck.

"No," said Rupert, "I don't think so. I believe you were asked to protect me from threats."

"Now that you mention it," said the wolf, "that might have more like it. He's a threat."

"Does he look like a threat!" said Rupert. "All I require is that he doesn't interfere. You've done enough."

"Are you sure?" asked another wolf. "It would be quite good practice for us. We haven't killed anyone for quite a while."

"Perhaps another time," said Rupert, with a friendly grin at Henry. "But for now I really need to get on."

"Excuse me," said Gervase from somewhere. "I'm a little confused. What point in this adventure have we reached?"

"The point where you keep quiet and come along with us," said Rupert.

"Absolutely," agreed Gervase, "but two wolves are currently standing on me."

"They're not really wolves," Rupert reminded him.

"I know that," said Gervase, "But they don't seem to."

"Move," ordered the leader of the pack and the two wolves moved. Gervase jumped to his feet and Henry thought he had better stand up too. Somewhat to his surprise, he did. The wolves watched him – wolvishly.

"That's all sorted then," said Rupert pleasantly. "Let's get going." He started to walk out of the trees, but then turned back to Henry. "Best stick with me —"

There was no need to say anything more. Henry was by his side in a trice, while Gervase strolled over to join them. Rupert smiled sweetly and started to walk along a path which led back to where Henry had been sitting earlier. This was not the way Henry wanted to go – homewards was very much the direction he would have preferred – but he was too frightened to set off on his own. Not that he found Rupert a very reassuring presence. What was his former friend doing talking to a pack of ersatz wolves, who were even now silently padding behind them, albeit at a respectful distance?

"Don't do anything to upset them," whispered Rupert. "They won't need much encouragement to turn on you."

"I'm not scared of them," declared Gervase, though in a whisper too. "If we'd only been armed we'd have kicked their lupine butts."

"Of course you would," said Rupert.

"What are they," asked Henry, impressed he could actually speak, "if they're not wolves?"

"The phouka, Prince Henry, you know," said Gervase.

"A type of fairy," explained Rupert.

"You're joking!"

"What do you want, gossamer wings!" Rupert shook his head. "Forget the fairy on a Christmas tree, or in a Walt Disney cartoon. They're nothing like real fairies. A lot of those are impressively treacherous or weird. The phouka are some of the nastiest. They can turn themselves into animals and when they do, they're extremely dangerous."

"Indeed," said Henry.

"I could tell you some stories —" began Gervase.

"Later would be better," said Rupert.

They continued down the path in silence. From the other side of the hill came the sound of laughter and music. Normal people were doing normal things. It was a bright night with a full moon. It was also very humid, with an occasional rumble of far-away thunder. The little breeze from earlier had given up its struggle with the heavy air and subsided until conditions were more in its favour.

"What's going on?" Henry asked Rupert. "Why are you here?"

"It's a bit like that Halloween, but a much bigger break through."

"Why tonight?"

"Midsummer's eve. It's the right time isn't?"

"Are you a magician?" enquired Gervase. "Prince Henry and I could do with a little magic."

"Yes you could," said Rupert. "Look around you. Perhaps this is magic?"

The path had been silvery in the moonlight. It now started to change its colour, to a sort of blue, which seemed odd. Henry inspected the moon. It wasn't blue, which in all the circumstances it might well have been. The path also seemed to flicker, as though it held an electric charge.

Rupert stopped abruptly. The undergrowth rustled and Henry jumped. A rabbit bounced out onto the path and paused in front of them. Rupert bent down and muttered to it, stroking its head. The rabbit twitched its ears.

"Yes," murmured Rupert, "I can feel it too."

The rabbit hopped back into the shadows.

"Thanks for the information," Rupert called after it. "Of course I already knew," he said to Henry.

"Are you telling me that rabbit has just spoken to you?"

"Why, did you hear it speak to me?"

"No, but —"

"Of course it didn't speak to me. It's a simple animal with a very small brain. It communicated with me."

"What - did it communicate?"

"You can see for yourself. The ley line is coming alive."

"O yes," said Henry drily. "I should have realised."

The path flickered and crackled a neon blue with tiny flames and spurts of fire. Creatures scurried alongside them, in front of them, across them, alarmed but not alarming, only rabbits, field mice, foxes, voles. Something brushed across Henry's face. It was a moth. There were lots of moths. Hundreds of moths were flying down to the pathway and burning to death in tiny blue funeral pyres.

Rupert led them off the path and began to climb

a hill, with the wolves still following. The line of blue spread up the hill to a mound covered by trees. They moved towards it. When they were nearly there, Rupert stopped. They all stopped.

"This is where I leave you," said Rupert.

It was not so dark that Henry missed the faintest tremor of anxiety cross Gervase's face. He himself was beyond anxious. He had given up.

"Please be good to each other," Rupert continued. "Of course, if these guys try anything," he said to the wolves, "feel free to rip out their throats. See ya."

He gave a funny little wave then walked up to the trees. The wolves surrounded Henry and Gervase, though made no attempt to approach. But they did start to slaver.

"I think I'll sit down while we're waiting," said Henry, finding his legs a little unsteady.

"Good idea your Highness," said Gervase, who remained infuriatingly chipper.

"All this exercise," remarked the wolf leader. "It works up an appetite."

"You're not scaring us," said Gervase.

"Listen," said the wolf, "Don't get smart. We may not be wolves for long, but while we are, it's seems real. We've got all their instincts and appetites, including the desire for raw meat."

"Understood," said Gervase.

"And we're hungry."

They waited, though for what, and for how long?

Not long. The bright blue started to illuminate the whole mound and they could clearly see the figure of Rupert through the few trees growing there. The blue grew even stronger and Henry thought there might have been two figures standing next to each other. No, there was only one. The glow lasted a few more seconds then began to fade. Rupert emerged from the trees, waved again, and set off down the hill, but not in their direction. Meanwhile the blue line became fainter.

"He's not interested in you two any more," said the wolf leader. "I think we can enjoy ourselves."

"Let's start with their eyes," said another. "I'm sick of the way they've been staring at us."

The wolves moved towards Henry and Gervase, who got to their feet.

"A hero's death, well of a sort," said Gervase. "It's an honour to die at your side Prince Henry."

"Thank you," said Henry, who suddenly found a little spark of dignity. He was so surprised to find it that for a moment he even forgot to be afraid. And that lack of fear was the last the wolves and Gervase saw of him, for they too faded, quickly and completely, leaving Henry alone on the hill, with no blue lines, no companions and no sign of Rupert.

He set off along the path, silvery once more, and made his way without incident. After ten minutes he approached the open gateway onto Spaniard's Road, passing other people strolling through the summer night. He made his way out of the Heath and began to walk down Heath Street, through the reassuring shops and restaurants, heading for home.

CHAPTER 6

Rumpelstiltskin

HENRY SLEPT, BECAUSE the walk and the shock had worn him out. When he woke up late the following morning he could see the puncture marks down his neck, so something *had* happened.

What part was Rupert playing in all this? He was very angry with Rupert, who had abandoned him. He could have been killed. He tried to contact Rupert and left messages, but there was no reply.

He got up. He told his mother the marks were insect bites. He pored over the newspapers and put on the radio, in case there was anything about strange phenomena on Hampstead Heath. There was nothing. He heard yet another item about the Chancellor of the Exchequer, whose profile was higher than ever. It was an interview with the man he had saved from bullying all those years ago. "'He has always been a hero to me' said the middle aged newsagent, 'and I have held him up to my children as an example of decent and honourable behaviour.'" All this about a minister who had been attacked only two months ago for increasing taxes.

He switched on his computer. Somehow he knew there would be a new story on the worldoflegends site. He was right:

> There are many strange characters in the world of legends. On the whole their appearance gives them away. There are obviously exceptions to this. The fair can be put under a spell, like the Prince who became a beast, or can pretend to be ugly when it suits their purposes. The hideous can also use magic to make themselves seem attractive and so trick the unwary. Children are naturally warned to be on their guard. But the general rule is that your true character is revealed by the way you really look.
>
> Rumpelstiltskin was a perfect example of this. He had been repulsive from the day he first came into the world, however that was. He might not strictly speaking have been born at all. There was a rumour that his mother was a mountain dwarf and his father was a troll, in which case he might literally have been a chip off the old block. Whatever the truth, he had been unsettling people from the very first moment he had been seen.
>
> He was clever and cunning, with two great gifts to compensate him for his unpleasant appearance. The first was his voice, which was soft and pleasing. He had often been able to use it to mislead travellers in the dark or trick the old and poor sighted. In addition, he was able to

charm and flatter those not put off by his repulsive features. His second gift was even more desirable. He was able to turn anything into gold for those prepared to pay a suitable price. Regrettably, he was unable to produce gold for himself. Whenever he tried, it never lasted. But it did for others, who were only too willing to make some very rash promises in return.

Currently Rumpelstiltskin was spinning some gold for a miller's daughter. Her father, seeking to talk up his daughter as a prospective bride for the King's son and heir, had boasted of her amazing ability to spin wool into gold. To encourage her to live up to this boast, she was being held prisoner. How she had fretted that first night. Rumpelstiltskin had latched on to that. However many leagues away he was, he could always sense a soul in misery. Perhaps this was a third gift. It certainly did him a lot of good.

He had now helped this young lady on two occasions and on the third night climbed in through the tower window to perform his bit of trickery for the final time. It was always a pleasure to see the desperation in the eyes of the person he was helping, or victim as he liked to think of them. This girl was no exception, but she was spunky, he gave her that. She showed no fear of him and her main emotion seemed to be anger at everyone concerned in this unnecessary episode.

"I've been thinking of what gift you might like to give me," he smirked.

"What have you chosen?" she asked.

"Well, I was wondering about your first born child."

"I don't have a first born child."

"No, but you will."

"That's unacceptable," she stated with a toss of her long blonde hair.

"You said 'anything' yesterday," grinned Rumpelstiltskin, wrinkling his horrid nose in a playful manner which caused a particularly large pustule to burst.

"Yes, but —"

"It'll be mine anyway," said Rumpelstiltskin. "I've decided to marry you."

"You have!"

"Indeed."

Rumpelstiltskin was very much enjoying this conversation. He was going to ask for a kiss as down payment and the girl's disgust would only make it the sweeter. Imagine his indignation therefore when he found himself transported out of the tower against his own wishes. The next thing he knew he was standing in a grove of trees, bathed in a brilliant blue light. As for the girl, she was aghast at his sudden disappearance. She certainly did not care for the prospect of marrying this ugly little creature, whose name she had still to learn and whose appearance both sickened and frightened her. Nevertheless, she was certain she could find some way round that. For the moment, her priority was getting a great heap of wool spun into gold. If that did not happen, her poor, stupid father would suffer a painful death. For that *matter, she was somewhat uncertain about her own survival.*

She was extremely relieved when the horrid little man suddenly reappeared in the tower.

"You vanished," she said. "You're the second person who's done that here."

"Really?" He was staring at her intently. "You are indeed a beautiful maiden. And that simple rustic blouse and skirt do more for you than a designer gown."

"Could you save that for later?" she answered. "There's an awful lot of gold to spin."

He kept on staring at her. Curiously he seemed a bit less ugly, but perhaps it was simply that she had got more used to him. That was as far as it went though. She could tell how dangerous he was.

"I said," she repeated, "there's an awful lot of gold to spin."

"May be there is," he said, "but I don't know how to do it."

"Her life's at risk!" cried Henry, then blushed, although he was alone.

He tried to make contact with Rupert again. He sent Rupert a text message that he would like to see him urgently. He sent him an e-mail saying the same thing and also left messages on Rupert's mobile and home phones. Nothing came back.

Dinner time and his father was in a particularly irritating mood, reminiscing yet again about his own student days and hinting at all sorts of adventures which his mother had no wish to hear again for several reasons.

Out of sheer desperation Henry said, "I had an adventure last night. I was attacked on my walk by a pack – by a group of thugs."

His mother looked worried. "Is that why you've got that mark on your neck?"

His father looked perplexed. "How did you fight them off."

"Well I'm not a complete wimp," said Henry. "Besides, someone came to my help."

"You should phone the police," said his mother.

"It's over now. These things happen. Don't go on about it."

He went upstairs to his room. These things happen! Yes, but they shouldn't. Especially not to him, who was supposed to be a dreary law student and asked for nothing more.

After this brief moment of triumph Henry had nothing left to do but think. First, but briefly, he considered again how to get into the site. But that way madness lay. He decided to leave it until after he had spoken to Rupert, in case he could persuade him to reveal the password. Next he turned his attention to all that had happened. He sat and stared into space for an hour or so. He tried out various theories, set up numerous hypotheses, went down several avenues. It all came to this:

He was mad.

1. He was the victim of a conspiracy, which was so unbelievable that to believe it also meant he was mad. Or

2. It was all true in which case he was likely to go mad.

3. To sum up then, his future could be described in one word, madness. It seemed – unfortunate.

The telephone rang. It was Rupert's mother. Rupert had not come home though he was expected. She wondered if he were with Henry. He was not. Henry allowed himself a passing reflection about Rupert's parents. What was it like to have such a curious individual as a son? On the other hand both Rupert's parents were deeply eccentric and Rupert's father made Rupert look almost normal – no that was going much too far. Less abnormal.

Henry went to bed.

At half past five the following morning he woke abruptly with the curious feeling that someone was watching the house. He got up and looked out. Someone *was* watching the house. Rupert was sitting on the low front wall and staring up at his bedroom. Even in the kindly light of a summer dawn Rupert was ugly. This morning in fact he was uglier than ever, a definite notch up the ugliness scale. He saw Henry and beckoned him. Henry put on some clothes, then made his way quietly out of the front door.

"Prince Henry," beamed Rupert. "It's an honour to meet you."

"Funny man," said Henry. "Why so early?"

"Early! Is it early? Is it late? I don't know. I've lost track of time. Or is it that time's lost track of me?"

Henry inspected Rupert suspiciously. "What have you been doing?"

"Wandering around," replied Rupert. "Ever since —" he chuckled. "Ever since I saw you on Midsummer night."

"That's over thirty six hours ago."

"An hour, a year, I'd have believed anything." His eyes were bright and excited. His skin was a pinky grey colour, which was the healthiest Henry had ever seen it.

"Have you taken something?" asked Henry.

"Not yet," answered Rupert with a happy grin. "But in the end it's all going to be mine!"

"What are you talking about?"

"Me," said Rupert. "I'm thirsty."

"Would you like some tea?" Henry had an instinctive understanding of how to cope with awkward situations.

"Tea. What's tea? O yes, I remember. No thank you. Some nettle juice, or squeezed crab apple. Or may be something stronger. Belladonna does it for me. Unlock the cupboard and let me have some."

"We've got some elderflower cordial," said Henry.

"It's a bit insipid," said Rupert, "but it's a kind offer and is gratefully accepted."

Henry went inside to get it. His parents were still asleep upstairs and happily their bedroom overlooked the back garden, so they would not be disturbed by the sound of talking. When Henry returned to the front garden, Rupert was lying on top of the wall singing happily to himself.

"It's a beautiful day," he said, "in a beautiful world, full of people, full of greed – full of opportunity."

"Where've you been?" demanded Henry. "I've been trying to get you. Your mother's been worried about you."

"My mother!" exclaimed Rupert. "I doubt it."

"Of course she was. You didn't go home last night."

"I don't have a home. Not as such anyway."

"Of course you do."

"Since I've left the mines, I go wherever there's an opening for someone with my particular talents."

"What are you talking about?"

Rupert sat up suddenly. "Sorry, just my little joke. I'll be going home after I leave you. But Henry, o Henry I must tell you, London is such an amazing place. I've been wandering round it. It's been a revelation. At first I was depressed."

"Why was that?" A niggling little suspicion was beginning to grow in Henry's mind.

"Noone seemed poor at first. That was quite a shock. I'd understood that life was a struggle for most people. But I couldn't see anyone dressed in rags or with bare feet."

"Did you try the underground?"

"May be one or two there, and the occasional beggar in a doorway. But everyone seemed so prosperous. What was there for me to do I asked myself? I felt cheated. My heart was heavy. Then I started to pay attention. I took in the advertisements, the newspapers, the magazines – the looks on people's faces. I focused on their inner desires. It was wonderful Henry. The more people have the more they want. There wasn't less scope for me here, there was more."

"Scope to do what'?"

Rupert smiled expansively. "Scope to make their dreams come true."

"That sounds like a new political slogan."

"A new what?" asked Rupert.

"It sounds like something you've spun for the Chancellor."

"I've spun nothing for anyone by that name."

"Come on," said Henry. "I thought he really valued your services."

"Why, does he need gold?"

"What's that got to do with it?"

"Humour me. Does he need gold?"

"Of course he does. I can't think of anyone who needs more gold than him."

"Really! In the entire kingdom?"

"In the entire kingdom."

Rupert squinted at Henry. "Then we were made for each other."

It was the squint. That was the moment Henry knew this was not Rupert. "I'm going to have a shower," he said. "Perhaps I'll see you later."

"O you'll see me later," smirked the ugly little man.

"Good," said Henry, "I'll go in now."

"Prince Henry, it's been an honour to meet you. But to be frank, you don't seem much of a threat."

There was no point pretending any more. "That could make me even more of a threat," said Henry.

"Nice little answer," said the other, "though I still don't think you are. So what I ask myself is, how come you've got such a tremendous reputation?"

"Must all be true!"

"Neither of us believes that for a second. Someone's promoting you. They've started to tell your story before it's happened. It's a bit of a risk. It might never happen at all." He laughed unpleasantly and Henry noticed how yellow his teeth were. In fact Henry noticed more than this. As the minutes drifted by, the person sitting on the wall grew even uglier, knobblier and hairier.

"Mrs Stiltskin isn't going to recognise you," said Henry.

"She'll see what she expects. I'm not that different."

"Why are you here?" asked Henry.

"Business expansion. New opportunities. Market need."

"And where's Rupert?"

"Where do you think?" cried Rumpelstiltskin.

He jumped onto the pavement and ran down the street. Henry let him go. He had no idea what else he could do.

Chapter 7

One riddle is solved

HENRY WAS NOT a happy individual. He had a gloomy breakfast, then went up to his room. He was beginning to accept that he was playing a part in what was going on, whether he liked it or not. That must be why Gervase was trying to find him, why the phouka were trying to stop him and why everyone kept calling him Prince Henry. He wanted none of this. His life might have been boring – well was a bit boring – but at least he had a plan and a realistic expectation that he would become a successful lawyer. He now felt that his safe, orderly progress to legal glory was being put at risk by a lot of unwanted and inexplicable events. This was completely unfair.

It was at this point, while his mind was grappling with such intractable problems, and so was entirely relaxed about web sites, that he realised how to get into the parallelreality.universe site . The solution just popped into his head. He had to open two browser windows. In the first he called up www.worldoflegends.com , then found the link for www.parallelreality.universe and the sign which read:

Find the password then enter a parallel
reality where magic and fable truly exist

PASSWORD:

In the second browser he again called up www.worldoflegends.com and the link for www.parallelreality.universe . This time there was nothing about a password. It was the same as three nights ago. He saw one word only. **ENTER.** He clicked - and he was in!

The solution was that simple. Opening a second browser window and finding the same site was like entering a parallel universe, so there was no password. Or may be the whole operation was the password. Whatever. He was there!

He quickly set up his webcam. He went straight to the 'The maiden in the turret'. Aurelia was asleep – a sleeping angel. He had better not wake her up. Henry was deeply disappointed. Still, he would explore other parts of the site. He wondered what had happened to Gervase, for whom he felt a vague responsibility, although this was extremely unfair. Henry had never wanted to take responsibility for anything except – at some vague point in the future – the English legal system. Yet without any choice in the matter he had been established as a hero and had failed to live up to this at the very first opportunity. True, he had not realised at the time he was supposed to be a hero, but even if he had, it would have made no difference. He would still have run from the phouka.

Henry guessed where Gervase should be if he had managed to escape. He clicked on 'hall of the swan Lords'. In a vast smoky space were ten young men who would look perfect in a rugby team. They were broad, battle scarred individuals with uncompromising body parts. They had muscles everywhere they could exist and in a number of places they had no business to be. Their fancy clothes and page boy hair styles were completely absurd on such enormous brutes. There was one other young man of much slighter build who seemed less absurd in that medieval costume, subject only to the wing peeping out of his left sleeve.

"So tell us again," demanded one of the bulkier brothers, "how you and the great hero overcame the phouka!" He could hardly speak for laughing.

"I've already explained," said Gervase, aggrieved, "we tried to beat a tactical retreat. To sort of regroup —"

"Regroup!"

"Yes," protested Gervase, "until we could find somewhere more propitious. I told you, neither of us had a weapon."

"What hero doesn't have a weapon?" demanded another brother.

"I don't know," said Gervase, "but this one didn't."

"He was a fraud," said a third brother, "You're too gullible."

"Leave him alone," ordered a young woman's voice from somewhere out of view. "None of you is the brightest candle on the mantelpiece!"

The brothers subsided a little. Gervase smiled good humouredly. "Don't you bother about me sis," he said. "I can look after myself."

"Of course you can," said the young woman moving next to him. She was wearing a pink gown with trailing sleeves. She had dark brown hair, rosy lips and was extremely pretty. "But that didn't stop me worrying about you."

"We were all worried," said the brother who seemed the eldest. "He knows that."

"Of course I do," beamed Gervase. "All right, I admit it was touch and go. One minute they were surrounding Prince Henry and me. The next minute it was just me, with no sign of Prince Henry —"

"That sounds like a coward, not like a hero," said a brother.

"— and then they had disappeared altogether and I was safe. And what's more, back in familiar territory. Say what you like, I'm sure Prince Henry had something to do with that. He saved me. I don't know how, but he did."

"Do me a favour," scoffed a brother.

"I just hope you're right," said the eldest brother to Gervase. "We need a hero."

"Not to see off the phouka," said the largest of the brothers.

"May be not," said the eldest. "But there are other things going on which worry me. A very serious dragon nearly got killed by a no account knight. A troll turned to stone —"

"They're more or less stone already," said the largest brother.

"Yes," agreed the eldest, "nine tenths. But not completely. They still need to move. Also a witch, trying to turn a prince into a frog, actually turned herself into a frog —"

"Nice one!"

"And a rebellion is brewing against that very wicked Queen, you know, the one with the magic mirror."

"But Adolphus," said his sister. "It sounds like good news."

"Sounds like, yes," said Adolphus. "I don't think it is. It's against the natural order of things." The nine bulky brothers agreed. "Evil does get defeated of course, but it doesn't simply collapse on its own."

"May be Prince Henry's behind it," suggested Gervase.

"May be," said Adolphus. "Because it isn't right this way."

"You just want a fight," said his sister, sounding angry.

"Nothing wrong with a fight," said Adolphus. "It's traditional."

"Traditional," said Henry scornfully, forgetting that he might be heard.

Gervase whirled round and gawped at him. "It's Prince Henry," he cried, "or part of him!"

The others all turned as well.

"Only his head and shoulders," observed the largest brother. "Perhaps he lost the rest. Or may be he's a ghost prince!"

"Or may be the rest of him ran away!" said one of the others.

"Let him speak for himself," said Adolphus. "I want to hear what he has to say."

"My name *is* Henry —" began Henry.

"Greetings Prince Henry," said Adolphus politely, whatever he was feeling inside.

"Prince is only my —" Henry started to explain and then decided not to. Before he disclaimed a title he thought he would see if it brought him any advantages. He might not be brave, but at least he would be cunning. "Greetings," he replied.

"Why do you not show all of yourself?"

"It's a bit difficult to answer," said Henry, "but I'm all here, I can assure you."

"We've only got your word for that," said the largest brother.

"See, here's an arm." Henry passed it in front of the webcam.

"That was an arm, I grant you," said Adolphus, "but it wasn't there for very long."

How could Henry possibly explain that he was in front of a camera and that they were seeing him on a screen which must exist only when the two worlds linked up - a screen which was so positioned to give him a much fuller view of them than they had of him.

"Prince Henry was definitely complete when I first met him," said Gervase helpfully.

"May be he's under a curse," suggested his sister. "You've all been there boys so you should be a bit more sympathetic."

"Well, it is a sort of a curse," said Henry, who was commenting more on the way his life was going.

"I was telling them," said Gervase, "that you must have done something to get rid of the phouka."

"That was kind of you," said Henry.

"In that case," said Adolphus," we are in your debt. By our code that debt must be repaid again and again."

"Well," said Henry, "I appreciate that. But there's nothing —" A thought struck him. "I suppose you don't know how to locate the maiden in the tower?"

"Which maiden would this be?" asked Adolphus. "There's quite a lot of that sort of thing."

"The - a - miller's daughter?"

"Sorry, no. We could try to trace her for you?"

"It doesn't matter," said Henry, feeling rather embarrassed, especially as the pretty sister was gazing at him intently. "It was good to meet you."

He went back to the main map. What explained the endless reference to him as Prince Henry? Was there someone called Prince Henry in that other world? Was it his double, like Rumpelstiltskin was Rupert's? Yet if there were such a person, Henry had the impression he would have come across that individual on the website or in a story.

Where to go next? He remembered what Adolphus had said about the wicked Queen facing a rebellion. He knew who that was and he was quite interested in seeing her, and also having another word with the magic mirror, which seemed aware of a world outside its own. Perhaps it would give up a few secrets. It might also know where to find Rupert, or the miller's daughter. He clicked on 'The magic mirror'. When the mists cleared he was gazing once more at the red and black room. It was empty, but outside he could hear the sound of a crowd shouting. A stone was hurled against the window, which seemed to crack but then restored itself.

"So you're back again," said the mirror, which was

clear. "And I can see you properly this time. Could just be better definition, but you don't seem quite so wishy-washy."

"You're in a better mood then!"

"I'm in a perfectly good mood, thank you, all things taken into consideration."

"What things?"

"Yes," said the mirror, "how can I help you?"

"Please," said Henry in a more emollient tone, "can you tell me my name?"

"That's a strange request," replied the mirror, then paused while another stone bounced against the window. "They're wasting their time. She's still far too strong for them — Your name. Where? Here or there?"

"Here."

"Prince Henry, though I can't find your kingdom at the moment. Perhaps if you came through your kingdom might turn up."

"Came through! How?"

"That's not the question you want to ask me most is it?"

"No," admitted Henry. "The miller's daughter – is she dead?"

"It should have been the question," said the mirror. "As for the miller's daughter, no she isn't."

The voice of a furious woman could be heard outside the door.

"It's the Queen," said the mirror. "Watch if you want but make sure she can't see you."

"Why should I care?" asked Henry, who was irritated with the mirror and had no intention of being lectured by it.

"Please yourself," said the mirror. "I'm only thinking of you."

For some reason, Henry accepted the advice and turned off the webcam. The door opened and a strikingly beautiful woman entered. She had pale, almost white skin, and lustrous black hair. Her eyes too were almost black, but sparkled amethyst, reflecting the lanterns and the candles. Her lips were like a hard scarlet carving. She was wearing a crimson robe and a tall, twisted silver crown. Henry had never seen anyone radiate so much power.

The Queen strode across to the mirror. "You can tell me how vulnerable I've become." Her voice was low and cold.

"Your Majesty," said the mirror, "every person who sees you is struck by the power of your presence."

"You aren't a person," returned the Queen, "and I expect the truth from you."

"There is no more powerful individual than you in this kingdom."

"That is simply playing with words. Of course there isn't. But that doesn't mean I'm as strong as I was. And what about outside the kingdom?"

"Who can say what goes on throughout —"

"You can. And you really have, so what is the point of pretending with me? Day by day I'm growing weaker and I can't understand why. They sense it. Who would have dared rebel a year ago?"

"There are always fools —" began the mirror but the Queen glared at him. "O all right, nobody."

"Quite so," said the Queen. "If this goes on, they'll win in the end." She stared hard at the mirror. "Tell me.

That image you showed me recently, that ugly face which gave you a bad feeling. Was that the face of someone who intends to destroy me?"

"Isn't it difficult to get questions right!" said the mirror in a musing sort of way.

"What's that supposed to mean?" snapped the Queen.

"Sorry," said the mirror, "I'm rambling. The answer to your question is – it's the face of someone who wants to help you."

"Can he?"

"Yes he can, your Majesty."

"Where is he? What is he?"

"He's on his way here. He's a sort of spinner and very clever indeed."

"Haven't I heard of him? It sounds like that vile little creature who makes people guess his name."

"It does, doesn't it."

"Well I know his name, so he needn't try that on with me."

"He won't, your Majesty"

"What does he want in return?"

"Opportunity," said the mirror.

Yet another stone bounced against the window.

"You're sure he can turn things round?" asked the Queen.

"Ooh yes."

"In that case I'm going to massacre those peasants. I so need a bit of light relief." She turned and walked swiftly out of the room.

Henry turned the webcam back on.

"Why didn't you want her to see me?" he asked the mirror.

"Why would you want her to, you silly boy? She's dangerous. At least you have some advantage over her at the moment. You've seen her fears and her power."

"Yes, but she's not in my world – OK, that isn't a guarantee we won't meet, is it?"

"Exactly."

"Will we?"

"I don't foretell the future," said the mirror. "I reflect the present, which is much more useful, though people rarely believe it."

"Then can you tell me who is coming to help the Queen? Is it Rupert?"

"That's not the name he uses and who can blame him! 'Rupert', I ask you!"

"Does he call himself Rumpelstiltskin then?"

"If he were Rumpelstiltskin, that's the last name he'd call himself."

"You can be such a pain," said Henry. "What's his name?"

" 'the Spinner'," replied the mirror. "And so can you."

"I'm sorry, but I'm just anxious —"

"I've been on too long," interrupted the mirror. "I'm running down. If you want to ask me anything else, make it another day – and for pity's sake, do try and keep it focused."

The mirror went cloudy. From outside somewhere came the insufficiently muffled sounds of screaming and violence. Henry went quickly back to the main map.

Since their last conversation the mirror must have

been doing quite a bit of thinking, or whatever reflective processes it went through, because it was no longer suspicious of him. It was also aware that he was known in two worlds. Not many people could claim that, thought Henry, although he would be more than content with one world, particularly if that world were sealed against intrusion by any other.

Henry let his eye wander over the map. He noticed for the first time there was more of it than he had appreciated. It was necessary to scroll down or across the screen. When he did, he discovered places like 'Sheherezade's bedroom', 'palace of the monkey King' and 'inside the genie's lamp', the last of which interested him greatly. He had never previously considered the extent of the world of legends, but obviously it covered myths and stories throughout the whole of his world. Did that mean anyone on the globe could contact this other world if they found out about it and then worked out, or were told, how to gain access?

Gain access. What did that mean? More than simply visiting it on a website? Yet when could the boundaries be crossed? The mirror had spoken of his coming through as though there was nothing wrong. Thanks all the same, but he had no wish to come through – except it would have been nice to meet —

He decided to check the 'The maiden in the turret' one more time. And she was awake! Gorgeous, golden, without the frightening perfection of the wicked Queen, but beautiful in a warm, attainable sort of way, which made Henry groan inwardly. After all, she was not attainable, she was in a different world. How sad she looked, leaning on the window, staring at a grey, rainy sky.

"Hello," said Henry. It was not an exciting sort of greeting but it was to the point.

The girl turned round, and a hopeful expression appeared in her eyes. That was nice. "Prince Henry! You're back again. Or at least part of you is. Are you going to help me?"

"I – hope so," said Henry. "What's happening?"

"It's all gone terribly wrong. I've been badly let down."

"The gold, you mean."

"Yes! How did you know?"

"Mmm – a little bird told me."

"Of course. They see everything don't they?"

"Yes," said Henry. "I thought something dreadful had happened to you."

"Well, it will soon," said the girl. "The King was furious when I didn't give him the third lot of gold. He was going to kill my father and me straight away, but I convinced him I was having an off day. He said I had better get things right tonight or my head will definitely have an off day tomorrow."

"What a swine," cried Henry.

"That's what I thought," said the girl. "It's not my fault that ugly little munchkin wouldn't make any more gold for me."

"I read - I mean, I heard he said he didn't know how to."

"But that doesn't make any sense. He's already done it twice."

"I'm afraid he might have been telling the truth."

"Oh damn," said the girl, "Then I'm done for – unless —" She smiled at him with complete trust, "you're going to save me. You are, aren't you, I can tell."

"I can't think of anything I want to do more," replied Henry with complete honesty, but did not go on to explain the substantial barriers in his way.

"What's your plan?" she asked. "Are you going to break down the door and fight the guards? In which case I suggest that all of you is required, not just your handsome face."

Handsome! "Well," replied Henry, "that is always a possibility." That was when his plan came to him. He knew it was wrong, he had no idea how to make it work, but he had to save that girl. "First though I'm going to try to get hold of some gold. I think I might be able to do that, although getting it through to you could be a problem."

"That's a bit less heroic," said the girl. "Still, as long as it works. And then we can live happily ever after."

"Yes please," said Henry, who liked that suggestion in principle although had little idea what it might mean in practice.

"Don't be too long," said the girl, "or I might not be in one piece when you get back."

"Before I go," said Henry, "Can I ask you your name?"

"Aurelia," said the girl, and smiled the most wonderful smile.

Henry blushed.

CHAPTER 8

The contract

YES, HENRY HAD a plan. All he had to do was to execute it. The first part required him to contact Rumpelstiltskin. He rang Rupert's mobile number. There was only Rupert's message. It then occurred to Henry that Rumpelstiltskin might have no idea how to answer a phone, or even know what a phone was. It depended on what he had learned before he came through – and if so, who had taught him? – and since his arrival.

He phoned Mrs Stiltskin. It seemed that Rupert had come home that morning, but then gone off to the Treasury, where he still was. What would they make of him there, Henry wondered? Mind you, everyone in government seemed so odd anyway, they probably wouldn't notice a thing.

Henry thought a bit further. If Rumpelstiltskin had gone off to the Treasury, this required more than boldness and cunning. Someone must have told him where it was and what he was supposed to be doing there. And someone must have told him how to find Henry's house.

That was a someone whose identity Henry could easily guess. Rupert.

Henry's phone rang.

"Hello," said Henry.

"Am I addressing Prince Henry?" asked a voice which sounded like Rupert's.

"Yes," said Henry.

"How exciting," said the voice which sounded like Rupert's, although it obviously belonged to Rumpelstiltskin. "To think that I'm speaking to you from so many leagues away."

"Miles," said Henry.

"Miles?"

"We measure distance in miles not leagues."

"O," said Rumpelstiltskin, "I thought I read something about kilometres."

"No," said Henry, "that's in Europe."

"I've also been reading about Europe. It's not the same as England is it?"

"Certainly not," replied Henry.

"Well, Prince Henry, how come you've summoned me?"

"I haven't summoned you. I simply left you a message."

"It sounded like a summons to me. And that can only mean one thing. You need my help. Prince, I am honoured. I am yours to command."

"I don't – need your – help," faltered Henry.

"That's not how you came across," said Rumpelstiltskin. "I can always tell when people are desperate."

"I'm not desperate. I simply want to enter into an arrangement with you."

" 'An arrangement'!" cried Rumpelstiltskin. "What lovely words!"

"Really, it's more a question of asking you to complete what you'd already started."

"Is that a sort of negotiating tactic?" enquired Rumpelstiltskin good-naturedly. "It won't work you know. I've got a pretty standard approach. And a set of standard fees and conditions."

"Look —" began Henry.

"That's exactly what I intend to do," said Rumpelstiltskin. "This is a useful piece of magic, but I won't make a bargain without looking you in the face. Would you do me the honour of coming round to my house. Where incidentally I am promised something called chicken karma for dinner. Why should I eat a chicken's destiny? I'd much rather eat the chicken itself."

"It's chicken korma," said Henry, "and I'd rather not come to your house. Can I meet you somewhere else?"

"Wherever you say, your Highness," said Rumpelstiltskin. "I am but a mere servant."

"How about in a pub?"

"Whatever is that?"

"An inn."

"That sounds an excellent idea. I have a prodigious thirst for ale."

"Can you find the Three Horseshoes in Heath Street?"

"The *Three* Horseshoes! What a cautious innkeeper. Are they lucky for him?"

"I'm sorry?"

"I'll be there your Highness. Trust me."

"No, I don't, but I'll see you there at eight."

And at quarter to eight Henry set off for the pub.

"Where did you say you were going?" asked his mother.

"I didn't," replied Henry.

"Well, where are you going?"

"The Three Horseshoes."

"Oh, that's unlike you."

"Are you a maudlin drunk or a happy drunk?" enquired his father. "Did I tell you about the time when I and three mates —"

"Give me strength," said Henry and left.

The interior of the Three Horseshoes was a Victorian reconstruction with no atmosphere which had replaced a down at heel bar with far too much atmosphere and very few customers. Henry had been too young to notice what it used to be like. Nor had he ever met the woman who ran the pub theatre upstairs. She would have told him the pub was on a ley line and that would have been useful information.

It was now a very crowded place and Henry was self-conscious about going in, which was stupid as nobody there knew him. It was just that there were lots of lively young people having fun, which was not something he did. Nevertheless, he could hardly stay outside, so he bought himself half a pint, which he sipped without pleasure as he disliked beer. He found himself a corner and waited. After about fifteen minutes Rumpelstiltskin sauntered in, wearing an ill fitting suit and trainers. He gazed about him with an air of such benevolence it was truly scary. Some drinkers smiled back at him, curiously unperturbed by his hideous face.

"Prince, I salute you," said Rumpelstiltskin with a bow and an unpleasant leer. "This is an excellent inn, extremely well situated." He squinted at Henry. "Though I suspect you are not bothered by that."

"What can I get you?" asked Henry.

"I see a sign about traditional ales," beamed Rumpelstiltskin. "A yard of traditional ale would be most restorative."

"I'll get you a pint," said Henry and went over to the bar. When he returned, Rumpelstiltskin was engaged in animated conversation with some people at the next table.

"Delightful people," said Rumpelstiltskin, turning back to Henry. "Very aspirational. Now how can I be of service to you?" He picked delicately at a large pimple on his nose and Henry felt sick. The sooner he got on with this —

"I need some gold," he said.

"Do you indeed!" cried Rumpelstiltskin. "Then I wish you good health." He picked up his glass and slurped down the whole pint at once, earning some applause from the people at the next table. "Another drink to celebrate!"

Henry duly fetched another pint.

"How much gold, your Highness?" enquired Rumpelstiltskin.

"Quite a lot."

"Then I wish you even better health." He also downed the second pint in one, though spilled a bit of it on his suit.

"I suppose you want another drink," said Henry.

"I do indeed, but I hate drinking alone. I'll get us both something."

Rumpelstiltskin made his way amiably to the bar, returning with another pint for himself and a glass of clear liquid, a piece of lemon and some ice for Henry, who did not normally touch spirits. A double vodka with lots of tonic is an insidious drink on a warm evening, especially when taken by someone who is hot and bothered. It soon disappeared and Rumpelstiltskin obligingly went back to the bar, informing Henry he had no real idea what that drink was, but the barman had promised it was both refreshing and suitable for someone who didn't like beer.

"You see Rumpel," said Henry leaning back in his chair, "I've got to help her. Just got to."

"Of course you do," said Rumpelstiltskin in an encouraging tone.

"If anything happened —"

"You must make sure it doesn't."

"I will. I certainly will. I may not have been much of a hero until now, but it's going to be different."

"Your Highness, I applaud you," and he raised his glass again. It seemed only polite for Henry to do the same. How easily it all slid down. Henry went over to the bar and bought the same again.

"And who is the object of your affections?"

"The miller's daughter. The damsel in the tower."

"Oh," said Rumpelstiltskin, "That's a tricky one."

"Yes," said Henry, "because she needs lots of gold."

"I was attempting to meet that need – third and final delivery, 10 bagfuls of best quality florins, as per order – when I was removed from the tower."

"I know," said Henry.

"For a moment I was speaking to my double in a blue glade. Then I found myself in your delightful world."

"Yeah, I know," said Henry, slipping slightly to one side on the plush, mock-Victorian banquette.

"Your Highness," said Rumpelstiltskin, "do I understand you wish me to spin the rest of the gold?"

"That's it Rumpel."

"I'd be delighted. Just lead me to a spinning wheel."

"Oh – does it actually have to be a spinning wheel – because I don't have any idea where to find one."

"That's the way I work," replied Rumpelstiltskin. "A loom might do at a pinch."

Henry looked sadly into his empty glass. Finding a spinning wheel would not be impossible, but would add a complication. "Hold on, what about a sewing machine?"

"What's that?"

"A machine – for sewing. It lets people sew – using a machine. It's not difficult."

"It sounds possible."

"Your – Rupert's – mother's got one. You could try it out."

"Agreed," cried Rumpelstiltskin. "A toast I think."

"Ooh yes," said Henry, "but I can't get up at the moment."

"Please," said Rumpelstiltskin, "permit me," and he made his way over to the bar yet again, returning with another pint and another double vodka.

"I'm just going to sip this one," said Henry.

"And now, my terms," said Rumpelstiltskin.

"Like a contract," smiled Henry. "I'm a brilliant law student you know."

"Your brilliance is legendary."

"Really!"

"Absolutely, although completely unproven. Let me explain what I require. It's a trifle." He beamed at Henry, and then beamed at everyone at the next table, who beamed back.

Henry did his best to beam too, though this was not a facial expression common to him. "Ask away – and I will give you my learned opinion."

"You have to guess my name."

"I know your name. It's Crumpelstiltskin."

"Not my first name, Prince Henry, my second name."

"O, your second name."

"And if you don't, there'll be a penalty clause."

"A penalty clause! It's a pretty serious contract then."

Rumpelstiltskin grinned at Henry who understood that grin meant unpleasant business, but was no longer in a state to be upset by it. He was interested only in the thought of signing a contract with a penalty clause, because that made him feel like a man. This was a bit sad really, as he recognised at a later stage.

"Incontrovertibly," exclaimed Rumpelstiltskin. "It's the fourth most serious contract there is. If you fail to comply, you give me your reputation."

"I don't have a reputation," said Henry.

"Then it's a very small penalty."

"What's the serious — est penalty clause."

"That you give up your soul. But I'm not authorised to ask for that – at the moment."

"I agree," said Henry. "A toast —"

"I congratulate you," said Rumpelstiltskin. "No havering about. Very princely behaviour." He produced an envelope from his jacket and pulled out two pieces of paper. On both were these words:

> *"I Rumpelstiltskin do undertake to produce for Prince Henry ten bagfuls of the best quality florins at the time of his choosing. Price: that he should guess my second name and tell me what it is at a time of my choosing. Penalty for failure to guess correctly: his reputation.*
>
> *Signed:*   "

"You've already drawn up the contracts!" said Henry. "How did you —?"

"A lucky hunch," replied Rumpelstiltskin and he produced a biro with a delighted flourish.

Henry leaned across the table, knocking over his glass, as was inevitable. Rumpelstiltskin obligingly mopped up the liquid with his sleeve, which he sucked at approvingly, then signed both copies. Henry did the same. Rumpelstiltskin pocketed one and Henry, after a vague attempt to do the same, stuffed his copy down the front of his T-shirt.

"All that remains," said Rumpelstiltskin, "is for you to tell me when you wish the goods to be produced. Two-o-clock in the morning is a good time, but I'm at your disposal."

"Two-o-thing in the morning," repeated Henry, more or less. "A very good time. But, a little bit early – or may be a little bit late, depending – How about nine-o-clock in the morning?"

"Excellent," said Rumpelstiltskin, jumping to his feet. "Pleasure doing business etc etc. I'll take my leave."

"But where —"

"You'll find it. Goodnight to you." He waggled his head in what was presumably a jocular fashion, bade farewell to the group at the next table as if parting from some very dear friends, danced his way to the door, gave a little twirl, received some applause, and left.

Henry wanted to leave too, but he found this was less easy than it should have been. Nevertheless, he did stagger to his feet, then bumped his way out of the bar into the street. The air outside was fresher than before and a real contrast to the warm, smoky atmosphere in the pub. It had quite an effect, because Henry very nearly passed out and would have fallen on his face on the pavement if people hadn't caught him. They took him round the corner, sat him on a bench, got him a large glass of water, then tactfully removed themselves when Henry was sick.

CHAPTER 9

Delivery problems

SOMEHOW HENRY GOT home. His parents were watching television. With immense effort he called out cheerfully, "I'm back mum and dad," – fortunately his parents were too engrossed in their programme to notice such atypical friendliness – and crawled upstairs to his bedroom. He threw off some off his clothes and went to sleep.

He woke up with a start only three hours later. It was half past midnight. It wasn't that he was feeling sick, or that his head throbbed. A dreadful thought had come to him. He had been tricked, or rather he had let himself be tricked. He had a made an arrangement with Rumpelstiltskin but forgotten to mention one crucial element. The gold was to be delivered not to him but to the maiden in the tower. Obviously Rumpelstiltskin had realised this, so even if it were not explicitly in the contract, it must be an implied term. Surely?

Henry dragged himself out of bed with as much difficulty as he had feared. He found his mobile phone. Never mind the hour, and anyway that tricky little monster should be sewing his gold – and how would that work exactly? Henry made the call.

"O dear," said Rumpelstiltskin. "What a regrettable omission."

"Yes, but you know that's what I meant."

"I only know what we agreed, Prince Henry. The gold will be delivered to you."

"But how can I get it to the tower?"

"Beats me."

"But you came from that world."

"So I did."

"In that case —"

"Your Highness, you're preventing me from fulfilling my side of the bargain. This sewing machine is a reasonable substitute for a spinning wheel, but the transformation takes a lot longer. There isn't a moment to waste." He rang off.

Henry groaned. The only person who must have the knowledge to help him was no longer in this world. Would Rupert even bother though? What was in his mind nowadays? Two nights ago he had given contradictory messages, at one point apparently saving Henry's life, but at another not seeming to care whether he was killed or not. There was only one way to find out. Henry would have to track him down in the world of legends. He turned on his computer and his webcam, then entered www.parallelreality.universe .

First of course he had to check on Aurelia. She was still in the tower, thank goodness, fast asleep on a straw mattress. The little angel. The next thing was to begin the search for Rupert. He could be anywhere, and not necessarily in a place where he could be seen on the website. The swan lords might have heard something about his whereabouts and be willing to seek him out. But there was a much better source of information. Henry clicked on 'The magic mirror'. He immediately jumped to one side and covered over his webcam, because the room was full of people.

The Queen was there, coldly beautiful as ever. She had guests. A hideous, whiskery old woman in a tall black hat; a white bearded, cruel nosed man, wearing a robe covered in silver stars and moons; a tall man in full evening dress, his eyes dead, his face white and bloodless: a young woman with greeny-grey skin and snakes instead of hair who sat on her own behind a screen. There were many others, some almost animals. Satyr, goblin, wraith – what were they? Their malevolence was so powerful it seemed to leak through the screen. Behind them hung the mirror, cloudy and unreflecting.

"This is the most protected room in my palace," said the Queen. "You can speak freely. How is it affecting each of you?"

"I cast my spells," replied the old woman, "but not all of them deliver. Another curse failed yesterday. The shame of it. Mind you," she cackled, "when I tried it again it worked. Oh the look of surprise on that man's face as the maggots burst out of his skin!"

"I stood in the shadows," said something with horns and a long tail, "and tried to frighten a child, but he just laughed at me. It was a real shock to both my systems. He stopped laughing though when I crushed his head! – Perhaps I shouldn't have done that?"

"I went to bite a neck," said the man in full evening dress, "and almost found a stake through my heart. How could such a thing happen? I've never failed to sense danger before. Of course, the danger was soon over – for me. I sucked her blood as slowly as I could to make sure she really suffered."

"Enough with the catalogue of failure," interrupted the white bearded man. "I get the picture that most of you are no longer regarded as invincible."

"We may not be regarded as invincible," said the creature with the horns, "but in practice we still are."

"But for how long?" asked the Queen. "That is the question. How long before one of us is too slow or fails to get it right at all?"

"In my case," asserted the white bearded man, "that isn't happening and it will never happen. There's no other wizard anywhere near my level. I'm quality, and when you're quality, nothing can take it away."

"Impressive," said the Queen dryly, "but I wouldn't bank on it."

"It's the look in their eyes that worries me," said the gorgon. "I can see them beginning to suspect I might be beatable."

"So true," said the vampire, "our reputations are beginning to suffer. And our reputations are an essential part of what keeps us on top."

"My point exactly" said the Queen. "And as I firmly believe that our powers are fading, our reputations are even more important than they were."

"Why should our powers fade?" asked the whiskery old witch. "I don't understand."

"Built in obsolescence," said the wizard complacently. "The quality's got to be there in the first place. When it isn't, things break down. No?"

"We can speculate all we like," said the Queen, "but so what? We need to take action."

"Find our why our powers are fading," said the gorgon.

"That obviously," said the Queen, "but it could take a bit of time. We can't wait. We must do something to protect ourselves now."

"Which is —?" enquired the wizard.

"Boost our reputations."

"How about a bloodbath," suggested the creature with the horns. "Just think if we were to all act together!"

"A bloodbath —" murmured the vampire.

"If we all act together," said the Queen, as if talking to a class of very small children, "all the heroic types will act together against us. We will win. But at a cost. Take it from me, some of us won't survive." There was a thoughtful silence. "I've brought in a specialist adviser. He's got another approach entirely."

The Queen went over to the door and opened it. She gestured to someone who now entered the room. He was small, ugly and wearing an unflattering orange tunic. It looked like Rumpelstiltskin. It was actually Rupert.

"Tell them your plan," ordered the Queen.

Rupert smiled charmingly and looked round the room, making eye contact with everyone present, except the gorgon. "Your Majesties, ladies and gentlemen, mm, others – my plan is very simple. I aim to make you popular."

"That I'd like to see," said the wizard.

"Well if not popular," said Rupert, unperturbed, "valued. For your unique gifts."

" 'Valued' is good," said the wizard less abrasively, "although some will be valued more than others."

"I have supper ready for you all," said the Queen, almost sounding genuinely hospitable. "While we eat, my adviser can tell us some of his plans."

She led the way out of the room. After they had left, the door shut and locked itself.

Boost their reputations. That reminded Henry. He had a reputation in that world and had already nearly lost it through feeble and cowardly behaviour in this. Now he had risked it again by his imprudent contract with Rumpelstiltskin. The thought of losing it bothered him a great deal.

What was Rupert up to? And what would happen if Rupert were successful? What would happen to Rupert if he were not?

"There you go," said the mirror, beginning to brighten up. "It's mindboggling. Especially that orange tunic. What's all that about!"

"You noticed me."

"O yes, Prince Henry, I noticed you. And that wizard might have done. I'm not sure. He really is very gifted."

"I've never seen a group like that before."

"They don't come any worse."

"I need your help," said Henry.

"I'm not a removal service."

"You know what I want?"

"I told you last time, I reflect the present."

"Can you help me?"

"Possibly."

"Will you help me?"

"A much better question," said the mirror.

"How do I send those ten bagfuls of gold through to the tower?"

"You don't."

"There must be a way. People travel between your world and mine."

"You want to come through as well?"

"No, I just want to get the gold to Aurelia." His heart was saying the opposite, because he so longed to meet Aurelia. But she might not like him in the flesh. Another thing was, he was uncertain about the world of legends. If he went in, he would want to be sure he could get out again, unless that is he really could live happily ever after with her.

"To sum up your thoughts," said the mirror, "it's safer to stay in your own world."

"Yes," said Henry, feeling ashamed of himself. He had shown himself up as a coward once more.

"Of course," said the mirror, "there'll be things you can find out here you might really want to know."

"Such as?"

"The answer to any riddle Rumpelstiltskin might have set you."

"There'll be ways round that. The internet might help."

"The what?"

Henry was about to answer, but stopped. "You've just asked me a second question. If I answer it, will you answer one of mine?"

"Is that the question you want answered?"

"No, and that's the third question you've asked me."

"We're very sharp tonight," said the mirror with what sounded like mild approval. "Though not sharp enough to pick up what I was telling you. Never mind. I'll give you one piece of information and it comes to you from your world."

Some writing started to form on the surface of the mirror. Henry stared at it in disbelief. It seemed to be an e-mail address: wilfred@yourservice.co.uk .

"That's – too weird," he exclaimed, sounding the least like a young lawyer that he had ever sounded.

"May be so," said the mirror, "But not as weird as that orange tunic. Good night."

"No please, I need to ask you some more."

"I know you need to. But I don't need to answer. More to the point, I don't want to answer. Come back to me when you've learned a bit more."

"I should have asked about Rumpelstiltskin's second name."

"You should indeed."

"Then I will."

"Good night sweet prince," said the mirror and gently clouded over.

Henry sat and looked at the screen. He had wasted that opportunity. And although he knew where Rupert was, how was he going to speak to him? He would have to approach the swan lords. In the meantime he had nothing except an e-mail address. He supposed he had better try it. He sent the following message: "I have been given your name as someone who might help me. Can you please tell me what service you provide?"

Almost immediately the following out of office reply was returned: "I am available between 10AM and 6PM and will answer all messages between those hours.

Wilfred's transport and delivery services, no job too small, no challenge too large. Telephone: — "

He would have to wait then. In the meantime, Henry was beginning to feel rather weak and dizzy. He remembered that he should have been drinking lots of water, so struggled downstairs, managed a glass and a half, struggled upstairs and went back to bed. He slept until just before 9. When he opened his eyes he was relieved to find that his headache had gone. He felt a great deal better.

He heard a van pull up outside his house. For a moment he drifted off again. His mother knocked on the door of his room.

"Henry," she said.

"Yes mum."

"Someone has sent you ten parcels. Very heavy apparently. Do you know what they are dear?"

"Em – it's Rupert. I think it's a little joke."

"Well, you have to sign for them. Then do something with them."

Henry got up and went downstairs. Nine parcels were lined up on the step outside the front door. The driver was staggering down the path with the tenth, which chinked as he came along with it.

"They're a bit serious," said the driver. "What you got in them?"

"Gold," replied Henry.

"O, nice one," said the driver.

Henry signed and the driver left. Henry tried to lift one of the parcels. It was extremely heavy.

"I'll move them after breakfast," he said.

He went upstairs.

Ten bags of gold. He could just keep them, in which case he would be set up for life – possibly. Henry was not too sure what that amount of gold would be worth, but it must be a healthy amount. Let Rumpelstiltskin take his reputation in the world of legends. Why did it matter? He never had to visit that site again. He could build up a more useful reputation as a lawyer in this world.

Henry had his breakfast. Then he considered once more the arguments in favour of keeping the gold. After that, as it was now one minute after ten-o-clock, he telephoned Wilfred's Transport and Delivery Services.

"Good morning," said an oldish voice at the other end.

"Is that Wilfred?"

"Unfortunately, yes."

"Have I caught you at a bad time?"

"It's the twenty first century. I'm suffering from stress. Of course it's a bad time."

"Someone said you might be able help me."

"Someone who dislikes me no doubt."

"I don't think so," said Henry. "You are open for business aren't you?"

"It's two minutes past ten. I've been open for an entire two minutes. It's kind of you to call so promptly."

"I need to transport some gold coins."

"From where to where?"

"From here in Hampstead," said Henry, "to – You're just not going to believe me."

"Let me be the judge of that," said the man. His accent was strangely old fashioned, he pronounced 'that' as 'thet', and although most of the time his voice marched briskly from word to word, sometimes it rested on a vowel which could not quite take the weight and wobbled slightly.

"To another world," said Henry.

"I take it I am speaking to Henry Prince," said Wilfred gloomily.

CHAPTER 10

Wilfred

WILFRED ARRANGED TO meet Henry that evening, remarking that this was not a job for normal working hours. Henry had to agree.

He dragged the gold round to the garden shed, accepting it would be insecure and open to inspection by his father. However, getting it upstairs seemed almost beyond him and, presumably, there was a chance Wilfred might be collecting it. Acquiring the gold, thought Henry, had put his reputation at risk. He wondered what sort of price Wilfred would be after.

He wanted to tell Aurelia help might be on its way, but decided it would be best not to raise her hopes. He put on the computer anyway. There was a new story on worldoflegends.com :

> *The Queen and the Spinner walked slowly through the palace garden. The flowers were all shades of black and red. Occasionally a bloom might foolishly start out as another colour. It*

changed pretty quickly when it realised where it was. All the flowers had a strong and sickly perfume which the Spinner found almost overpowering. There were no birds or butterflies. They irritated the Queen.

She listened to the Spinner with interest. Some of what he said was difficult to accept, because his ideas so challenged her way of doing things. She kept her reactions hidden of course, as she did her fear. She was not ashamed of her fear. She understood fear, she caused it in others and she respected it. She met it face to face. But it could not be openly acknowledged, because people would think it a weakness.

The Spinner was excited. He was confident that he could help. He had been promised riches if he were successful – and a variety of unpleasant deaths if he failed. He was neither interested in wealth nor scared of failure. He relished the opportunity and the pleasure of showing how clever he was. He wished his skills to become legendary.

"Now, your Majesty, let's take a look at the main rival for your throne."

"Snow White," said the Queen. "Just saying her name makes me nauseous."

"Am I right in thinking you plan to poison her?"

"Who's been talking?" demanded the Queen. "And how could they? I haven't told anyone. Nobody left alive even knows she's my daughter."

"An educated guess," said the Spinner. "But

if anything happens, people will suspect you and that might lead to a rebellion."

"Not a problem. I can still deal with one of those."

"My point is you'd do much better by announcing she's your daughter then discrediting her."

"How? Snow White is in the dictionary as a definition of goodness."

"First of all, she's royal and she has obligations to her people. Yet she's living a carefree life in the forest. You on the other hand are here day in day out, weighed down —"

"Nothing weighs me down."

"— devoted to ruling the kingdom."

"True," agreed the Queen.

"It's always better when it's true," said the Spinner. "I like to start with the truth. If that doesn't work, then a version of the truth and so on down to an absolute lie if necessary. "

"What else?" asked the Queen.

"Next, your Majesty, consider the background of these dwarves. Miners. Working class. How fitting is it for a Princess to be living with seven members of the working class - cooking and cleaning and washing their clothes? It's not on. Your people are traditionalists. They expect royalty to know its place."

"True again," said the Queen.

"And another thing, has she got a chaperone with her?"

"Of course not."

"Exactly. That's more than enough to damage the reputation of your daughter. Now we have to improve yours."

The Queen inspected the ugly little man in his vile orange tunic. She felt he was getting rather over familiar in his tone. However, she would let it go for the moment.

"What you need," said the Spinner, "is to present a kinder, more compassionate image."

"I don't do kindness and compassion," said the Queen, stepping on a bee which had unwisely landed on the sunny path in front of her.

"But it would help if people thought you might. A few simple acts could go a long way."

"Like —"

"Well, take the next person to be rolled to his death in a spiked barrel."

"You want me to remove a few spikes?"

"Actually, your Majesty, I suggest you don't roll him at all. Commute his sentence to —"

"Regular torture?"

"Well, yes, if you don't feel you can go any further. Something to give people a bit of hope."

"What else?"

"Kiss a few babies."

"I don't like jokes."

"I'm not joking."

"This is going to be even more difficult than I thought," said the Queen.

Rupert was plainly still in the palace. Perhaps the mirror would have an idea how to contact him, so

Henry attempted to enter the parallelreality.universe site. One of those messages came up to say that the site was temporarily unavailable. This did happen to sites of course, but Henry was anxious. He became more anxious as the day progressed and the site remained off-line.

He turned on the six-o-clock news simply to occupy his mind. The second item was about public expenditure. Very shortly the Chancellor of the Exchequer would announce what money the Government would be spending on all areas of its business over the next three years. The Chancellor was seen leaving for the country house where he would finalise his decisions. There was just a glimpse of a passenger in the front seat. It looked like Rumpelstiltskin.

"It had been expected," the news reader was saying, "that little extra money would be available. But a rumour is beginning to spread that the Chancellor will be fairly generous."

The news reader consulted the chief economics editor, who was slightly puzzled, as he could not work out where the money would come from and up until now the Chancellor had a reputation for financial prudence. The news reader then consulted the chief political editor, who was equally startled, but thought it might have something to do with the Chancellor's desire to become Prime Minister. Even so, if the money were not really there, too much generosity would only damage his chances in the long run.

Henry turned off the news. What did he care about the Chancellor's political ambitions? He was far too preoccupied with his ten bags of gold.

At half past six, shortly before dinner, a battered van

drew up outside. Henry opened the front door. Standing there was an old man wearing a crumpled linen suit. He was almost bald except for a determined circle of white hair.

"Good evening," said Henry. "Are you Wilfred?"

"I have to say, I do feel particularly stressed this evening," announced the old man. "Can you see that? You can, can't you, it shows in my face." And he did have a pair of very tense nostrils.

"Yes," replied Henry, who understood that no other answer would do.

"Life has taken its toll. Show me the merchandise."

Henry led Wilfred round the side of the house to the shed.

"Please open a bag."

Henry did so.

"May I inspect the contents?"

Henry agreed. Wilfred pulled out a handful of gold coins, all of which bore the portrait of Queen Elizabeth II.

"I'll say this for him," observed Wilfred, "he's a genuine craftsman. He didn't have to bother with that."

"Are they real gold?" asked Henry.

"O yes," said Wilfred mournfully. "We'd better go."

"To where?"

"To the despatch point, where else? Or have you changed your mind?" He inspected Henry beadily.

"No, but I'd like to know your fees before we go ahead. I'm only a student."

"You want student rates?"

"No. Yes. What are they?"

"There aren't any student rates."

"Oh."

"There aren't any rates at all. This is a free service."

Henry dragged the first bag round to the van. Wilfred sat down in the driver's seat and waited. This went a long way to explaining why this might be a free service, thought Henry, wiping the sweat from his brow. As he put the last bag in the van, his father came out.

"What's going on?" he enquired.

"I've got to deliver some packages," said Henry, perhaps a little furtively.

"What's in them, dangerous drugs?"

"Gold," said Henry.

"No need to be sarcastic," said his father.

"Wasn't that what you were being?" said Henry.

"Your mother says dinner's ready."

"I've got to go in the van."

"Is this some sort of summer job? Surely you could have got something a bit better?"

"The best jobs are all gone," said Henry. "Later."

"Later what?"

Henry grinned at his father, who was looking extremely puzzled. "Goodbye Dad."

The van set off along a familiar route, and Henry himself became puzzled.

"This the way to – um —" he said.

"Rupert's house," said Wilfred.

"Why are we going to Rupert's?" asked Henry anxiously.

"We're not," said Wilfred and turned into the driveway of the huge Victorian house that was crumbling away next door.

"What's going on?"

"Perhaps you'll kindly take the bags inside," said Wilfred.

"Rupert might see us get out."

"Unlikely. Rupert is no longer there and Rumpelstiltskin is at a country retreat with the Chancellor of the Exchequer."

"How do you know all this?"

"I feel a migraine coming on," said Wilfred. "I need some paracetemol and a cup of herbal tea, may be a short lie down. I'm doing too much."

He got out of the van, walked up a few steps and opened his front door. Henry followed him, dragging the first bag of gold, and stood again in that long, cold hallway. This time he could see the heavy furniture covered with yellowing paperbacks, pots of leggy, over the hill plants and all sorts of dusty ornaments.

"You can wait in there," said Wilfred, "I'll be with you in half an hour." He indicated an open door then pulled himself up the staircase to the next floor. Henry hauled in the rest of the gold, shut the front door and went into a living room, where the plants were less frail and the books were less yellow. On the other hand the chintzy armchairs seemed lumpy. There was a huge window at the far end, but the room was dark because of some overgrown bushes pressing against the glass. Henry relaxed in his armchair, which was more comfortable than expected, and gazed at the room. Most quaint were the paintings, all busy scenes from an England which no longer existed except in the minds of American visitors – happy peasants outside a thatched cottage, knights jousting near a castle, merry men in Sherwood forest, a Victorian seaside. But they were pleasing. So was the room, now that he grew used to it. It was decorated in a mellow green and was not so much dark as restful, like a glade in a forest, with a little dappled sunlight squeezing in through the bushes outside the window. Henry slumped into the cushions and dozed off.

He woke up when Wilfred brought in a tray with two cups of tea and some sandwiches. It was actually over an hour after he had arrived

"Everyone tells me I'm overdoing it," said Wilfred.

"I'm sorry to hear it," said Henry.

Wilfred shook his head. "They've got to be stopped."

"Who?"

"Rumpelstiltskin and Rupert. They're going to unsettle things."

"I can see that."

"What are you going to do about it?"

"Me? What's it got to do with me?"

"You're a friend of Rupert. You're in a jam with Rumpelstiltskin. You're supposed to be a hero. It's got a lot to do with you."

Henry did not like the way this was going so he changed the subject. "Can I ask how you know all this?"

"It's my job," answered Wilfred, "and that's all I'm saying. Rupert just thinks I'm an eccentric old fool, which I hope I am, so he pays me no attention. On the other hand, he worked out this house was on a ley line, which is why he liked coming here as a boy. I never let him in again after that Halloween."

"When Rumpelstiltskin came through for the first time?"

"Yes. I had no idea Rupert already knew so much,

even though I was watching him. I've been watching him ever since."

"Why?"

"I recognised how clever he was. I realised that one day he'd break through the barrier. It happens on occasions. And at the moment the barrier is weak. The difference between the two worlds is no longer so clear. The old legends are losing their strength and this world is losing touch with reality. Now that Rumpelstiltskin and Rupert have transferred, the barrier will grow even weaker." Wilfred rolled his shoulders. "Can you see all the tension there?"

"Yes," said Henry, who was beginning to feel quite tense himself.

"What Rupert doesn't understand," continued Wilfred, "is that he's damaging the very place he loves so much. He wants to do things that happen in this world but should never happen there. You'll have to tell him and make him come back."

"I suppose I could when I can get him on a screen."

"It would be far better face to face."

"How can I do that?"

"You can go through and bring him back."

"No," said Henry. (Could he!) "I simply want to get the gold to Aurelia."

"That's not very princely," said Wilfred.

"I'm not a prince."

Wilfred smiled sadly. "You must do what suits you best."

"Why does it matter so much to you?"

"It should matter to everyone," said Wilfred. "Now you've had some sandwiches and built your strength up, you'll have to do some more work. The gold has to go up to the top of the house."

So Henry had to drag the gold up two flights of stairs to the room where he and Rupert had first seen Rumpelstiltskin. The first floor landing had many shelves stuffed full of books and a precarious stack of old newspapers. The second floor landing was gloomy, with more books and various unrecognisable items. He put the gold in the same dilapidated room where Rupert had conjured up, or whatever the technical term was, Rumpelstiltskin. It was stuffy and oppressive. Several dead flies and the odd wasp lay on the window sill. The piles of abandoned clothes were still there. It was a very warm evening and by the final journey Henry was beginning to get extremely irritable. This was all getting out of hand. Once the gold got through, that would be that. He would leave the world of legends alone and go back to his studies. He was a fool to have let himself be led astray.

It was only half past eight and light outside. "Do we have to hang around until midnight?" he asked Wilfred.

"Certainly not," said Wilfred, "I'll be in bed long before then. I need nine hours sleep. Which I never manage because I can't relax enough."

"I thought mysterious happenings had to occur after dark!"

"Perhaps you don't watch Prime Minister's question time," said Wilfred. "The correct place is more important."

"Can I ask you something?" said Henry. "Why are you helping me?"

"I'm not," said Wilfred. "I'm helping to complete the

story of the maiden in the tower. It won't be quite right, because she won't have to solve a riddle, but she's not supposed to die and she needs the gold to prevent that. Please move the gold to the middle of the room and put the bags as close together as possible."

Henry started to do as requested and noticed Wilfred open a fragile notebook. "Ah," he said, with the tiniest hint of scorn, "an incantation?"

"No," said Wilfred. "I'm simply checking to see if all the arrangements are in order."

"Such as —?"

"Such as you standing over the ley line next to the bags."

"Am I?"

"Yes, you are," said Wilfred. "Remember two things, trust in your own legend and listen, really listen, to the mirror.

"That sounds like something out of 'Lord of the Rings'," said Henry disparagingly.

"Doesn't it," said Wilfred. "Enjoy your journey."

"What journey?"

"The one you're going on now."

"What — NO!"

And he was still shouting no as Wilfred and the room faded away.

CHAPTER 11

Arrival and departure

THE FIRST THING he noticed was the smell. It reached him before he saw where he was or had any emotions about it. It was the smell of an unclean body, mouldy straw and damp stonework. It made him feel sick.

Next he took in where he was standing – the turret. Aurelia was staring at him with an expression combining amazement and admiration. She was even prettier in the flesh, but his mind was not prepared to deal with that. It was too busy with masses of panicky thoughts. He was in another world. How could he cope? How could he get back? Could he ever get back? He was absolutely scared out of his wits. "Why me, why me, why me?"

"Why you what?" enquired Aurelia.

Henry was unable to reply.

"Wicked spell," she said. "Well, no, great spell, as it brought you here with —" she opened one of the bags, "— all this gold!" Her voice almost squeaked with excitement.

Henry remained unable to reply.

"Has it taken away your power of speech?" She seemed rather concerned. "Perhaps the spell was stronger than necessary. Or may be one of the ingredients wasn't pure. That can cause unpleasant side effects."

Henry lurched over to the open window, looked down to the moat below and was sick.

"Sit down," said Aurelia kindly, leading him to the one chair. "You're obviously not used to magic."

"No," croaked Henry, but this really meant, "No, I shouldn't be here."

"Well you wouldn't be. You're a man of action."

"No."

"Don't be modest. You have a brilliant reputation."

Henry looked up at her lovely face and somewhere inside a little self-preservation chip kicked in. "Yes."

"I want you to tell me all your adventures."

"Now?"

"No, not now. Now I want to leave this turret, have a bath and make myself beautiful for you. Oh and have my father released."

"Good – plan."

"The King will be here any moment. He comes here every day after breakfast."

"But it's the evening."

"No, it's the morning. You really are disorientated."

"If only that."

From outside the turret door could be heard the sound of footsteps and bolts being unlocked.

"You must stand up," said Aurelia.

"Must I?"

"Yes. It's the King. You must look like a hero – which

now I come to consider it, you don't quite. Why aren't you wearing shining armour or expensive raiment?"

"Raiment?"

"Clothing."

"A side effect of the spell."

The door opened and the King entered, together with a few soldiers. When he saw Henry he cried, "An escape attempt. It won't work. Overpower him."

"This is Prince Henry," said Aurelia.

"Ah," said the King a little less certainly, "you've got some sort of valiant deed planned, I'll be bound."

"If necessary," said Henry surprising himself. "However, let's hope it won't be."

"Absolutely," laughed the King.

"You wanted ten more bags of gold. I've provided them. Now please let this young lady go free."

"Not a problem," said the King. "She's – you've fulfilled her side of the bargain."

"She wants a bath," said Henry, and blushed, "and a, em, gown."

"Silken gown," said Aurelia.

"Silken gown."

"My pleasure," said the King

"And her father —" added Henry.

"Good as done," said the King.

This was all rather easy.

"Come," said the King expansively, "Let us leave this wretched turret. And allow me to say, Prince Henry, I'm greatly impressed with your feat of bringing one two, three — *ten* heavy — yes indeed — bags of gold —" which the King took the precaution of checking "— into the tower unseen by any of my guards outside. I should be angry, you breaking in like this, but, ha ha, of course I'm honoured that my castle should be the scene of your latest exploit. How many times did you have to climb up here, I wonder?"

"I can't reveal that," replied Henry with what he hoped was an enigmatic smile.

"No indeed," said the King. "Mystery is part of the legend."

That was useful information.

The King led them down from the tower and Aurelia was taken away to be reunited with her father, followed by a bath, or possibly the other way round. The smell of unwashed bodies was still fairly pervasive, although the King himself was drenched in some sort of fragrance. They went into a large hall where a sullen young man greeted them. It was the King's son, the Crown Prince, who it turned out was anxious that he would be forced to marry Aurelia.

"Right," said the King to him, "get used to the idea that you're about to be married."

"Are they engaged, your Majesty?" asked Henry.

"Not formally, no, but it's how things are done around here. We put a maiden in the tower on some excuse or other, and should she produce what we ask – gold, silver, diamonds, whatever – she marries the current Crown Prince."

"Do the maidens always manage to come up with the goods?"

"No," said the King. "More often than not they don't. We've had any number of Crown Princes who don't get married until they're really quite elderly monarchs. So," he said to his son, "you should be relieved."

"Well I'm not," said the Crown Prince. "She isn't my type."

"Anyone who produces thirty bags of gold is your type," said the King. "Take it from me." He turned to Henry. "Perhaps you'd care to join us for breakfast. There's a little matter I'd like to raise with you."

"Oh." Henry did not care for the sound of that. He was also put out at the thought of Aurelia marrying the Crown Prince.

"Yes," resumed the King, as they sat eating a variety of cold cooked flesh, crusty rolls, honey and seasonal berries, "it's not something which will cause you any trouble, but would be of great assistance to me. There would obviously be a reward, suitable for a man of your rank and reputation."

"Some sort of derring do required?" suggested Henry, with a tiny laugh.

"Naturally," said the King.

"A violent deed?"

"Momentarily, yes, but nothing you won't have done before."

"Involving —?"

"What you'll like about it is that it's a matter of honour."

"I'm pleased to hear it. And the task is —?"

"It's to avenge one of my knights. He was smashed to death."

"Oh. Dear. Unpleasant."

"And unexpected," said the King.

"I imagine that sort of thing always is."

"I'm not making myself clear," said the King. "He should have been roasted and then eaten."

"Should?"

"That would have been normal. But he was simply discarded. That's quite an insult."

"How, em, did this happen?" But Henry had already guessed.

"He was trying to kill a dragon."

"A dragon."

"Don't be alarmed," said the King. "I wouldn't insult you with an ordinary dragon which any novice knight could dispose of. It's Deathbreather."

"That would be the ancient and legendary dragon which guards so much treasure."

"As it happens, yes," said the King. "Acquiring that great hoard would be an incidental advantage of Deathbreather's death."

"He is pretty vicious," said Henry.

"Indeed he is," agreed the King, "But as you point out, he is very old now and is vulnerable to someone with your legendary skills."

"Naturally," said Henry. "And I will certainly get round to him."

"Your reputation is that you never reject a challenge."

"And I'm not," lied Henry, "but em —" Inspiration came suddenly. "— I'm on a quest to find the Spinner. I can't interrupt a quest midway."

"The Spinner," repeated the King. "I might have heard of him."

At that moment Aurelia was led in, wearing an emerald silk gown and a delightful silver necklace which Henry suspected was a royal family heirloom. She looked ravishing but this still did nothing to cheer up the Crown

Prince, who slumped forlornly in his chair. Aurelia's father, a fat and foolish man, followed behind and was prevented from approaching the King's table.

Henry was in a state of great confusion. One part of him relished sitting in this great hall, with colourful banners over his head and servants attending to his requirements. He was admired by all as a hero, very ego boosting. It was fun, and difficult to take too seriously. It was like being in a pageant or a play. The other part of him remained in the panicky state which had gripped him on arrival. This was another world, very real, with rules of its own. He was known as a Prince. If he were exposed as a fraud, he hated to think what they would do to him, yet how could he possibly carry out heroic deeds or go into battle? He had to find Rupert, or may be the mirror, and get them to help him go back. He glanced at Aurelia. She smiled angelically at him. Perhaps he could take her back as well.

"Good news," said the King, "I remember where I heard of the Spinner. He has travelled to the next kingdom where he is advising the Queen, although no one quite knows what she requires of him. Happily the mountain where Deathbreather lives is directly en route. You would hardly have to make a detour at all, just half a day to climb the mountain and kill the dragon."

"That's fortunate," said Henry, as a tiny piece of him died inside.

"You're going to kill Deathbreather," cried Aurelia. "That's so brave of you."

"Isn't it," said Henry.

"And what reward will you claim?" enquired the King.

"Aurelia," replied Henry.

The King glared at him. "That's an abuse of my hospitality."

"Your Majesty," said Henry, "if, when, I kill Deathbreather, you will have an enormous treasure at your disposal. Why do you need to marry your son to a miller's daughter?"

"It's a break with tradition," said the King, "but when you put it like that, you do have a point."

"In fact," added the Crown Prince, "I won't really need to marry at all."

"We have a dynasty to maintain," said the King.

"I've got two brothers," said the Crown Prince. "I'm more of a bachelor boy." He smiled charmingly at Henry and also at the royal page pouring him a goblet of ale.

The King gave him a filthy look then turned back to Henry. "Prince, we must get you prepared – unless you have your armour hidden somewhere."

"No," said Henry, "and I do need my armour, which – er – has special strength. It brings me luck."

"I quite understand," said the King, and Henry breathed a sigh of relief, "but you need have no worries, as I will lend you my own armour, which was forged by master craftsmen and has never even been dented in hundreds of years."

"That's very reassuring," said Henry. "Does that mean I am leaving immediately?"

"I thought you would prefer that in view of your quest," said the King.

Henry gave up. He took such pleasure as he could from Aurelia's admiring glances. He wondered whether this would be like a dream, where you can have all sorts of unexpected skills and strength, but somehow he doubted that. This was real life, for the moment anyway. He followed a servant out of the dining hall and on to the royal armoury, where the King's armour took pride of place. It was certainly impressive, golden and elaborate, with intricate patterns and the royal coat of arms etched into the breast plate.

"It's splendid isn't it?" said the Crown Prince who had taken an obvious liking to Henry and had decided to come along.

"Yes," agreed Henry, "and it must be strong as it's never been dented in hundreds of years."

"I don't think it's ever been used in hundreds of years," said the Crown Prince. "It's only for show."

"Oh."

"But don't worry. It was forged by dwarves and so on, so it should be very strong."

"Might it be better," suggested Henry, "if I wore some armour that the King has tested in battle?"

"Definitely," said the Crown Prince, "but I don't think we have any. My family don't seem to do any fighting. It's not part of our tradition. We're known for living off our wits."

"Plus the treasure brought to you by royal brides?"

"And that."

Perhaps the best thing about the armour, thought Henry as he was strapped into it, was that it was unbelievably light. That might mean it would be no protection at all, but at least he could walk in it.

"There's a set for your horse too," explained the Crown Prince.

"My horse?"

His horse. There was no way Henry could bluff his way out of that. He had no idea how to ride and was nervous at the very idea of getting on a horse.

"Although," continued the Crown Prince, "riding is not the quickest way to the mountains. It would really be much faster if you went by boat down the river until you reached the foothills."

"Then that's what we must do," said Henry. "You know I'm in a hurry."

"You wouldn't be able to take any horses with you."

"It's a sacrifice I'll have to make."

"But what about after you've killed the dragon?"

That was not a very relevant consideration. However — "I'm sure we can find some horses locally. I'll worry about that when I need to." Never.

Henry clanked gently back to the King. Aurelia was now sitting at the royal table and seemed to bear the King no ill will for her ordeal in the tower. She looked at Henry approvingly.

"That's much better," she said. "As soon as you've killed the dragon we can think about living happily ever after."

"I thought," said Henry, "we were going to do that as soon as I helped you get out of the tower."

"We were," she replied, "but you've accepted another test. I'll be waiting for you."

"Aurelia," said Henry uncertainly, "before I go, I would like to have a few minutes alone with you. Perhaps a little stroll in the garden?"

"Of course," said Aurelia. "That would be delightful."

The castle garden was inside a courtyard with

very high walls and, to Henry, walking round it was like walking round an exercise yard in a prison. It was very formal, with little square or circular flower beds surrounded by tiny box hedges. In the centre was a square pool with some sort of heraldic beast, a griffin may be, spurting water out of its mouth. There were four other heraldic statues at each corner. It was a quaint and delightful garden, thought Henry. If only he weren't in it.

"It's —" began Henry, then stopped. He tried again. "I'm —" He smiled hopelessly.

"You're very uncertain for a hero," said Aurelia.

"It doesn't do to be too brash."

"No, but I always imagined heroes would be more self assured."

"Well, you can't believe all you read in books."

"I can't read," said Aurelia.

"Oh," said Henry. "I'll teach you."

"And what about the protestations of courtly love?"

"I'm working on that."

"You see," said Aurelia, holding his arm, "I was expecting someone more polished. I don't blame you. I'll do what I can to help, but I'm not certain at the moment. A hero, especially a Prince, should have professional standards which should be taken for granted. That's the starting point for all his adventures, romantic or heroic. There isn't time to learn on the job. You make me nervous. I thought you'd had more experience."

"It's true I'm still fairly new at this."

"That's why I'm not sure we're at the happily ever after stage. Not yet. Once you've killed this dragon you might gain a lot more self confidence."

"That's definitely a fair comment."

"I'll be thinking of you. And worrying about you."

"I'll be worrying about me."

Aurelia looked tenderly at him. Like a sister might. They went back inside.

Preparations were vigorously in hand to speed Henry to his death by roasting. The royal barge was being prepared. A squad of soldiers to act as escort, though only to a prudent distance from the cave, was standing by. Provisions were going on board. Henry felt sick. He badly wanted to relieve himself, but wondered where. He rather suspected that any corner in the castle was probably acceptable. However there must be a privy, even if flush toilets were unlikely to exist in a medieval fairy tale world. Then he forgot about that as a desperate hope grabbed him.

"Before any adventure," he said, "I like to meditate briefly alone. It helps balance my energies and gets my ying and yang into a state of equilibrium."

"Excuse me?" said the King

"It helps prepare me."

"I understand," said the King. "That's most appropriate behaviour for a hero facing death – facing down death I mean. Why not return to the garden?"

"I like to be somewhere – higher. The turret where you kept Aurelia would be very suitable."

"Surely not. It's not been cleaned out."

"It will be fine your Majesty," insisted Henry. "I like the view."

"You can actually see the top of Deathbreather's mountain on a clear day," said the King, "so may be you have a point."

Henry was led to the base of the turret, then climbed alone to the cell at the top. It was true, no amount of fresh air blowing in through the window could disguise the vile smell of that straw. He looked out briefly to see several mountain peaks in the far distance. He inspected the walls. There was nothing there to explain how Aurelia could have seen him when he was still safe in his own world. He was obviously not expecting a visible screen, yet he was expecting some sort of clue as to how the link worked. May be a screen came out of the wall when the link occurred. If so, he could see no crack or place where this might happen. Yet he knew that anybody in the turret could be seen through the web site.

He also knew that it was possible for someone to look into the turret without being seen themselves. After all, he had done it. He wondered if anyone were watching him now. In particular, Wilfred. Wilfred, who had done this dreadful thing to him. There must be a reason. If anything the old man had seemed well disposed towards him, yet sending Henry through against his will was a definite breach of his human rights and probably a criminal offence, although Henry couldn't entirely work out what. It was a mixture of false imprisonment and kidnapping.

Perhaps Wilfred was keeping an eye out for Henry. It was a long shot.

"Wilfred, are you there. Please speak to me if you are." Nothing. "I want to come back. You had no business to do this to me." Nothing. "Can't you at least tell me how long I'm supposed to be here?" Nothing. "Or give me some hints on how to survive – like how to kill a dragon for example?" Nothing. "At least find a way to reassure my parents, though Heaven only knows how you're going to do that. But please try." Nothing. "Is anybody there? Anyone? Turn on your webcam and speak to me. Please."

Nothing. Henry gave up.

He stared bleakly out of the window. He was supposed to be contemplating the saurian encounter ahead. Three possibilities occurred to him. First, he would be burned quickly to a crisp. Hopefully he would feel no pain. Secondly, he would be clawed at or torn to shreds, then eaten or burned to a crisp. This did seem possible if the dragon was up for a little fun. Henry gave two loud sobs before managing to stifle the noise in his hands. Thirdly, he would find a way to kill the dragon. This must surely be completely out of the question unless the world of legends had really transformed him into a hero in a way he could not believe.

His soul and his bladder were distinctly uncomfortable. He could do nothing about the former, but he emptied the latter into the straw, then went back downstairs, his energies about as unbalanced as they could be.

Preparations were complete. All he was required to do was to walk out of the castle gate down to the river and board the royal barge. It was now midday. The sky was blue, the sun was shining and Henry was unbelievably hot in the golden armour. The roasting process had already begun. However, there was an awning over part of the deck, while a cool breeze blew on the river. The King, the Crown Prince, Aurelia and a vast crowd were waiting to see him off. A minstrel was beginning a ballad in his honour which was to be finished with the account of how he killed Deathbreather, or, said the minstrel, with his glorious death in the unlikely event that he died in the attempt. Either way, the ballad would only add further lustre to his already glorious reputation.

The barge set sail and Henry, exhausted, stared at the sparkling water until he fell asleep.

CHAPTER 12

Deathbreather

HENRY WOKE UP. There was no wonderful moment when he forgot where he was or thought it might all have been a dream. He remembered exactly the predicament he was in.

It was late in the afternoon, although Henry's body clock told him it was the early hours of the morning. He was suffering from a sort of interworld jetlag. He looked about him. He was alone under a scarlet awning. The soldiers were sprawled in the sunshine. The barge was actually a vast galley, with at least thirty rowers, so regrettably they were making very good speed. It was gilded and extremely ornate, with carvings of nymphs and sea monsters on the outside, and the huge figure of an ocean goddess at the prow. In fact, Henry discovered, the barge never went to sea, in case its elaborate perfection was damaged by the waves, but it was and looked completely seaworthy, as befitted a vessel belonging to a King.

He was deeply troubled. He was confronted with bizarre codes and conduct suitable for a world based on legend. In other circumstances he would have found these rules fascinating. He was a lawyer and rules were to be his life's work. However, these rules were working against him as they demanded his taking part in an adventure for which he was completely unsuitable. There was no way he could avoid it unless he ran away, and then he would have to survive on his own. And if people found out who he was, and he suspected they would, he would be branded a coward so life would be unendurable.

The gentle strumming of a lute, a pleasant tenor voice – the minstrel was making progress with his ballad. Henry shook his head and looked across at the banks. The river was flowing through a green summer forest, with trees so tightly packed that those nearest the river found themselves edged into the water. Some relished this and grew more strongly, while others seemed less certain and were like timid children dipping their toes into the river then recoiling anxiously.

Henry smiled wryly. It was predictable, it always happened in stories, but there were shadowy figures slipping almost unseen through the forest and watching the progress of the barge. Everyone on board could spot them occasionally.

"They aren't trying too hard," said the commander of the guards. "They don't seem to mind that we know they are there."

"Who are they?" asked Henry.

"Fairies or elves, your Highness. I think they're warning us."

"About what?"

"Trouble ahead, which they intend to cause."

The barge started to slow down. It had been heading

up stream from the start but the river had been wide and the current sluggish. Now the forest died away, the banks grew rockier and the river was narrowing as the barge headed into the mountains. The current was stronger and the rowers were tired, even though they worked in shifts. The banks turned into the steep sides of a gorge. The sun was hidden from view and the air grew chilly. They were drawing very near to the mountain where Deathbreather had his cave and although the dragon was less active in his old age, he still came out from time to time, searching for prey. The King's barge would offer him a wonderful opportunity to show he could still manage a mass killing, something which gave him especial pleasure. Nor was Deathbreather the only danger. The mountains were home to other murderous creatures, all of whom would relish the opportunity of taking human life.

"Prince Henry," said the commander of the guards, "this is where we will drop anchor."

"Rest here for the night, you mean," said Henry.

"Yes," said the Commander.

"That sounds sensible," said Henry.

"It's far too dangerous for us to leave the barge after dark."

"Naturally," said Henry.

"We will wait here for you."

"I'm not going anywhere."

"Your Highness," said the commander with a laugh, "we will have to add sense of humour to your many qualities. Minstrel, note that please."

It was more prudent, apparently, for Henry to approach the cave under cover of the night. That way there was less chance that Deathbreather would notice his approach. There was of course every chance that Henry would meet many other creatures of the night, but once they realised who he was, said the commander, they would probably run away or swiftly regret that they had not.

What was the point of even arguing, thought Henry. One way or another he would be dead by morning.

The barge had started to pull into the shore, when the helmsman cried out a warning. Twelve riders were making their way towards them down a tricky path on the side of the cliff. The soldiers drew their bows and the commander drew his sword, then looked expectantly at Henry, who drew his.

"Approach no further," called the Commander, "until you identify yourselves as friends. And understand this. We are led by the great hero Prince Henry, and we outnumber you, so if you have any plan to attack us, you should think better of it."

"We have no plans to attack you," shouted the first rider, "and we are well aware you are led by Prince Henry. We have come to enter his service, if he is willing."

"Identify yourselves," cried the Commander.

"We are the eleven Lords who once were swans – by daytime that is."

"And their sister," added a female voice.

"Yes, sorry Elise – and our sister."

"We've heard of you," said the Commander, "but how can we be sure that you are who you say you are?"

"I should be able to recognise them," whispered Henry.

"That is a useful first step," the commander whispered

back, "but just because a person looks familiar doesn't necessarily mean that he is who he says he is."

"I think I know a way to test them," said Henry, feeling for a brief moment pleasantly on top of things. Furthermore, ten of those twelve were beefy fighting men who might relish the chance to help him overcome a legendary dragon.

"You may continue to the shore," said the commander. "The Prince will do you the honour of addressing you."

The twelve horses bore their riders safely to the river's edge. Adolphus and Gervase dismounted. Henry came out from under the awning, as he felt this was more fitting for a Prince, and leaned against the rail.

"Greetings Adolphus and Gervase," he said.

"Greetings, Prince Henry," returned Adolphus.

"I knew it wouldn't be long before we found you on a great quest," said Gervase excitedly. "And this time you have your sword with you. I hope you don't mind me asking, but is your sword really called Fleshbiter?"

"Yes," said Henry. It was so much simpler. "Please tell the commander when and how you last saw me."

"A few days ago," answered Adolphus. "And we only saw part of you, and a brief glimpse of your arm."

The commander's expression suggested that he assumed Adolphus was out of his mind.

"It's certainly them," said Henry.

The commander ordered the rowers to take the barge as near in as they could. The anchor was dropped and a little rowing boat was launched to bring the two brothers on board. A few minutes later Henry stood facing Adolphus's chest and Gervase's beaming face.

"How did you know we'd be here?" asked Henry.

"Your Highness," explained Adolphus, "it was most curious. This morning an old man appeared to us, in the same way you did, and told us that you were on your way to kill Deathbreather before continuing on a series of great adventures."

"Yes," said Gervase, "he told us we should accompany you. We didn't need telling twice."

"We didn't need telling at all," said Adolphus. "We wanted to come. It's a very great honour for us."

That, Henry decided, meant Wilfred was looking out for him. Better if Wilfred had not put him into this position in the first place. "This very evening," he said, "I will be setting off for Deathbreather's cave."

"Then we will accompany you, if we may," offered Adolphus.

"Certainly," said Henry graciously. Heaven be praised!

The remaining brothers and Elise were also brought on board and introduced. Up close Henry realised that Elise was even prettier than she was on the screen, even if she did not have Aurelia's staggering beauty. She was wearing a dark green riding outfit which suited her very well. Her eyes were hazel and humorous. With eleven brothers a sense of humour was probably essential.

"Well your Highness," she said, "I expect you rescued the miller's daughter?"

"Yes," replied Henry.

"She must have been very grateful."

"I believe she was."

"So you will be living happily ever after, interrupted only by the occasional heroic foray?"

There was something about Elise. Henry did not

wish to lie to her. "That's what everyone he expects," he said.

Fires were lit. They ate supper and Henry drank two goblets of wine, which helped to relax him a little. Gervase was all for asking him to recount some of his adventures, but Henry requested the minstrel to perform, explaining how this helped to nourish his soul before a major feat. On the other hand, the minstrel chose to sing about glorious battles and heroic deaths, so Henry tried not to listen. The sky became dark. Constellations of unfamiliar stars began to flicker. A chilly wind blew over the river and Henry recognised that the time had come for him to leave. He had another goblet of wine.

He learned why the barge had stopped where it did and why the swan lords had met them at this point. They were at the foot of Deathbreather's mountain. It seemed that that the path down which they had ridden led upwards into the foothills before climbing conveniently to the very mouth of the cave. Indeed, on that mountain all paths led up to the dragon, such was the lure of this ancient monster. Over the centuries any number of people had climbed to the cave, hoping to defeat him, meeting only their end, speedily if they were lucky.

A difficulty was that there were only twelve horses, but thirteen riders, including Henry. The brothers tried to persuade Elise to stay behind, but she refused. Each of them offered to give up their horse to Henry, but he refused. He insisted that he would walk, but that offer was also refused. Such generosity and nobility were almost too much for the minstrel, who, like a news reporter, felt it incumbent on him to keep up a sort of running commentary, but was unable to rhyme fast enough. As he was irritating everyone, he was thrown into a cabin, although his desperate outpourings could still be heard.

The matter was resolved when the brothers decided that each would take it in turns to walk, so freeing a horse for Henry, who had no way of avoiding this. The first problem was mounting, but there he was fortunate, because tradition dictated that an armoured knight was always helped onto his horse. The next problem was staying on, yet curiously this was not a problem after all. The horse had been selected by Elise, who insisted on this particular animal, and Henry found him mild and steady. Because they were proceeding up hill or mountain paths, there was no question of going faster than a walking pace so there was a real possibility he would remain in the saddle.

By the time Henry had settled down enough to look about him, they were already some way above the barge, which soon disappeared from view. The wind was stronger and he pulled a cloak around him. The night was clear with a full moon, which seemed to give a great deal more silvery light than on his world, making the path easy to follow. The brothers were alert, for there were pitch black shadows and many suitable places for an ambush. And where were the elves or goblins who had travelled with them along the river bank?

For the first hour or so the path rose steadily through sloping grass land and stubby trees, but then started to climb more steeply as they headed up the side of the mountain. The path was uneven and stony, forcing them to go carefully and occasionally a horse stumbled. This was just absurd, thought Henry, who was uncomfortable and sore. It was a scene from a film. What was he doing in it?

The path became narrower and Henry became seriously unnerved. There was a rock wall one side of the path and a nasty drop on the other. He was, notionally, leading the way, but his sole preoccupations were gripping the sides of the horse with his knees and trying not to hold the reins too tightly, for he recognised that was both a cruel and a foolish thing to do. His eyes were set firmly on the path ahead for he dared not look downwards. His tense body and arms were hidden beneath his cloak as otherwise Adolphus, riding behind, must surely have realised how uncertain he was. But his horse seemed untroubled by his lack of confidence. This was truly a miracle, as was the fact that the horse was the real leader, never diverging from the path in the foothills or refusing to continue once the going became so treacherous.

After a couple of hours of this torture, Henry came to a small plateau and Adolphus politely requested him to stop. This was fine, but how could Henry bring this huge determined animal to a halt? He had to try. He tugged gently on the reins and said, "Stop please." The horse stopped.

Adolphus was obviously puzzled by this sort of polite relationship between a hero and his steed, but said only, "Let me help you dismount Prince Henry."

Somehow Henry managed to swing his leg over the back of the horse, but would undoubtedly have sunk to the ground if someone had not gripped his elbow. It was Elise. She said nothing, but he could read the look in her eyes, which forbade such weakness. He walked over to a boulder and sat heavily on it.

"A little refreshment," said Adolphus, and went to get some wine while his brothers dismounted.

"You can do this," whispered Elise.

"Of course," said Henry.

"They don't see it but I do. You doubt yourself. I don't understand who you are, but think what you've done already. Three hours on a horse when you've never ridden. Be strong." She moved away.

Adolphus brought him a goblet of wine.

Gervase came over and gazed at him with envy and excitement. "I wish I was coming with you," he said.

"Aren't you?" Perhaps the others had decided Gervase was too inexperienced. That was probably right, but how safe was it to leave him on his own?

"We'll be waiting here for you," said Adolphus. "We will listen for the sounds of struggle and envy you the battle."

"Oh? Don't you intend to come with me?"

"Your Highness, that it is such a generous offer, but we wouldn't dream of sullying the purity of your heroic deed. We'll be here until noon in three days' time."

"Will I be gone that long?"

"Who's to say? Great fights can last a day or more until their resolution. Whatever happens, we'll ensure your story is spread throughout the world."

That was it really. The little sparkler of hope fizzled out. Henry was on his own. After five minutes he struggled to his feet and went over to where the path continued. Nobody could convince him to remount. He said that he preferred to be at one with the environment. Not all the brothers understood what that meant but they respected his wishes. He smiled bravely, heartened a tiny bit by so much good will and admiration. Then he turned away and began to trudge up the mountain path.

The bitter wind blew the prospect of failure into his face. He cried. He cursed. He despaired And all the time he climbed higher and higher, nearer and nearer to his inevitable extinction. Now he was no longer on horseback, he did look down, clasping a rock to support himself. There was only mountainside, shining whitely in that extraordinarily bright full moon.

For the final half hour the path was far too precipitous for any horse to manage, and Henry had quite a scramble to haul himself up it, not helped by sheer exhaustion and the weight of the armour which, though light, was not insignificant, and he was not especially fit. He made it though, to another small plateau, where several other pathways ended and an abandoned skull, not tidied away by the dragon, lay next to a huge cavern.

So what was he supposed to do next? Walk into the cave until he came across the dragon and challenge him? Move silently through the cave, hoping to take the dragon by surprise and thrust his sword into the dragon's heart, but where was that? The difficulty with either choice was that the cave was dark, he knew that from the webcam, so he would be unable to see the dragon. A much more substantial difficulty was the sheer power of the creature, illustrated by the first story he had read on the worldoflegends.com website. He had no prospect of killing Deathbreather.

It was at this point Henry noticed he was no longer alone on the plateau. Quietly surrounding him were several horrible figures, part human, part wolf. One of them drew back its lips and showed a mouthful of large pointed teeth. Scared witless, Henry moved into the cave out of instinctive self-preservation. He saw them approach the opening so went in deeper himself, hoping to find somewhere to hide. He moved gingerly, edging into complete blackness, until he saw neither the entrance behind him nor anything ahead. He was terrified.

The stench was overpowering. It was far worse than the straw in the turret. It was a mixture of powerful chemicals and excrement. Henry gagged.

"Midnight," rumbled a huge voice from above Henry, "and I'm hungry. It's always a pleasure when dinner delivers itself."

Henry wanted to run, but it was impossible to run if you could see nowhere to run to.

"I have to say I admire your sheer cheek," said Deathbreather, "coming right up to me as bold as anything."

That was certainly foolhardy, agreed Henry, though not aloud.

"Hardly any have ever dared," said the dragon, "so I hope today isn't starting a new trend."

Henry had to say something, if only to defer the moment of incineration a tad longer. No, not only that, but also to preserve a little self respect. He found a tiny bit of strength.

"Well – em —" ("Well" came out rather shakily, which was unacceptable.) "Well, none of the others has been me."

"Logically and grammatically impeccable," said Deathbreather, "but I fail to see the relevance of your remark."

"I mean none of them has been a hero."

"O no, I'm not having that." The dragon sounded extremely angry. "It completely demeans me and my accomplishments. Some of my challengers have been exceptionally heroic." A few irritable spurts of flame briefly indicated where the dragon's unseen head was. Basically, far too near Henry.

"May be, but none of them has been Prince Henry – me that is."

"I'm honoured," said the dragon.

"You've heard of me no doubt?"

"Indeed," replied the dragon. "And I recognise you now. You were here before, quite recently, in a sort of vision. Good of you to turn up in person. Actual food is much tastier than virtual food."

"It seemed more – heroic."

"You seem very keen to point out your heroic status. Is that to inform me or convince yourself?"

"To warn you," said Henry. Where was this conversation going, he wondered? He never found out, because a large lamp was lit. It illuminated some of the piles of treasure and more significantly the huge scaly head of the dragon. The lamp was held by Rupert, who was standing to one side of Deathbreather, a truly enormous creature – the length and height of a doubledecker London bus. Most of him was in shadow but his vast outline was all too clear.

"Smart armour," Rupert said to Henry. "It'll look good in the great Deathbreather's collection."

"So will your head," returned Henry, drawing his sword, much to his surprise, for there was no way he was going to take that threat any further.

"Henry," said Rupert, very nearly in admiration, "that's a very spunky reply!"

"You are in my cave," growled the dragon, "and you are at my mercy. I expect respect. You will talk to me, not each other."

"Forgive me, most ancient and legendary of all great dragons," said Rupert smoothly, "but Prince Henry and I have known each other for many years."

"That alone will not stop me roasting him," said Deathbreather.

Henry had caught something in the dragon's voice and remembered some more of that first story. Deathbreather was anxious. Of course the dragon remained enormously powerful, but he had recently glimpsed his own mortality. Henry became bolder, although he was still extremely scared.

"I'm not planning to be roasted," he said. Perhaps he could have sounded slightly more defiant, but the point was made.

"Once again," returned Deathbreather, "accurate, no doubt, but irrelevant."

"Mighty dragon," said Rupert, "I know you will remember what we were discussing even as Prince Henry entered the cave."

"Yes," said the dragon tersely.

"The great Queen —"

"Our world is full of Queens who think they're great," interrupted the dragon. "That epithet fails to impress me. She's a Queen. She does a bit of magic. End of story."

"Indeed," said Rupert, unruffled. "The Queen urges you to consider my expert advice."

"You expect me to act against my nature."

"I have your interests at heart."

"At heart, no," said Deathbreather. "In mind, possibly."

"Definitely," said Rupert, "for all the reasons I put to you."

"I doubt if this great hero will accept your proposal."

"Believe me," said Rupert, "Prince Henry will accept it."

"What are you talking about?" asked Henry who remembered what Rupert had said to the Queen in the garden of her palace and sensed a lifeline.

"The mighty Deathbreather," answered Rupert, "is aware that he is considered somewhat of an outsider. He's decided that the time has come to become part of the community."

"No," said the dragon.

"Well," continued Rupert smoothly, "to co-exist with the community. This is a very generous gesture, bearing in mind how many people have tried to end his life."

"The dragon as victim," murmured Henry before he could stop himself, but fortunately Deathbreather's hearing was not acute enough to pick up what he said.

Rupert shook his head, as if dealing with an idiot, then went on, "Deathbreather has decided he will no longer kill human beings."

"No," said Deathbreather, "I have decided I won't kill human beings during an experimental period. At the end of the period I will review the success of the experiment and my situation generally. If I am then convinced this policy is sound, I may turn it into a long term strategy."

"Understood," said Rupert, "but I suggest it isn't

necessary to go into that sort of detail. The point is, as of now, you're not planning to kill anybody. That's the message."

"Apparently," said Deathbreather, without enthusiasm.

"In the circumstances," Rupert pointed out, "it would be inappropriate, your Highness, for you to challenge Deathbreather."

It was with immense effort that Henry restrained himself from agreeing wholeheartedly. He was beginning to learn a bit about image and, when all was said and done, he was quite intelligent. "You may choose to alter the rules," he said, "but that doesn't mean I have to do the same."

"True," said Rupert, "but how noble and magnanimous is it to attack an opponent who has —"

"Don't you dare say 'refused to fight'," interrupted the dragon, "for that isn't my position at all."

"Certainly not," said Rupert. "I was going to say, 'offered to negotiate an arrangement of benefit to all interested parties.'"

"You need to put a bit of flesh on that," said Deathbreather. "On the other hand I could take a bit of flesh off you!"

"What I'm proposing," said Rupert, "is for you to publicise the arrangements you've got on offer."

"Remind me what they are," said the dragon.

"You will forego the standard offering of one damsel a year. You will not accept contracts for disposing of unwanted knights. You will no longer set fire to villages and towns, and in consequence their inhabitants, which have incurred your displeasure. You will confine yourself to killing livestock or wild animals. All this," explained Rupert, "will cease to make you a threat."

"It will make me a laughing stock."

"With respect, no it won't. It will make you more of a nuisance."

"Is that the best you can do?" snarled the dragon. "Reduce me to a nuisance? In that case I will go on as before and preserve my honour"

"It's not the best," said Rupert, "I want you —"

"Want!"

"— would like you to be regarded as a valuable member of society by performing certain services."

Deathbreather did not react well to that. Rupert had obviously been protected by a spell, otherwise the burst of flame would have destroyed him. Henry was fortunate not to have been in the direct line of fire.

"I don't perform services," said Deathbreather.

"I put that clumsily," said Rupert, unperturbed. "Certain specialist tasks."

"Such as?"

"Stubble burning or transport, for which you will expect a fair price —"

"No," said Deathbreather, "for which I will expect a substantial price."

"Transport," repeated Henry. "You mean, like Dragonair!"

Rupert smiled at him lethally. "I turn to you, Prince Henry, fearless and accomplished warrior. You have heard the terms on offer by the magnificent Deathbreather. Do you find them acceptable?"

Obviously he did, but to accept at once would be demeaning and suspicious. "They are certainly worth considering," Henry said, "but em —" What? Then he remembered the King's desire for more gold. "I suggest the agreement should be marked by a suitable payment to the King, to indicate goodwill."

"There is no goodwill," said Deathbreather.

"What Prince Henry is saying," explained Rupert, "is that a small contribution from your treasure would be a positive sign —"

"How small?" asked the dragon, who clearly found parting with any of his gold and jewels deeply painful.

"A chest-full," proposed Henry.

"And we would call it payment for the lease of the cave," added Rupert. "Strictly speaking these mountains do belong to the King."

"Leave me to think about it," said Deathbreather. "I will give you my decision at dawn."

Rupert led Henry back towards the entrance of the cave. In the lamp light Henry could make out the discomforting sight of bones and smashed pieces of armour.

"Incidentally," said Rupert, "not all of the bones are human. Some belonged to animals. Or creatures of the night."

"Most reassuring," said Henry, and stopped. He had remembered the terrifying figures who had followed him to the cave mouth. "Outside are some werewolves. I don't think we should go any further."

"Werewolves won't be a problem to a major hero like you!" Rupert laughed. "I wouldn't worry. I'm sure they were only the phouka. They're my bodyguards – making sure you didn't run away."

"I wasn't going to run away," said Henry.

"Yes, I accept that. You've definitely come on a lot. Though," –Rupert grinned – "not enough to really challenge Deathbreather. Fortunately he believes you truly are a famous hero."

"I suppose you just saved my life," said Henry grudgingly.

"That's exactly right. You should sound more grateful."

"I am grateful — What did you mean about the phouka making sure I didn't run away?"

"I needed you to come into the cave."

"How did you know I was coming? — I realise the barge was watched, but even so, how did you know I'd even come through to this world?"

"This is a magic world. Do you think it goes unnoticed when the great Prince Henry rescues a maiden in the tower! But how did you manage to get there? I didn't think you had any idea what to do."

"Sorry," replied Henry, "I just did and that's all I'm saying for the moment."

"You must have been helped, which is very interesting. My guess is you can't do it by yourself and what's more, you don't know how to get back again."

"Do you?"

"Of course," said Rupert and patted him on the arm. "I'm sure you'll learn to love it here."

"You still haven't explained why you needed me to come into the cave."

"Your reputation for valour and honour! Because you're graciously prepared to withdraw your challenge on the basis of Deathbreather's offer, it makes him feel more confident that he's not doing anything too shameful.

Of course, if you actually were the hero he thinks you are, you would never have agreed. I wanted you because you're a frightened law student, completely out of your depth."

"I'm —" What was there to deny? Henry let that go. "The truth is, although you may have saved my life, it was only because it suited you, not out of friendship."

"Is that so? And are you such a good friend to me?"

The actual answer was that Henry had lost any feelings of friendship a long time ago. So he didn't give that answer but asked, "What are you up to Rupert?"

"Enjoying myself. I've got a chance to exercise my talent here in a way I could never do in the other world. I'm a spin doctor Henry, and here I can spin myself into legend."

"As a great liar?"

"Don't be so naïve. It's not lying. It's presentation. It's story telling and what better place for what I do?"

"But aren't you doing harm by interfering with the natural order of things?"

"I thought I was preventing harm. Aren't I about to stop Deathbreather from murdering human beings? I should get a medal! And I'm going to check lots of other evil-doers from indulging their blood-thirsty desires. But that won't be news to you. I rather suspect you've seen me or read about me on the web sites."

"Yes," said Henry.

"So you're concerned for the natural order of things! That's a selfless thought which doesn't come from the Henry I know."

"I'm not that incapable of noble deeds and thoughts," Henry objected, but recognised how flabby that sounded.

"After all, the reason I came through was to help Aurelia." That was so near what actually happened it was almost an honest account. "You left her stranded in the turret."

"I was confident someone would rescue her," replied Rupert. "Someone always does."

Rupert led Henry out into the icy, moonlit night. There were no werewolves about, only one thin figure, with a goat's head, tangled hair, long slender limbs, and gleaming, white eyes. He was wearing the sort of outfit expected on a fairy or elf. He grinned speculatively at Henry.

"My chance to greet you, great Prince," he said in exactly the same voice he had when transformed into a wolf on Hampstead Heath. It was the leader of the phouka. "You didn't stop to say hello on your way in."

"I mistook you for something threatening," said Henry, attempting an insult.

"Likewise," returned the leader, succeeding. "Do you want us to give him some traditional phouka hospitality?" he asked Rupert.

"No thank you," said Rupert. "Prince Henry is helping me at the moment. I don't need to bother you. I'll contact you at dawn once the great Deathbreather has made his decision."

"Feel free to change your mind," said the phouka and loped over to the edge of the plateau, where Henry saw a lot of similar creatures sitting quietly.

"They won't trouble you," said Rupert to Henry, "unless I say so that is."

"But they're dangerous?"

"O yes, I told you before, very dangerous."

Rupert sat down by the cave entrance and suggested

Henry did the same. There was nothing else to do but wait and freeze in the vicious wind. Rupert had on what seemed to be the same orange tunic which had so offended the magic mirror. It was hardly keeping him warm yet he seemed not to notice the cold. Henry did and was embarrassed to hear bits of armour knocking together as he shivered.

Eventually the sky paled over a nearby mountain top, which turned, as it was supposed to, a pleasing pink. The sun was rising. The phouka stretched expectantly. From within the cavern came the sound of something vast stirring. Rupert stood up slowly. Henry stood up quickly. They both moved away from the entrance. Very slowly Deathbreather hauled himself out of the cave, an ancient bringer of evil surveying yet another dawn.

"Very well," rumbled the dragon, "I agree." He stared over at the phouka. "What are those things doing here?"

"My bodyguard, great Deathbreather," answered Rupert.

The dragon sent a great spurt of flame over towards them. Two phouka ignited then fell over the edge of the plateau. "One last time eh, before giving up!"

"O my —" Henry managed to stop himself. He saw the shock in Rupert's face, though he hid it quickly.

"I take it," said Deathbreather to Henry, "you don't feel obliged to seek revenge for the deaths of two low-life fairies?"

"No," said Henry, who could barely reply for trembling.

"No," repeated Deathbreather, "the laws of chivalry could never require that."

"We need to announce your decision," said Rupert.

"The nearest humans are Prince Henry's honour guard, who are waiting for him further down the mountain."

"Then Prince Henry can tell them," said Deathbreather, who was idly inspecting the remaining phouka, who, to give them their due, had made no attempt to move. However, their goat's heads were all turned towards the dragon. The mixture of fear and hatred in their white eyes was clear.

"He certainly could," agreed Rupert, "But it would be so much more impressive coming from yourself. It would be a magnificent gesture."

"I understand that," said Deathbreather. "I could fly down to them. It would create a stir. I love creating stirs. Mind you, if anyone there tries it on with me, I'll have to burn them up."

In view of the reason for his agreeing to this arrangement, Deathbreather must have been anxious about facing a group of brave fighters, but this morning he successfully concealed any doubt he might have.

"It would be better to avoid any incidents," said Rupert. "I suggest that you and Prince Henry arrive together."

Deathbreather glanced at Henry. "I've seen more imposing heroes. I have my image to maintain."

"To be seen in my company," said Henry, "can only enhance your reputation."

"What I propose," continued Rupert, "is that you let Prince Henry climb on your back and then fly down with him to his attendants."

"I don't think so," said Deathbreather. "That would be a symbol of my subjugation. Once Prince Henry has joined his guards, I'll make my appearance. It's an awesome sight."

That was it. There was no point delaying, so Henry began the awkward scramble down to the swan Lords, wondering how he could convince them he had just done something heroic. Rupert, accompanying him to the edge of the plateau, told quietly him not to worry, because his reputation would protect him. Rupert also said he would follow him down once Deathbreather had left, but thought it best to remain with the dragon until then in case any further convincing were needed.

CHAPTER 13

The gathering of heroes

IT HAD INDEED been an awesome sight. Henry had returned to a group of concerned and admiring people, who had become rather puzzled when he started to explain what had occurred, or a version of it. Before he had finished, Gervase had spotted Deathbreather flying down to them, his scales sparkling like bronze in the early morning sunshine. How beautiful evil could appear in the right setting.

The dragon had landed. The brothers had gathered together behind Henry but had not drawn their swords. Elise had been placed in their midst, for her own protection they said, ignoring her protests. The dragon had spoken, Henry had agreed, and Deathbreather flew back to his cave, leaving the treasure chest he had been gripping in his talons. The deal was done.

Rupert never turned up. Henry was not surprised. It was left to him to defend his own deed, except that he realised a defensive approach was a sign of weakness. Instead he proclaimed his action – not at length, because he did not have the confidence, but he was a lawyer and there was a case to be argued.

"Killing Deathbreather would be the – my – usual approach to a monster of this sort. It would certainly have rid the world of a foul creature. But keeping him alive to atone for his crimes is a sign of real strength. Furthermore he can perform some important services —"(Happily the dragon was not there to hear this offensive word.) "— for the community. Should he lapse, then he can be dealt with, or rather, I can deal with him."

The ten eldest brothers were distinctly dubious, but who were they to disagree with a hero of Henry's great reputation. If this were how the great Prince wished to play it, there it was. After breakfast, when Henry politely sipped a revolting drink called sedge tea, they saddled up and once again assisted Henry onto one of the horses. He was exhausted, but after his encounter with the dragon, a stolid, peaceful horse no longer caused him any bother. His only worry was that he might fall asleep and tumble off.

Towards noon they reached the foothills and Elise rode up beside him.

"Were you very frightened?" she whispered.

"Yes," he replied.

"But you came through."

"O yes."

"They don't like your arrangement, but I admire it. A solution without killing, it's very brave."

"It's not very traditional."

"So?"

"And it might be a mistake." He looked at the

admiration in her eyes and felt absolutely disgusted with himself.

"You're done in," she said and made them stop for an early lunch. Henry then lay down in the shade of a tree and fell into a deep sleep. It was late in the afternoon before they woke him and they continued their descent to the barge, which they reached in the mellow evening sunshine. The news of the deal once again took everyone by surprise. However the treasure chest – bearing a King's ransom as one soldier said, shortly before he was locked in the brig for even breathing the thought that the King might need a ransom – was received with great excitement. This would put the King in a very good mood.

Henry was expecting to go back down the river with the treasure, but this was not to be. He had been summoned elsewhere. A message had arrived, announcing a council of many of the world's significant individuals to discuss a matter of serious concern, undisclosed. Transport would arrive first thing in the morning. Really, things were just going from bad to worse, yet may be, if the council members were that significant, someone might have a clue how Henry could contact his own world, though raising this delicate subject would be extremely tricky.

The minstrel had been allowed out again and was busy updating the endless saga of Henry's bravery. It was clear to all the minstrel was in difficulty. Praising a non-event was outside the mindset of a travelling troubadour, used to vaunting feats of great nobility and courage. His desperate attempts to explain what happened in high flown language -

"On this brave dawn," the hero shouted, "noone dies

When from the jaws of death I pull a compromise."

- moved even the hardest heart. Eventually the minstrel abandoned the task, turning instead to songs of failure and defeat until he broke down in tears and was led gently below.

It was too bad, thought Henry, when he had to feel guilty about driving a minstrel to despair. He sat under the awning wrapped in a cloak. Gervase approached him respectfully, nervously rubbing his hands together, for in this world his wing did revert after sunset.

"Your Highness —"

"Yes Gervase."

"I have a request. I know it's a real cheek, but, well, it would be such an honour." His eyes were full with how this was a make or break moment and this was the biggest favour he had ever asked.

"What is it?"

"Do you have a squire?"

"Excuse me?"

"Of course, you're a Prince and have all sorts of servants, obviously, but I sort of wondered if you had – a special squire?"

"No, Gervase, I don't."

"Ah, the thing is, you see, I wondered if I could, sort of, be him."

"Oh."

"It's impertinent of me isn't it? Please forgive me Prince Henry, my family would be horrified that I've troubled you, because I *am* such a schlemiel and not really up to the role of squire."

Of course, that was what did it. Henry understood all about not being up to the role. Probably Gervase would be rather an irritating companion, but he should be given his chance. Furthermore, while no less baffled than his brothers by the arrangement with Deathbreather, he had never questioned it. He was completely loyal to Henry.

"It's not impertinent," replied Henry. "I really appreciate your offer —"

"But the answer's no."

"The answer's yes," said Henry, "though I don't have any money. I'm a penniless Prince!"

Gervase was untroubled. His cup of joy was full.

Henry managed to shake him off. He then relieved himself over the side of the boat, rubbed his teeth with a cloth and some sweet smelling herb Elise had given him, and went down to the royal cabin, graciously made available by the King. On the deck above Gervase was burnishing the golden armour to unimagined shiny perfection. Henry stripped down to a shirt and leggings, also donated by the King, and lay on the bed. Several large candles were burning, but the cabin was dim. He should have offered the cabin to Elise, he realised, but he was too exhausted to get up again. He slept. There were many disquieting dreams. He was stranded in the world of legends for the rest of his life. His parents were trapped in the magic mirror and he had no way to help them escape. Elise was tied to a cliff top and Deathbreather was coming for her, burning everyone in his path. Henry was waiting for the dragon, armed only with a toy sword, and he was petrified.

"Wake up, Prince Henry," said Gervase. "They're coming."

"Dragons!" muttered Henry in alarm.

"No your Highness. You should greet them."

It was morning, sevenish. Henry got himself out of bed, reluctantly allowed Gervase to strap on the accursed armour, then climbed to the deck, where he found the entire ship's company staring up at the sky. It was a clear summer morning, with a sun so friendly that it almost had a face with a smile. Henry pulled himself together. It was simply the sun. Over the river hovered a cloud of what looked to be extremely large insects with iridescent wings. Gorgeous as they were, Henry did not care for insects, especially the sort you were only supposed to see in a rain forest, so thought perhaps he might return to the cabin until whoever was arriving had arrived. He turned away, but felt a hand on his arm. It was Elise.

"You mustn't turn your back on them," she whispered. "If they don't get respect they'll leave."

"Good," said Henry, "I can't stand insects."

"They're not insects. If you insult them, your reputation could take a real knock."

Nothing got Henry's attention like a reference to his reputation. He squinted at the flying creatures, who had the sun behind them.

"Bow," hissed Elise.

"What?"

"Just bow!"

Henry bowed. A tiny figure landed on the rail in front of him and politely bowed in return. It was a tangle haired, handsome man, about thirty centimetres high, wearing an elaborate costume. His eyes were disproportionately large and bored like two little emerald drills into Henry's inner core.

"Fascinating to meet you, Prince Henry," said the small man in a remarkably strong voice for someone of his size.

"Likewise," replied Henry, who felt those eyes going deeper and deeper. There was no reply and Henry understood that he had not finished this greeting. He could only guess what he had omitted. He added hopefully – "Your Majesty."

That did the trick. "Your name is so celebrated, yet nobody seems to have come across you. I decided this was a perfect opportunity to see what you were like."

"I'm delighted," said Henry.

"Not a typical hero figure."

"I'm sorry about that."

"I wasn't expecting it. Callow and youthful was the rumour and callow and youthful you are."

"Well," said Henry, remembering something he had read on the web site, "although one should usually judge by appearances, they can be deceptive."

"Certainly, and sometimes they can even mislead the deceiver. Are you ready?"

"It depends on what I'm supposed to be ready for," replied Henry

"A hero should be ready for anything."

"Then I must be ready."

"Good. Which two will you be bringing with you?"

"I beg your pardon?"

"Which two attendants?"

"Oh – I do have a, well, a whole honour guard you might say."

"Naturally," said the tiny King. "But the arrangements limit you to two. Otherwise some participants will come alone while others seek to bring entire armies. It gets out of balance and those with armies get too demanding. And there's the whole question of provisions. Use us, but don't abuse us. The limit is two."

If he had been sensible, Henry would have chosen Adolphus and the largest brother. Instead he decided he would keep loyal to Gervase, who was after all his squire, and for the second —- "Elise, if she wants to come along."

She did, although this was surely a blow for women's rights from which her brothers might never recover. As for the little King, he smiled and said, "An unusual warrior who chooses the weakest fighters."

"But they —" began Henry. What?

"Care for you the most. So how generous are you really being to them?"

Henry did not answer that. Instead he said, "They'll enjoy coming along."

"Despite the risks?"

"What risks?"

The little figure bowed and flew away.

"What risks?" repeated Henry.

"There are always risks," said Elise. "I don't care. I'm grateful. And," she mouthed at him, "you need my help."

Gervase rushed over. "Oberon himself. What an honour!"

"Oberon," said Henry. "As in Oberon and Titania?"

"In theory," said Elise, before embracing Adolphus, who was an anxious man.

"They'll be fine with me," said Henry. "They're in

my – protection." Whereas, if anything, it was the other way round.

The cloud of fairies dropped from the sky, surrounding Henry, Elise and Gervase. They divided into three groups and attached themselves to various bits of body. They rose into the air once more, unsteadily at first as they adjusted to the weight, then more confidently, so that Henry began to relax into this unexpected and breathtaking mode of transport. He grinned at Elise, he laughed at Gervase, who kept saying, "Wow," and for the first time since he arrived in this world he saw it as something other than hostile.

They flew away from the river and the mountains, crossing different landscapes which changed quickly and abruptly, so one moment they were over a plain, next marshes, after that a desert where they landed at an oasis and had refreshments brought to them by waiting Bedouin. They took wing again and crossed over a desert town with soukhs and minarets. From an open window high in a shining white palace a young man stepped on a flying carpet, which followed them on their journey as once again they crossed into a different landscape. Henry wondered about these sudden changes, but felt unable to ask anyone except Elise, and for the moment had no opportunity to speak to her alone. Even at the oasis they had been surrounded by fairies while Oberon was always watching him with those intrusive emerald eyes.

The changes were not only abrupt, they were also misleading, because they gave the impression they had travelled a substantial distance over a great deal of time. In fact, when Henry thought about it, they had probably not travelled more than a few miles. How could it be otherwise when the fairies were so small? There were two possible explanations he decided, and may be both applied. First, as this was not a world subject to rules he was used to, distance and time might work differently. Secondly, as each bit of the world was home to a separate legend, existing side by side, the boundaries between them were sudden and absolute, so that once you had left one legend, it was not possible to look back at where it took place. This was the sort of concept he had come across enough times in stories or films. Its effect was to suggest a much lengthier journey.

Henry decided not to waste any more energy on this puzzle until later. It was much better to enjoy the experience, in every sense the most uplifting thing which had ever happened to him. The air was pure, the sun was hot but never burned him, a cool breeze refreshed him. He wanted to be like this for ever, relaxed and totally alive. When he looked at Elise and Gervase he could see they felt exactly the same.

They passed above a region of sharp black mountains where even in the afternoon sunshine a lonely castle threatened nights of danger. They skimmed over a turquoise ocean where the song of the sirens almost lured them too near until Oberon urged them to safety. They drifted on warm thermals through a flower filled valley where a pegasus flew with them. The young man on the flying carpet followed them through every change. Others joined them, borne also by a cloud of fairies through the long summer afternoon.

Finally they came to a wood where everyone was brought to the ground. The shadows were lengthening, but the light was still golden. Ahead stretched a wide path curving out of sight. On one side the ground sloped upwards and the gnarled roots of ancient trees pushed out of the grassy bank then disappeared into the path like big stitches holding everything together. On the other side the ground sloped downwards. Henry thought he saw figures lying between the trees, but realised their bodies were formed out of mud, trunks and stones. They were covered with ferns and grasses which looked like clothes or hair. May be they were alive. Who was to say in this world?

The fairies left them, drifting away into the wood. Everyone walked in silence, enjoying the peace, recognising this was planned for the journey's end to put them into a reflective and tranquil mood. It had the same feeling as the mellow green room in Wilfred's house.

The path turned suddenly and passed through some tall, wild rhododendron bushes, covered with pale mauve blossom. Ahead was a lake, where swans and mallards floated contentedly in the early evening. In the middle was an island which had to be their destination. Twenty or more slender boats were lined up at the water's edge. As they all climbed in, Henry saw the almost transparent naked shapes of young men and women who took hold of the boats and pulled them across the lake. Still noone spoke, and in their boat Henry, Elise and Gervase lay back against the cushions watching the ripples spread round the almost invisible swimmers.

They reached the island all too soon, because people, and they were mainly all people, started talking again and Henry understood that he would have to resume the role of famous hero, expected to take part in this council. Furthermore, a nasty little thought which

he had managed to keep to the back of his mind now
came boldly forward. He had a very good idea who all
the others might be, and when he put it quietly to Elise,
she confirmed this. He was at a gathering of legendary
heroes and heroines, all of whom deserved their splendid
reputations. Surely he would be exposed as a fraud? He
was also struck by the horrible realisation that Elise was
herself a heroine and deserved to be there in her own
right, not as an attendant to him.

The island consisted of a large open clearing, edged
by willow trees and bulrushes. At one side of the glade
were long tables laden with food and drink, and no
amount of concern kept Henry away from that. He was
ravenous, as were Elise and Gervase, as were apparently
all the others brought along to the council. While he ate
and drank – from silver plates and crystal goblets, what
else! – he anxiously inspected his fellow delegates. There
were several classical looking warriors, wearing helmets,
breast plates, short tunics and elaborate sandals. They
each looked unnecessarily fearless and muscular, and
extremely noble. They were the very personification of
nobleness. Henry kept out of their way. There was also
a young woman dressed in the same style – perhaps
that was Atalanta, the famous runner? There was a tall
striking man dressed in the lavish robes of the ancient
Assyrian empire. Elise said that he was King Gilgamesh.
The young man who had flown on the carpet was now
clutching it, rolled up, under his arm, and grinning as he
tried to eat at the same time. He could not be persuaded
to put the carpet down. Someone who might well have
been Beowulf was talking to a woman who was dressed
like the image of Britannia, so presumably she really

was Britannia. She seemed to be accompanied by an eighteenth century sailor and a First World War pilot. There were others too, who would have been from every part of the human race, and who represented legends unknown to Henry. There were also a few non-humans, including an elf, a hobbit possibly and a centaur. It was in effect a combination of scenes in many fantasy novels, totally fascinating, and Henry wished sincerely that he was somewhere else.

"It's brilliant being here," enthused Gervase, like a child in a fast food restaurant with several free offer tokens.

"Isn't it," said Henry with a wan smile.

"It is," said Elise to him, "and you'd better be a part of it. You're obviously supposed to be a part of it, so the sooner you accept it, the sooner you'll settle in."

"Yes, but —"

"Somehow you're here too early, but I believe in you. Or in what you're going to be. I might even make you a special shirt, and don't underestimate that offer. I promised myself I'd never touch another knitting needle for the rest of my life!"

That was a gesture of love, but a sisterly one. Undoubtedly.

A summoning drum began a slow beat. The drummer was a young black boy. Next to him stood a tall, black man in leopard skin robes and heavy gold jewellery. He seemed imperious, yet he was holding out both his hands in a benevolent gesture.

"Who is that?" asked Henry.

"Mwindo," said Elise.

There was no point pretending. "Who is Mwindo?"

"Where do you come from!" said Elise. "Mwindo is a very great ruler. He's been on a mission of vengeance against his father who tried to have him killed as a baby."

"I think my father wishes he'd done that." Unfair. And right now both his parents would be demented with worry. "Why's he the one taking the lead?"

"He's the senior hero present."

"It's brilliant being here," repeated Gervase, who had been too agog at the whole scene to take in what Henry and his sister had been saying.

The drumming stopped. There was a reasonable degree of quiet. Mwindo spoke.

"You heroes and heroines whose deeds are justly celebrated,

You heroes and heroines are in the presence of Mwindo.

Mwindo 's legend is oldest of all.

Your legends are burnished by the polish of mine.

You heroes and heroines are in the presence of Mwindo."

There were a few polite acknowledgments from those present. The classical heroes raised their eyebrows but said nothing.

"He's got a very good opinion of himself," said Henry quietly to Elise, though not quietly enough. The young man with the roll of carpet was standing next to him and laughed.

"He's better than he was, but he just adores the sound of his own voice. And he's such a poser. We think he might calm down once he's worked things out with his father!"

Mwindo continued.

"Each one who is here is chosen for his valour.

Each one who is here understands the nature of evil.

Each one who is here will never retreat from danger.

Each one who is here will fight for his brothers and sisters.

Each one who is here is chosen by Mwindo

Each one who is here must now make his own choice."

At this point a classical hero asked permission to speak, and when this was graciously given, said, "We all know why Mwindo invited us here. There is something very strange going on. Many of the most wicked people and creatures we know, whom we have fought or are pledged to fight, have turned away from their determined pursuit of evil. This is seriously weird."

"And, you might add, Perseus, highly suspicious," said another classical hero.

"Highly suspicious, Jase," agreed Perseus. "I went after Medusa the other day and when I caught up with her she warned me to look away. Then she offered to check out all our cellars and turn the rats and mice to stone."

"I went after the fearsome Bull of Heaven," said King Gilgamesh, "and found him harnessed to a plough, singing nursery rhymes to the farmer's children. It made me physically sick, but what could I do?"

"And I was all ready to fight Abanazer," said the young man with the carpet, "when he smiled and returned my magic lamp which he said he had mistakenly picked up instead of his own lamp. During the time he had it, I discovered, he'd asked the genie to feed all the poor and the needy. I tell you, there was a real risk of the townsfolk preferring him to me!"

Henry felt relieved at hearing this. If all the others had found their enemies behaving in this odd way, it was only to be expected that Deathbreather would be acting the same. Should anyone have heard of Henry's agreement with the dragon, he could imply that it was the identical sort of situation. It was, almost, subject only to the fact that he had never intended to fight the dragon in the first place.

"May be the bad have changed," suggested the individual who looked like a hobbit and who Henry sensed was not fully accepted by all present.

"Hardly," said Beowulf dismissively.

"I don't think they really have," said Perseus, "but they're putting us in an impossible position. If they're doing no wrong, how can we fight them? And if we can't do that, what's our purpose?"

There was an uncomfortable silence.

"I'm sure they haven't changed," said Jason. "They're up to something."

"In that case," said King Gilgamesh, "we should attack them anyway."

"Is that fair?" asked the hobbit.

"When are they fair to us?" replied Gilgamesh.

"It may or may not be fair," said Perseus, "But it's justified. If they're planning something big, then we're entitled to a pre-emptive strike. It's really only self-defence. Why should we wait to be attacked?"

"It pains me to say this," – Aladdin shook his head sadly – "but I think we need proof first."

"I agree," said Britannia. "I couldn't support an attack otherwise. It just wouldn't be British."

There were some others of a similar view. Mwindo summed up the situation and his own opinion.

"We are like minnows in a pool
First we swim one way, then the other
Some are determined, some are frightened.
While we dart about, the fish swallows us."

"Give me strength," muttered Jason. "Why can't he just say what he means?"

Henry was certain only he knew who was responsible for this world-shaking behaviour. He felt obliged to enlighten the gathering. He would tell them an edited version of the truth.

"May I speak?" he said.

Mwindo gestured at him to do so.

"When I – didn't fight Deathbreather recently, I met someone near his cave. Someone who had persuaded Deathbreather to restrain his usual behaviour." He had their attention. "He was called the Spinner." The name was not a complete surprise to all. The rumours of the Spinner had started, although nobody had any idea of what he was spinning. "He was first employed by a great Queen."

"Which great Queen?" asked the centaur. "This —"

"Yes, I know," said Henry. "This world is full of great Queens. It's —" He had to describe her, yet he had no idea of her name. "It's the keeper of the magic mirror, the mother of Princess Snow White."

"Always bad news," said Jason, scratching himself on his groin.

Henry suddenly remembered how the ancient Greeks

never changed their underwear, or was that only during the winter? He pulled himself together. "She was anxious that her powers were waning, and it turned out some of her, em, kindred spirits felt the same. The Spinner is helping them appear less bad."

"In that case it's a trick," observed Gilgamesh. "There's no reason for us to hold back."

"In fact, there's every reason to attack them," said Jason, "if they are weaker and less confident."

"It still seems iffy to me," said Britannia. "I mean, if they're not a real threat at the moment —"

"Of course they are," interrupted another classical hero, "It sounds like another wooden horse deal." It must be Hector. "Who knows what magic they're hiding or armies they're concealing!"

Perseus spoke. "I'm going to say something which noone else has. If I'm alone in feeling this, then you may wish me to leave. I've felt my own powers waning recently. When I met Medusa last, I realised I could not resist her. If she hadn't told me to look away, I'd have been a statue."

There was an uneasy pause. Then one by one others also admitted to feelings of doubt or moments of weakness. Mwindo once again summed up the position as he saw it.

"We face the dwindling of our power.
If we lose our power do we lose our lives?
Better lose our lives than lose our enemies.
If we lose our enemies we lose our legends.
Without our legends our names are unheard.
When good and evil both do nothing, evil wins."

That must be the right approach normally, thought Henry, at any rate here. However, both the good and the evil had a common enemy to dispose of first or else this world was likely to collapse altogether. If Rupert could be sent back, the evil would probably revert to type without his guidance, then the timeless battles could continue. Even if both sides were less powerful, the balance would return. Henry had to explain this to them.

It was the end of twilight. Coloured lanterns were shining in the branches of the willow trees. The lanterns nearest to Henry seemed to be attracting a forest's worth of moths, all enormous, one of which hovered in front of him. He recoiled automatically before recognising it as a fairy.

"Prince Henry," said the fairy, "I would invite you to come with me."

This sounded more like an arrest than an invitation.

"I've got something to say to everybody," said Henry.

"They'll be here all night," said the fairy. "King Oberon asks that you visit him straight away."

"You'd better go," Elise advised, with a concerned expression. "Oberon is not a gentleman to be ignored – unless you don't mind living for a hundred years in a giant spider's web crawling with huge spiders or existing as a microbe in the crater of a volcano."

"You should bring your attendants," said the fairy.

A cluster of fairies once again attached themselves to Henry, Elise and Gervase, bearing them across the silent lake to the wakeful night time forest. The full moon had risen, so the ground not in shadow was almost bright. They flew back over the pathway and Henry saw again those curious reclining figures, but now their eyes were glowing. So were their wide open mouths. Perhaps they were some kind of dangerous spirit who came to life after dark. In a large open glade stretched a figure far larger than the rest, a giant, with enormous eyes and a huge mouth – and other glowing areas along the side. When the fairies dropped down beside the vast body, Henry realised what the figures were - the homes of the fairies, and this must be Oberon's palace. As they landed, Oberon walked into the glowing mouth, his arm round the shoulders of a female slightly smaller than him, barely covered in a gauzy wrap. He pushed her gently away into the glade.

"There's been a manifestation," he announced. "A head and shoulders have appeared, asking for you."

Henry's heart did a triple jump of pure joy.

"Is it the head of an old man? Called Wilfred?"

"No it's not Wilfred. It's the top part of Rumpelstiltskin, which is more than enough. In your own interests, you need to speak to him."

Henry's heart had made a false start. He was about to be disqualified. "Where is he?"

"Inside, in my bedroom. His sheer cheek beggars belief. When I think what I — You'd better come in."

"But how can I do that?"

"Your reticence does you honour, Prince Henry," replied Oberon, misunderstanding him. "Please enter."

The next thing Henry knew was that he was standing with Oberon, now more or less the same size, in a large room. It was filled with the perfume of flowers much bigger than they were, and the sheets on the bed were cut from scarlet poppies. But these and other wonders of the overblown furnishings passed Henry by, even the fact that he had shrunk to thirty centimetres in height. The only matter of interest was the head and shoulders of Rumpelstiltskin floating against the gold leaf on the walls.

"Prince Henry," grinned Rumpelstiltskin, "this is such a pleasure."

"It's certainly a surprise," said Henry.

"I bet it is," said Rumplestiltskin. "It's time to collect my payment for the ten bags of gold."

"But I haven't had the opportunity to ask around."

"I can't help that," said Rumpelstiltskin.

"This isn't fair."

"Au contraire," beamed Rumpelstiltskin. "It's in the contract. Tell me my second name."

A thought struck Henry. "I need two more days."

"So you might," said Rumpelstiltskin, "but you're not getting them."

"Don't you always allow three attempts over three days? It's an implied term in the contract."

"Very clever," said Rumpelstiltskin, winking at Oberon. "He's a bright boy, this one." He leered down at Henry. "No, there aren't any implied terms. Tell me my second name or take the consequences."

"I want to challenge that interpretation in court," shouted Henry desperately.

"By all means. What's my second name?"

"I don't know it," said Henry bleakly.

"Then I'll have your reputation. Thank you friends and goodnight. Rumpelstiltskin has left the building!"

Rumpelstiltskin disappeared.

"That's very powerful magic," murmured Oberon. "Who's helping him?"

"What's going to happen?" asked Henry.

Oberon's great emerald eyes showed a trace of compassion. "At this moment," he answered, "all those attending the gathering of heroes will see you as a fraud. They're very angry."

"But there are things I still need to explain to them."

"Keep away. They won't listen. Someone there might even kill you."

"Can I explain everything to you? May be you could speak to them."

"No, that's not my role." There was a momentary blur and Henry found himself outside once more. "What I will do though," said Oberon, from several metres below, "is take you away from here. Choose a place. When you're ready, let someone know."

He called out, "Cobweb", and the pretty little fairy barely dressed in gauze reappeared. She giggled. Oberon gave her a kiss and led her inside.

"What's gone on?" asked Elise, deeply concerned.

"I've – Can't you tell? The whole world knows by now."

Elise frowned. "Oh. Nobody believes you're a hero any more."

"I never was a hero," said Henry. "That's the whole point."

Gervase seemed extremely confused. "But you were. I'm sure you still are. Perhaps you're under a curse?" he suggested helpfully. "Elise and I know all about curses. There's always a way to remove them."

"Yes, I'm under a curse," said Henry, "but it's my own fault."

"That doesn't mean you can't get rid of it," said Gervase.

"Yes it does when the curse is me."

"Prince Henry," said Elise, "that sounds clever but quite honestly I don't know what it means."

"My reputation was false," said Henry, "and now Rumpelstiltskin's taken it from me – because of a foolish contract I made with him."

"If it was false," said Elise, "then it wasn't worth anything. Go out and get a proper reputation."

"Doing what?"

"Well, the sailors on the boat said you were on a sort of quest."

"I am."

"A quest," repeated Gervase with the clear message that he intended to be part of it.

"I'm sure that's the way forward," said Elise.

What could Henry do? He had tried to speak to Rupert, who showed no readiness to listen. He supposed he would have to try again. If Rupert weren't prepared to stop what he was doing, perhaps he would be prepared to send Henry back. So that was the solution, he had to find Rupert.

"I'm searching for the Spinner," he said. "He's endangering your own world by interfering with good and evil."

"That sounds like some pretty major stuff!" exclaimed Gervase. "I'm with you on that."

"No," said Henry. "I don't want you to put yourself

at risk," especially when Henry was thinking largely of his own escape.

"I'm your squire. It's my place to be at your side." That stupid loyal idiot.

"I want to come Henry," said Elise.

"No, I made a mistake. I might have to pay for it. I don't want you two in danger." A warm glow of self-satisfaction came over Henry. That was a pretty selfless act.

"I insist," said Elise.

"OK," said Henry.

"So do I – with all due respect," said Gervase.

"OK," said Henry.

Well, he had tried. And he needed some friends.

CHAPTER 14

Friends and enemies

HENRY SPENT AN uncomfortable night out in the glade, dozing fitfully and watching his companions sleeping the sleep of the just. Shortly before dawn they were brought some berries and edible fungus, also some honey sweetened drink. Henry rid himself of the accursed armour, which only mocked his current predicament, though he was persuaded to keep the sword buckled on. After that the fairies carried them to the land ruled by the Queen who had first employed Rupert. Oberon was certain Rupert was there. However, they were not taken directly to the palace, which might simply land them in trouble. Instead, they were left in yet another forest, not far from a smallish cottage. This was serious chocolate box – walls covered by honeysuckle and climbing roses, diamond paned windows and a chunky thatched roof. A strong smell of bacon and eggs was drifting out of the open doorway.

It was a delightful morning with a heavy dew. Birds were singing to sickeningly good effect and a high soprano voice was warbling away inside the cottage. Just his luck thought Henry. This had to be Walt Disney's version of Snow White. No wonder her mother wanted to kill her. Henry was shocked at himself.

They walked up to the doorway and looked in. A young girl, no more than sixteen, was standing at a range, trilling cheerfully as she cooked breakfast for seven small individuals, all bearded (please note Disney) and all watching her with adoring eyes. The adoration was clear even though the dwarves had their backs to the door.

"Good morning," said Henry.

"Why, hello!" cried Snow White, pleasantly startled. The seven dwarves turned and inspected the new arrivals mistrustfully.

"Hello," said Henry and stopped. He had run out of ideas.

"Hello," said Elise. "We were directed here by Oberon. He thought you might help us."

"He would," said a dwarf darkly. Obviously not Happy then.

"Don't be so grouchy," chided Snow White.

May be Grumpy? No, decided Henry, this had to stop right now.

"Of course we'll help you." Snow White radiated goodness.

"But you don't know who they are," protested another dwarf.

"It doesn't matter," said Snow White. "It's the right thing to do. And I can tell they're kind, lovely people."

"You think everybody's 'kind, lovely people'," said a third dwarf. "That's nearly got you killed twice."

"But she was such a sweet old woman."

"She almost strangled you the first time," said the dwarf.

"And almost poisoned you the second," said another.

"I've promised not to let anyone in when you're at work," said Snow White. She smiled at her visitors. "Now who are you?"

"I'm Henry," said Henry, deciding to drop 'Prince'.

"I'm Elise," said Elise and, seeing that Gervase was standing open-mouthed in admiration, introduced her brother as well.

" 'Henry'," repeated a dwarf. "Not a common name round here. It wouldn't be Prince Henry, would it?"

Damn. "Yes, as it happens," said Henry uneasily.

"One of our little bird friends has sung us a song about you this morning," that dwarf continued in an unfriendly way.

"O my," exclaimed Snow White, "was that why the blackbird was such a noisy little chirruper when Mr Sun showed his head!"

"Yes," replied the dwarf. "He told us that Prince Henry had been exposed as a fraud."

"It's true," admitted Henry.

"It's not," said Elise. "Prince Henry was tricked by Rumpelstiltskin into losing his reputation."

At the mention of the name 'Rumpelstiltskin', all seven dwarves sent great gobs of tobacco coloured spittle into a brass spittoon.

"Now boys," objected Snow White, "what have I told you about those dirty habits?"

The dwarves looked shame faced. However, one said, "Rumpelstiltskin is as nasty a piece of waste as you'll ever come across." Furthermore, the dwarves became a lot less hostile.

"That's better," said Snow White. "Now let's all sit down and have breakfast."

As they ate, Henry was forced to explain why he had entered into a bargain with Rumpelstiltskin. Was it his fault that the story which came out was somehow to his very great credit? He had to think of something quickly, and while he was trying to explain himself, and edit the bits about changing worlds, people somehow leaped to the wrong conclusions. What almost everyone believed by the end of breakfast was that he had heard about Aurelia's imprisonment and knew that Rumpelstiltskin would enter into some outrageous bargain with her. In the circumstances he had met Rumpelstiltskin, made his own contract to protect Aurelia and then took the last ten bags of gold into the tower. Because of the immediate need to go after Deathbreather and then attend the gathering of heroes, he had been left with no time to find out Rumpelstiltskin's second name. He had sacrificed his reputation on the altar of duty. Only Elise's slightly quizzical expression suggested a certain doubt, but she said nothing. Henry smiled at her sadly.

"Such rotten luck," said Gervase, managing briefly to take his eyes off Snow White.

"That Rumpelstiltskin," said a dwarf "is a disgrace to the family."

"Are you related to him?" asked Henry.

"Unfortunately, yes. He's part dwarf and a sort of cousin. He's been trouble from the day he was – well, from the day he was."

"Does that mean you know his second name?"

"No," replied the dwarf, "but I should be able to find it out."

"Mind you," said Henry, "it might be too late now, strictly, but it could be worth trying if I see him again."

"I'll send word to his mother," said the dwarf. "She'll help. She can't stand him."

"No wonder the poor creature is so mixed up," said Snow White, "if his mother doesn't love him."

What could anyone say really? And who could tell what each of them knew about Snow White's past?

Henry explained that he had to find someone called the Spinner who was probably at the palace, but it was far too dangerous to go to the gate and demand admittance. There the dwarves were able to assist. As miners they had considerable knowledge of a whole system of underground caves and passages, one of which led under the palace and came up somewhere inside it, although a prudent regard for the Queen's evil powers had prevented any of them from finding out exactly where. One of the dwarves offered to lead Henry underground and point out the way.

Henry, Elise, Gervase and the dwarf set out on their journey, leaving the other six dwarves to march off to work, not singing though. Henry had wondered whether to warn Snow White about strangers and apples, but decided he should intervene as little as possible into what was happening in this world, and anyway Snow White's story had a happy ending. From the look on Gervase's face, that happy ending should have been with him, but unfortunately Gervase was not a prince, so he was going to be disappointed.

They wandered through the sunny forest, Gervase

chatting to the dwarf about life with Snow White, while Henry and Elise walked behind them.

"Prince Henry," said Elise, "may I be frank?"

"Of course."

"You're keeping a lot hidden. That's up to you. But you don't have to claim credit for things you haven't done, because you're going to get your reputation back. And that'll be from things you really have done, although you haven't done them yet." She patted him on the arm. "You're a sort of hero in waiting!"

Henry sighed. "I didn't set out to mislead, but I didn't want to reveal where I come from. It's too complicated."

"You can trust me."

Henry had understood that from their first meeting. "I'm not from here."

"Neither am I."

"No, I don't mean this isn't my country, I mean this isn't my world. I'm a visitor, I suppose."

Elise took this in her stride. "From the moon?"

"No, from a parallel universe."

"I'll tell you something," she said. "I haven't the slightest idea what you're saying – yet again! On the other hand, it does sound like it would explain why there's so much you don't know."

"Indeed."

"Well, you might not have come from this world, but I'm positive you're going to stay here."

Help, really! "Can you read the future?"

She smiled.

In her way, Henry decided, she was equally as beautiful as Aurelia, less from the point of view of looks, more as a whole person.

The forest petered out. They began to walk along a narrow country lane which wound through some lush farmland. They climbed a gate and started across a wide field full of buttercups at one end and cows at the other. Gervase and the dwarf remained deep in conversation. Gervase might be a little dim but he had definite charm. The dwarf was laughing a lot. He stopped laughing. The cows were moving resolutely towards them. Well, that was hardly a problem, they were only cows, although they seemed rather big cows. In fact they were bulls, huge, black and thundering across the field, viciously determined.

"Run," shouted the dwarf, "it's the phouka."

"How does he know that?" asked Henry.

"Who cares! Run," cried Elise.

They ran, but could never run fast enough, especially the tubby dwarf. And Henry suddenly felt responsible for what was happening. Why should his companions be harmed on his account, for clearly he was the person the phouka were trying to kill? He did something which made no sense at all. He stopped still. Then he turned and faced the phouka and saw the fury in their eyes as they charged towards him. He should have been scared, but was excited on one level and, deep inside, quite calm. Time stretched, giving him ample room to plan, to act – even to enjoy himself.

The first bull snorted past, unable to pull up short. Henry waved goodbye. He somersaulted in front of the next bull, who lunged at him, but missed. He stood in front of a third, throwing himself out of the way at the last moment. He avoided the others, all going too fast to stop so quickly. However, they checked themselves further on, returning purposely to where Henry stood. Elise, Gervase and the dwarf ran on until they realised they were no longer being followed. They turned round. They stared in horror.

Henry stood with his arms folded. The leader of the bulls came forward on his own.

"It ends here," he said, his red eyes full of malice. "In the heat of the afternoon. Mano a mano."

"You haven't got any manos," said Henry.

"No," said the bull, "but I've got horns."

"I'm not frightened of you," said Henry, taking off his tunic and holding it like a matador's cloak.

"A piece of advice, my son," said the bull, "Don't mess around. Die with dignity."

He charged at Henry who swept his tunic in front of the bull and cried "Ole". Fun no doubt, but Henry knew the bull was too powerful for him to play at being a matador. The bull came at him again. Henry did something extraordinary. Where did the thought come from? Where did the skill, where did the strength? He ducked out of the way, twisted round beside the bull, grabbed his neck, pulled himself onto his back. The bull started to slow down, preparing to buck, throw Henry to the ground and gore him. Gripping on with one hand, Henry pulled out the sword and pressed it into the bull's neck.

"Call this off," he gasped, "or I'll kill you."

"So kill me," said the bull, still rearing up, "if you can."

It defied belief that Henry managed to stay on. "I can and will."

He would have. The bull understood this. He

quietened. "Kill me if you want," he said. "But how will you kill all the others?"

"Of course I can't manage that," replied Henry. "But if they attacked me, how would that meet your code of honour?"

"What code of honour!"

"Was all that mano a mano stuff just for affectation?"

"No," said the bull. "Kill me. You've earned the right. The others won't touch you."

"No," said Henry, "that doesn't meet *my* code of honour." He slid off the bull. "Wanton death is unacceptable."

"I agree," said the bull turning back into his real shape with his white goat's head. The other bulls did the same. "I saw how you looked when Deathbreather incinerated our brothers."

"If that's your view," said Henry, "why were you trying to kill me and my companions?"

"You represent a threat," answered the leader of the phouka.

"Who told you that?"

"Those who protect the Spinner."

"A threat to what?"

"Our world,"

"That's not true. It's the Spinner who's the threat."

Elise, Gervase and the dwarf jogged up to them.

"Wow," exclaimed Gervase, "that was truly excellent. Have you taken them prisoner?"

"No of course I haven't," said Henry.

"Because," added Gervase anxiously, "the alternative

would be for them to take us prisoner. They do pretty much outnumber us. Are we going to fight them?"

"No," said Henry, "they're leaving us."

"Not completely," said the leader, "we're going to watch you while we think this through. But we won't interfere with your journey."

The phouka drifted off.

"What made you take those risks?" asked Elise.

"I was angry," Henry replied. "With me basically."

"You're back on the track. You've begun to restore your reputation."

"From that?" Henry frowned. "Who's going to know?"

"You'll see," said Elise. "It won't be enough, but it'll confuse people and make them cautious. So should you be. Heroism doesn't mean behaving like a prat."

"I'm one of those confused people," said Henry. "I thought the phouka were vicious killers. I don't seem to have got that quite right."

"They can be," said the dwarf. "They're treacherous and mean-minded to those who don't like them or they don't like. But they're very friendly to those who accept them."

Gervase, in squire mode, handed Henry his tunic. Henry put it on, only too aware that for a hero he had rather a scrawny frame. They walked though the field, and the next one, until they came to a small hill.

"If you went to the top," said the dwarf, "you'd see the town and the palace. But we'll go in here," he indicated a narrow entrance "and move underneath them."

"Another cave," murmured Henry. "No good comes from caves."

"I wouldn't quite put it that way," said the dwarf. "I would agree that good isn't always found in caves. We'll just have to be optimistic."

"You're not about to start singing are you?" asked Henry.

They passed through the opening. It was a small cavern without unpleasant smells or bones, which was a good start. The dwarf lit a lamp, then led them to an even narrower opening at the back of the cave. They squeezed through that and found themselves in a long corridor-like tunnel, lighted by brasiers. The walls glittered with little specks of gold embedded in the rock. The dwarf extinguished his lamp.

"It's a fine sight," he said from his perspective as a miner.

"It's a worrying sight," said Elise. "It means this corridor is in use. We can guess who uses it and keeps these flames burning constantly."

Henry did not accept he would ever be a hero. His reckless behaviour with the bulls must have been temporary madness rather than genuine bravery, but he had to protect his companions – sweet, innocent, immensely breakable – and make sure nothing he did interfered with their preordained lives. "This is too dangerous for anyone else. Please go back to Snow White's cottage."

They protested.

"I'm your squire," said Gervase. "I have to be at your side. End of story."

Exactly. That's what was bothering Henry.

"If you don't take me with you, your Highness, it shames me."

"Noone could blame you at the moment," said Henry. "My name is mud."

"But that won't last," said Gervase, "and if I haven't stuck with you through the bad times, then my name will be mud. My brothers will say I wasn't up to it."

"I doubt it. They'll be furious with me and worried about Elise. This is a tricky world. I need you to protect your sister."

That was unanswerable. Gervase and the dwarf returned to the cave.

"Em —" Henry was not too certain how to put this to Elise. "Would you do me a favour?"

"Of course."

"No, I mean would you give me a favour?"

"That's hardly loyal to Aurelia."

"There's no reason to be."

"Oh." She gave him a scarf, she gave him a kiss, then she left him. Henry wondered if he would ever see her again

He made his way along the tunnel for several minutes without incident, then he turned a corner and reached a narrow bridge over an extremely deep drop. He had so hoped to be spared this, but it was obviously an essential part of any legend which took someone through underground caverns. Granted, the hero always made it across, and this particular bridge did have a railing, yet it had to spell trouble. Even if all went smoothly on the way in, there was bound to be a major problem on the way out.

It seemed quiet enough. No roar from an approaching monster, no rumble as falling boulders crashed down from above, no screech when some evil flying creature swooped up from below. He might as well cross.

He walked gingerly on to the bridge, which was firm and made of stone, but did not fool him for an instant. It might snap upwards, or split into two, or disappear altogether, each of which would send him tumbling into an abyss, a fiery furnace (though he could see no flames), a pit of huge serpents – demons even, demons were making quite a comeback in popular mythology. He held on tightly to the railing. Much good that would do him if it all went pear-shaped! However, the bridge stayed where it was.

Two metres from the other side a smallish young man emerged from an archway and grinned at him. He was wearing a longish orange robe.

"Prince Henry!" cried Rupert. "So kind of you to come to tea!"

"What's with the orange?" asked Henry, sounding like the mirror. "It really isn't your colour."

"It's bright. I like it. Perhaps I shouldn't be calling you 'Prince' any more."

"As it happens," said Henry, "I now believe you should."

"Even after you've been exposed as a cheat to a hefty percentage of this world's major heroes?"

"I was tricked, as you know."

"Tricked out of something you never had in the first place!"

"It isn't quite as simple as that, is it, because someone had to give me a reputation here for me to lose it. Which means either I earn it eventually or someone wants to protect me."

"You clever old thing," said Rupert. "Are you coming off that bridge? Bridges and unhappy love affairs, it's always best when you're over them."

Henry decided to take that advice and walked onto the other side. "Why were the phouka turned against me?"

"Because of your reputation."

"What was my reputation? I've never found that out. No one I spoke to ever seemed to know."

"You didn't speak to the right people. Only the most powerful had an inkling of it. They can tell, while a reputation is still growing, before everyone else learns about it. And even they didn't really understand. What they picked up, though, was you could be a great threat to them at a time their power was waning. The wicked ones decided to nip you in the bud so to speak. How were they to know you stupidly nipped yourself in the bud by a foolish agreement with Rumpelstiltskin? Even I didn't know that until yesterday. What an idiot!"

That was true, therefore Henry decided to let it pass. "Is that why they sent the phouka after me the night you crossed over?"

"Yes. They weren't to realise you were a timid little student. They thought you might actually do me harm. The word 'Please!' comes to mind."

"Why were they so keen on you?"

"Because I offered them a way forward. And once again, though they couldn't quite work it out, they understood I could help them."

"But —"

"Enough, enough," said Rupert. "We've got so little time."

"For what?"

"For me to send you back."

"To our world?"

"That's exactly right," said Rupert.

"You've got to come back too," said Henry.

"I don't think so."

Rupert turned and started to walk down the passage. Henry followed, posing more questions, trying to reason with Rupert yet having no solid basis on which to argue.

"What's your reputation here?" he asked.

There was the slightest of pauses before Rupert answered. "It's fairly obvious isn't it? You know what I do best. You heard me with Deathbreather. You were at the gathering of heroes. I'm spinning for the bad guys. I'm making them change their ways. I can't believe you could object to that. Think of all the good I'm doing, the lives I'm saving!"

"Yes," said Henry, who had to accept the validity of that argument. "But isn't there a balance of good and evil here? You're disrupting it. And the barrier between the worlds —"

"You've been listening to Mr Senility Wilfred. Forget about him. He lives in the past. He wants everything to stay the same but this world has to evolve too."

They climbed a staircase up to an ancient carved door. It was all very predictable.

"Now this," explained Rupert "leads into the palace and I'm going to take you to the room with the magic mirror."

"O yes," said Henry, remembering a conversation a week or two ago, "the one you told me I shouldn't bother with."

"I lied," said Rupert. "The mirror says hello!"

"How can you get me into that room? It's the Queen's private chamber. She's not going to invite us in."

"She's away this afternoon, visiting an orphanage. She's working on her image. With luck the children won't realise that most of them are only orphans because she murdered their parents."

"Even so —"

"She doesn't realise that mirror responds to anyone else. We can go in. Mind you, if she finds us there, I mightn't be able to explain my way out of it."

He unlocked the door. "A magic key Henry, a gift from a grateful client who was otherwise dangerously close to death by drowning. Think how much the burglars on your world would give me for this!"

"My world? Our world."

"Sure."

Rupert took Henry into yet another passage, although this one was deep inside a building. It led past a torture chamber, which was not empty. A starved grey body was stretched out on rack, stinking, moaning, dying. The body turned its head as they passed and mouthed "Water."

"This is too bad," said Rupert. "She promised me she was going to give up torture. May be this one was already on the go and she just forgot about him. Come on."

"Hell, Rupert," said Henry with real anger, "We've got to set him free."

"But he's in chains. What am I supposed to do?"

"Use your bloody key."

Rupert looked at Henry. "Only works on doors. Give him some water and I'll speak to the Queen later."

Henry found some foul water in a cup, but the prisoner was grateful enough. They passed on and up through the palace until they reached the state rooms. They were all decorated in crimson and black. It was a hot evening and the reddening light spread across the furnishings like poisoned wine. This was a sick, evil place. Henry had wondered whether any servants would try to challenge him, until he saw them. They were in a trance, pale faced, glassy eyed, going about their duties with no awareness of anything else, or simply standing, waiting until required. Henry had a feeling that some of them had been in the same position for days on end. They must have been drugged, or rather, under a spell.

Rupert opened a door and Henry found himself in the familiar room. Even through a computer screen he had sensed the stifling hostility to anything pure, but the cloying smell of burning herbs was unexpected. Each breath he took was like inhaling wickedness and it was impossible to believe that anyone staying in that atmosphere for very long could avoid its corruption.

Rupert was untroubled by the room. He walked across to the mirror.

"Mirror, mirror on the wall,

Who's the smartest of them all!"

The mirror unclouded itself. "O hooray. Mr Self-satisfaction. And with a friend I see."

"Good evening," said Henry politely.

"Manners maketh the man, they say," observed the mirror. "Good evening, Prince Henry."

"He wants to go back," said Rupert.

"Does he?" asked the mirror. "Do you, Prince Henry?"

"Well," Henry replied, "this isn't my world. I shouldn't be here."

"Shouldn't you?" said the mirror. "Why so definite?"

"I don't belong."

"Do you belong in your own world?"

Good question. He felt pretty much of an outsider there. But at least he knew its rules, he functioned, after a fashion, he had a career planned —

"Now mirror," said Rupert, "if Henry would like to go home, we shouldn't stop him, should we."

"True," agreed the mirror. "And I won't. But we'd better get on with it or else *she* might."

"You mean the Queen's returning?"

"Yes," answered the mirror, "and she's not in a good mood. An afternoon with thirty two children under twelve is very much at the limit of her tolerance. It was touch and go."

"In what sense?" asked Rupert.

"She nearly brought a child back to the palace."

"O," said Rupert. "If she starts eating children, that's a really unwise move. Where's the good news story in that?"

"I do want to go back," said Henry.

"That's good bye to sweet Elise," the mirror pointed out.

"I realise that," said Henry, "but I shouldn't be interfering in her life."

"Is that her view?" asked the mirror. "Is that even your view?"

"No," said Rupert irritably, "Henry's view should be of himself in you. Take a look Henry."

"I don't reflect anything unless I want to," said the mirror, "remember that. However, do take a peek."

Henry looked in the mirror. He saw his tired face and the absurdity of his pretending to be something he was not.

"Yes pretence is absurd," said the mirror, answering his thought, "but are you really sure you know what you are and what you aren't?"

A good question, for which Henry required a long time to work out the answer.

"Which of us does?" Rupert cut in quickly, "We can't hang about. The Queen's on her way. Go home Henry. I may not be able to help you again."

"How can I get back?"

"Ah well," said Rupert, "we have the technology!"

"O, a joke," said the mirror. "Isn't he cute!"

"You are going to help, aren't you?" said Rupert in a much harder voice.

The mirror clouded slightly. "This hasn't been an easy decision. I've got divided loyalties. If I could only see the future —"

"You can see the present," said Rupert. "If he had a place here, he's lost it. What's more, I was brought here to do a job and — I don't have to say any more do I?"

"No," sighed the mirror. "You'd better leave. If she finds you here she won't understand. Even your silver tongue won't be enough to save you."

"It's a challenge I look forward to," said Rupert, "but perhaps not today." He turned to Henry. "Goodbye old chum. Give me a call some time, if you can find me. Otherwise my advice to you is, get on with your life and don't interfere. Because, if you do, I won't protect you."

Henry was extremely confused. He found it difficult to work out whether Rupert had any real feelings of friendship for him. He'd been convinced there were none, recent events hardly suggested otherwise, and he had killed off his friendship for Rupert. He understood that Rupert's prime motivation for sending him back was self-interest. Yet there seemed to be some genuine concern in there too. Henry was not at all certain he should be leaving, even if this were truly possible, but what he wanted so badly was a period of calm reflection, which seemed completely impossible if he remained here.

Rupert smiled and went out through the door.

"She's going to freak," said the mirror.

"When she finds out what's happened?"

"She won't be quite sure what. But she'll know something has. And I'll be too drained to speak for hours."

"She'll threaten to smash you again."

"She won't."

"Before I go, can you tell me —?"

"You always leave everything too late Prince Henry. I've got less than a minute. Stand in front of me."

Henry did as asked. The mirror started to cloud over, then the mistiness dispersed and Henry was amazed. He seemed to be looking into a computer screen and Wilfred's gloomy face was staring back. Henry started to speak, but as on the previous occasion the room stared to fade away. On this occasion though he could watch the room door open and the Queen enter. The last thing he saw was her glare of puzzled fury.

CHAPTER 15

Partial explanations

HENRY WAS SITTING on the dusty floor in the room at the top of Wilfred's house. Wilfred himself was inspecting him mournfully from his chair next to an old desk where a laptop was open but off.

"I've got appalling hay fever," he said, shaking his head. "Of course the dust doesn't help." His eyes inclined towards a patch of damp. "Or the mould."

"You shouldn't have just sent me without asking permission," said Henry. "It was a breach of my human rights."

"As it happens, you're very grateful. It's such a pity you didn't stay."

As it happened, Henry was very grateful. Was it a pity he didn't stay? "You know how to send me through. Presumably you could send me there again if necessary, though I think it would be pleasant if I had more of a say about timing. And I don't want to go."

"Look at yourself in the mirror," said Wilfred.

"I didn't just come through that, did I? 'Henry

through the looking glass'. I don't think so. But what about that magic mirror? Is it a computer screen. If so —"

"I want you to take a close look at yourself." Wilfred interrupted.

"I've just done that."

"Not in this world."

Henry did as bidden. He still saw his tired face, but noticed something he had completely missed before. A certain amount of self-confidence.

"That is new!" he said.

"A pity you didn't see it earlier," said Wilfred.

"Like you often are," replied Henry, who was resenting Wilfred's judgemental attitude, "I was stressed."

"Do you understand the harm he's doing?" asked Wilfred.

"I understand the theory of it," Henry replied. "But what I kept hearing was how all these evil characters had stopped —" he remembered the tortured man in the Queen's dungeons, "or at any rate reduced their killing and maiming, their reigns of terror and so on. It seems difficult to quarrel with that."

Wilfred put his head in his hands. "What I require is a week in Torquay, in a small private hotel, with no children, no animals – and no Americans until possibly dinner on the last evening."

"Do you want me to make you a cup of tea or get you some water?"

"No thank you. The mistake you are making is to see the world of legends as operating by the same rules as our world. It obviously has some of them but it's much more extreme. Remember what it reflects - moral tussles, battles between good and evil, dreams, nightmares, repression, desires of every sort —"

"The actual battles which go on inside us?"

"Absolutely. It all seems to be real, and it is in its own terms, but in essence it's – it's a manifestation of the human psyche."

"So people are required to die horrible deaths?"

"That's part of it yes. And sometimes they have wonderful, happy lives, the sort nobody on this world will ever have."

"I see that Rupert's blanding out some of the extremes. By holding back the evil beings he's diminishing the role of the good ones. But he doesn't seem to be changing anyone's basic character. It's more that he's not really letting them fully express themselves."

"But that's the whole point Henry," cried Wilfred. "They have to express themselves as they truly are. Otherwise they become increasingly like us and the barrier weakens even further."

"Can you explain again why that matters?"

"Because, Henry, in the first instance it will allow more and more inhabitants of that world to cross over into this. For a period there'll be mounting chaos and confusion. Ultimately, we'll deal with it, then the other world will be gone and we'll lose our past, our memories, our depth, our culture —"

"How are you so sure?"

Wilfred sneezed. "This room encapsulates all the disadvantages of my house, which are many, and none of its comforts, which are few, and are all found on the ground floor." He stood up. "A few drops of Echinacea and a herbal infusion, followed by a light supper – and an early night. Though if I sleep in this weather it will be a minor miracle."

"How are you so sure?" repeated Henry.

"You should contact your parents," Wilfred advised. "They'll be concerned about you."

Henry was horrified. He had forgotten all about them. "O my God! How long have I been away?" He considered. He had arrived in the world of legends in the early morning. There was a night on Deathbreather's mountain, a night on the royal barge and a night outside Oberon's palace. Now it was – he looked through the window – early evening, early morning? "Three days, four days?" His parents would be frantic with worry.

Wilfred had the grace to appear a little embarrassed when he answered. "Rather more, I regret to say. Time doesn't synchronise as I believe I mentioned."

"How long then?"

"Regrettably, nearly five weeks."

Henry jumped to his feet. "Didn't you care about them?"

"Did you Henry?"

"You sound like the mirror. Of course I do. I've got to get home." He stopped. "What can I tell them? If I tell them the truth, they'll think I went mad." He paused, aghast. "No they'll think I was on drugs. It will be even worse than when I was thirteen."

"I e-mailed your father at work," said Wilfred. "It said you were unhappy and were going away for a bit."

"How did you get the address? Oh, I suppose that must be fairly easy for you."

Wilfred chuckled.

It was a hot July evening, but Henry ran home,

looking very fetching to several young ladies as he was wearing a white silk flowing shirt, only slightly grubby from a night in the forest and the encounter with the bulls, some tight suede breeches and fancy brown leather boots. Neither he nor his parents were ever to mention this outfit, but there were many occasions in the future when he wore those items singly, and with surprising pleasure. In fact, he became extremely interested in clothes.

He rang the bell and pounded on the door. Both his parents answered, their faces drawn and scared. His mother burst into tears and so did his father, much to his amazement.

"I'm sorry —" he began, with little idea what to say next, but there was no need.

"You're home, you're home," his mother kept saying. That was all that was bothering her.

"Are you hurt?" asked his father. "Are you in trouble with the —" he managed to stop himself.

"No," said Henry. "I just —"

But his father always knew best, even when he wanted to be loving, which he definitely did. "I've been thinking," he said. "I've not been taking you seriously. I've not been giving you space. When I was a boy —" etc etc.

The upshot was his father blamed himself. Five weeks' disappearance was a good length. If it had been only five days, his father's anger would have triumphed conclusively over feelings of guilt. Discussion about Henry's reasons and whereabouts was postponed until later and later never came. Instead there was a shift of attitude between Henry and his father. They became more tolerant of each other.

Henry had a bath, had a dinner cooked by his mother and went to bed, where he slept until late the following morning. His plan was to sit quietly in the garden – he hardly dared leave the house until his mother calmed down – and ponder. Very deeply. First though, in an effort to return to normal, he had breakfast and read the morning paper. It slowly dawned on him there had been unfortunate developments:

CHANCELLOR'S SUMMER BONANZA

It is widely thought that yesterday's announcement in the House of Commons was a direct slap in the face for the Prime Minister and was effectively the official declaration of a campaign by the Chancellor of the Exchequer to take over at Number 10. There are rumours of rows in cabinet earlier in the week when the Chancellor indicated he wanted to disclose the contents of his goody bag before the summer recess rather than waiting for his autumn statement. However, with the government's low standing in the polls, it is thought that the Chancellor obtained a huge majority in favour of his announcement. In effect the Prime Minister was outvoted and his authority might well be fatally undermined. [leading article, page 27].

The Chancellor announced a huge increase in Government spending on the Health Service of ten percent a year over the next five years.

Similar amounts were announced for the police, transport and, unexpectedly, the armed forces. The Chancellor said that he would make further announcements in the autumn statement.

Some economic experts are at a loss to know where all this money is coming from during a global recesssion. ['Money' page 1] Other experts take an opposing view, suggesting that the Chancellor was showing an astute forecasting eye or may be taking a bold gamble.

Watchers of the normally dour Chancellor have been impressed recently by his good humour and an almost devil may care attitude.

Henry read the leading article. He read the money page. He put down the newspaper. He had absolutely no doubt who was behind all this. Rumpelstiltskin. This meant the Chancellor must have promised Rumpelstiltskin something, and it must be of enormous significance if Rumpelstiltskin were prepared to churn out so much gold.

Henry cleared his mind of Rumpelstiltskin and let in the thoughts he had pushed to one side ever since his return. They were mainly about Elise. He wondered whether she was safe, whether she and Gervase had made – would make – it safely back to their own home? He really cared about her, and it wasn't the sort of crush he had on Aurelia – and what was Aurelia doing? He could check the web site, but was almost too nervous to do so.

The telephone rang. It was Wilfred, who had not, as expected had a good night.

"There's a lot more I want to ask you," said Henry.

"I would like you to go into the web site," said Wilfred.

"Is Elise safe?" asked Henry, with dread in his heart.

"Yes," said Wilfred. "She's not home yet, but you can read about her. Then I would like you to find 'Britannia rules the waves'. She'll be expecting you. After that I need to put something to you."

"OK," agreed Henry, without quibbling, much to his own surprise.

He went into www.worldoflegends.com . There was a short new – what he used to accept as a story, but it was of course a report. Who was responsible for them? It had to be Wilfred and the mirror working together. He read:

> Elise and Gervase crossed the boundary from Snow White's country to their own kingdom. In fact, the climates and flora and fauna in both kingdoms were all broadly similar. Even so, the transition into another land was fairly abrupt, as one moment they were walking through forest and the next they were standing on a desolate moor. The transition would have been even more startling if they had not anticipated what would happen, because of their journey to meet Henry and their experience of flying over so many lands on their way to the gathering of heroes. Although people did travel in the world of legends, it was usually only major heroes and villains, or fairies and the like.
>
> Gervase was cheerful and excited. Everything he had done recently, his brothers had not done. For the first time in his life he felt he was no longer

simply the youngest and a target for his brothers' affectionate joshing. Elise was pleased to see him happy, but she was pensive, concerned about Henry. He was completely unlike anyone else she had met, which had caused her initial interest. He was certainly weak and irresolute at the start, but even then she sensed all sorts of hidden depths which were never found in the men in her family. Her brief encounters with servants, gardeners, peasants and townsfolk did not encourage her to think that the other men in her world were any different.

Elise considered that Prince Henry had changed amazingly over the last few days. He had survived an encounter with a dragon, which must put a lot of minor problems into perspective. He had faced up to the loss of his reputation. Most significantly, he had turned and faced the phouka, knowing full well how dangerous they were, because he wanted to protect her. Reviewing the situation in its entirety led Elise to only one conclusion. She was very attracted to Henry – handsome, sweet and noble Henry. But would she ever see him again?

"Prince Henry's a very unusual hero," said Gervase, "but I'm not bothered in the slightest. He's been kind to me and he's my liege lord. As far as I'm concerned, he's the business."

"Yes," agreed Elise. "I'm afraid he makes a lot of other men look very shallow."

"Including me?" asked Gervase anxiously.

"You're special," replied Elise, as she had done

*since he was a baby. It usually worked, but Gervase
had also grown up a bit in the last few days. He
smiled though.*

" 'Handsome, sweet and noble'," thought Henry.
"Cool!" Of course he hardly deserved such compliments,
but even getting them was an extremely unfamiliar
experience. And she was very attracted to him. So was
he to her. Yet how could they be together unless one or
other crossed over? A permanent arrangement on those
lines had any number of problems and popping through
for the odd night out seemed, well, unrealistic.

He turned on the webcam, then got into www.
parallelreality.universe. He found 'Britannia rules the
waves' and clicked on it. The usual mist cleared and he
found he was looking down at what was almost a large
Cornish port. On the horizon the sea was blue and
sparkling like no English sea ever is except in postcards.
The houses edging the harbour were mainly whitewashed,
with flowers overflowing from hanging baskets and
window boxes. Other houses were scrambling up a steep
hillside. In the harbour were brightly painted fishing
boats. There was also a large eighteenth century style
flagship with fluttering pennants and – o yes – Henry
could hear jolly sailors singing sea shanties. A large gull
flew across the screen and squawked.

Henry was wondering about his vantage point when,
for the first time in this site, the webcam, or whatever,
moved. The harbour slid off to the right and from the left
came the background of a little stone castle, with more
flags, including the cross of St George. He was gazing
at a courtyard garden which must face the sea. On one

side was the front part of a Spitfire, which the Second World War pilot, the one seen at the gathering of heroes, was lovingly buffing up. He was whistling 'We'll meet again'. Directly in front of the screen stood Britannia in a flowing robe, breastplate, and a helmet over her long red hair. She was, in his father's phrase, although Henry didn't think in those sort of terms, a damn fine figure of a woman. She smiled at him.

"Super morning," she said in a resonant voice. It was upper class, but with the slightest trace of a Cornish accent.

"Yes," agreed Henry warily.

"Did you see my flagship?" she asked. "Splendid isn't she. I so wanted to take you on board."

"That's very kind of you."

"Today it's calm as anything, but I love it when it's a force ten gale. She loves it too. She's invincible."

"I can well believe it."

"You've had a bit of hard time, Prince Henry," sympathised Britannia.

"I have," said Henry, "but honestly, a lot of it's my fault."

"I spoke up for you. Don't like to see a man kicked when he's down. Or condemned without a fair trial."

"People must have said I was a fraud."

"They did, but a lot of us wouldn't stand for it. Not without proof. And the very next day we heard tell of your bullfight. Such fun!"

"I'm not quite sure I'd put it like that," said Henry.

"Very brave, anyway," said Britannia. "And a good sign. Your reputation's growing again."

"What was my reputation exactly?" asked Henry.

"World saver. Pretty serious stuff. Back against the wall. True Brit. You know."

"Queen and – erm, King and country?"

"Natch. And we're all here for you."

"Thank you," said Henry, who did not care for any of that.

"But you don't seem to be all here for us. Where's the rest of you?"

"I can promise you every bit of me's present and correct."

"Good, because you'll need more than your head and shoulders if you're going to save the world."

"About that," said Henry. "I'm not against it in principle, obviously. But a few clues as to what's required wouldn't go amiss."

"Damn right," said Britannia.

"So?"

"Oh I don't have them. What I do have is a strong sense of being under threat, everything I hold dear at risk. Fairness, tolerance, courtesy, pragmatism, cussedness, the BBC, peaceful country villages —"

"Warm beer and cricket?"

Britannia's eyes twinkled. "Sure, for those who like that sort of thing."

The pilot strolled across to her side and smiled at Henry.

"Good to see some of you again. That's quite an amputation!"

"No really," said Henry. "I'm all here."

"That's the ticket." The pilot saluted and wandered back to his plane.

"But you don't know what's causing the threat?" said Henry.

"No," replied Britannia, "yet I can already tell that others sense it. There's a heavier mood about." She turned round and called to a maid in the sort of uniform seen in an Agatha Christie film. "Put on that record, dear, it always cheers me up."

Meanly Henry assumed that he was about to listen to 'Rule Britannia' or at the very least 'Land of hope and glory'. What he heard was something much more lyrical. Both he and Britannia became silent as they listened to a piece of music which celebrated the English spirit, 'The lark ascending' by Vaughan Williams. Every other sound – the screams of the seagulls, the voices of the sailors, the whistling of the pilot – fell away as the music soared. The view slowly returned to the sunny harbour. By the end of the piece Henry knew he had no choice. The whole incident was sentimental, and a deliberate set up, but it had worked. This was not the real England, but nor was it all lies. It was a necessary fairy tale and it had to be saved.

At five past six Henry telephoned Wilfred. He got only an answer-phone message.

"If you really must contact Wilfred's transport and delivery services, please explain why after the tone." The tone was actually the first four notes of "Rule Britannia".

"I want to help," he said. "I'm not sure how, but I do. First though I really must know more about what's going on."

Ten minutes later Wilfred called back.

"Must you know more?" asked Wilfred. "It's very wearing having all these demands made on me."

"You haven't told me exactly who you are, or how you discovered and contacted the world of legends, how you are working with the magic mirror to set up the web site and provide the reports, and how you know about the barrier."

"Oh," said Wilfred, "that's an awful lot of information."

"Yes," said Henry. "That's exactly my point!"

"Surely a young man with your intelligence can work out a great deal for himself."

"May be, but —"

"We've got masses to do," said Wilfred, "and we need to start by finding out what the Chancellor of the Exchequer has agreed with Rumpelstiltskin. When we do, we have to solve the riddle and stop Rumpelstiltskin from doing whatever nasty little deed he has in mind."

"Have you any idea what they agreed?"

"I have, but we want the facts. We must ask the Chancellor."

"Why should he even speak to us?"

"The desire to share a remarkable secret with someone who'll believe him? Fear may be. Even guilt. I think that he'll be only too happy to talk."

"Rumpelstiltskin might have already claimed his price."

"Perhaps, but I don't think he's called it in – or if he has, I don't think he's doing too much with what he's been given, because I'm sure we'd have seen the consequences."

"And what about Rumpelstiltskin?"

"We must get him back to his world. Once he's there, he won't be able to call in the debt – unless the barrier collapses."

"He called in my debt when we were in different worlds."

"Of course. Everything that happens in that world is caused by something in this – but not the other way round."

"But," Henry objected, being sharp on the whole, "my reputation started to improve again because of something I did there, not here."

"No Henry. It was because you have started to rebuild your reputation in this world and that seeped into the other."

"What have I done exactly?"

"Well, you're a nicer person. Slightly."

"Thank you," said Henry. "How are we going to attempt to contact the Chancellor?"

"I've been sending him e-mails. Our correspondence has reached an interesting stage. I will send them on to you."

"How did you find out his private address?" asked Henry, then realised what a foolish question that was.

Wilfred rang off. Shortly afterwards there was a ping on Henry's computer. Wilfred had forwarded the exchange between him and the Chancellor.

Wilfred had written:

Dear Chancellor
   Forgive me raising this unpleasant matter
for the third time, but you have not yet replied to
my two previous messages. I repeat, I am aware

*that your spin doctor, referred to publicly as
Rupert Stiltskin, has been doing a different sort
of spinning for you. Technically, this is actually
sewing, is it not? Perhaps we might discuss the
consequences of this interesting occurrence?*

The Chancellor had enquired:

Who are you?

Wilfred had answered:

*No friend of Rumpelstiltskin. Please suggest a
place where we might meet.*

The Chancellor had replied:

We can't meet.

Wilfred explained:

*It would be so much easier if we did.
However, in the mean time please tell me what
price Rumpelstiltskin asked for working on his old
sewing machine.*

The Chancellor answered.

*I brought him a brand new sewing machine.
He's been much quicker. It's astounding what he
can produce. As for his price, I thought it was a
joke, or symbolic, like a peppercorn rent. He said
he had a second name and I had to guess it at a*

time of his choosing or else I would have to give him my reputation. That was absurd. How can one person take over another's reputation?

This was where the exchange had been passed to Henry with a request that he intervened. So Henry wrote:

Good evening Chancellor. I used to be a friend of Rupert's. I made a similar arrangement with Rumpelstiltskin and I have now lost my reputation.

There was no reply that night.

CHAPTER 16

The Chancellor

THERE WAS NO reply in the morning either.

Henry checked the website once more, but did not turn on his webcam, wishing to be unseen. He found the 'hall of the swan Lords'. They were all back, including Elise, and were in the middle of an argument about him. Plainly his reputation was not restored completely in that quarter, although things could have been worse. Elise and Gervase, naturally, and Adolphus, surprisingly, were all speaking on his behalf, while the attitude of the other brothers was not so much outright anger as confusion. They liked their heroes to be uncomplicated, and who could blame them!

Henry tried the 'The magic mirror'. There was noone in the room. He called out to the mirror, he even turned on the webcam in case it helped, but got no response. He had a look at 'The maiden in the turret' to make sure Aurelia had not been imprisoned again. No Aurelia, but a new maiden. What was all that about? Was this King particularly greedy?

Finally, just out of interest, he clicked on 'Dracula's castle'. The mists swirled away and he could see into a dark hallway, lit by candles sputtering in a draught. Outside a wolf bayed and Henry was sure this was not one of the phouka, but a real, Transylvanian type wolf. The Count, who was the vampire he had previously seen with the evil Queen, was standing by the great doorway of the castle. Several people were sitting on a neat row of chairs. Good grief, did the Count now line up his victims like drinks on a bar? On the other hand, none of the people looked in any way frightened. What they looked like were patients in an outpatients department.

"First," the Count was saying, "I will attend to the young girl bitten by a snake. I will suck the poison out of her – not an exact science of course, so I might take a little more blood than necessary."

"That's fine," said the young girl's mother. "She's ever so feverish."

"Secondly," continued the vampire, "I will clean away all that blood from the unlucky gentleman who fell off his horse." He licked his lips appreciatively. "Then I will try a total transfusion for —"

That was enough. Count Dracula as medical saviour!

It was towards the end of July and Parliament was due to adjourn for the summer recess. However, Henry read in the paper that the Chancellor was going to answer questions in the House of Commons. He thought it would be interesting to see the Chancellor in action, and found a website where the session could be viewed. He noticed at once how cheery the Chancellor was. Actually, it was more than that. The minister was almost manic.

The shadow Chancellor stood up. "Right Honourable and Honourable Members will have been impressed by the extraordinary generosity of the Chancellor in the last week, but with whose money? Has my Right Honourable friend given up all idea of balancing the books? Perhaps he's chosen to juggle them instead?"

"I should have remembered," replied the Chancellor, "that my Right Honourable friend was interested in the circus. Wasn't his approach to the economy described by one newspaper as clowning around." [much laughter]

"Perhaps," resumed the shadow Chancellor, "my Right Honourable friend would care to enlighten the House as to how, four months after a budget in which he warned us about grave financial difficulties, he can manage to produce billions of pounds out of thin air."

"Ah," said the Chancellor, "so now I'm a magician rather than a juggler!" [more laughter]

"I note," observed the shadow Chancellor, "that my Right Honourable friend is refusing to answer the question."

"Not at all," returned the Chancellor. "The answer is simple. I operate the sort of prudent yet imaginative financial management the opposition has never understood."

"Imaginative yes," said the shadow Chancellor but his voice was drowned by Government cheers.

Like overgrown children, thought Henry. The Speaker had to remind everyone to calm down and the camera swung onto him. That was when Henry saw a familiar figure, sitting in a box for Government officials. He was grinning. It was Rumpelstiltskin, keeping his eye on a major investment.

Henry phoned Wilfred, who was out or refusing to answer. Henry left him a polite but frosty message reporting no progress and demanding more information. He paced irritably round the house and garden. How he had changed. He longed for some sort of action.

At last, at 5-o-clock, the Chancellor sent Henry an e-mail:

"Please let me have a phone number."

Henry did as requested. Five minutes later his mobile rang.

"Who are you?" asked the Chancellor. "Who is Wilfred? How do I know you aren't playing some stupid game?"

"You met me once," said Henry "outside Rupert's house, when Rupert was still Rupert. I said I wanted to be Lord Chief Justice."

"Yes," said the Chancellor. "I remember. You're just a student. Not a very impressive one either. What reputation can you possibly have lost?"

A very reasonable question and difficult to answer. Best not to answer it then. "You've seen what your spin doctor can do. And you must have discovered it isn't Rupert any more."

"O dear Lord," groaned the Chancellor.

"How did you start the arrangement with him? What

made you even listen to Rupert – the person you thought was Rupert?"

"We were alone in my office one evening. When he produced his old sewing machine I thought he was mad. When he produced gold from it I thought I was mad."

"You were mad to agree with him. What exactly did you think he was?"

"I didn't know. I just saw —"

"A great opportunity."

"All that gold," murmured the Chancellor to himself. "So much good I can do with it."

"How did you explain it to, I don't know, people who had to move it? Or the Bank of England?"

"There was such a lot of it. You can buy people. But most of it, it's not for me, it's for the country."

Not for him! Except it would help him to become Prime Minister.

"I might be able to find out his other name," said Henry.

"You must," said the Chancellor, sounding desperate. "He told me this morning he wanted an answer at midnight tonight. He leered at me. 'Otherwise,' he said, 'no more gold.'"

"I have to do some research," said Henry, "But when I reply, will you come back to me quickly?"

"At once," said the Chancellor, sounding most unministerial.

Henry went over to his computer and entered the site. He had remembered correctly. It was possible to get to 'Snow White's cottage'. He clicked on the link. The first thing he heard was her singing. How did they put up with it? Snow White was busy at the kitchen range. The dwarves were with her.

"Heavens to Betsy!" exclaimed one of them. Henry had not noticed the pronounced American accent before. "What's happened to you?"

Snow White spun round and gasped. "O you poor thing!" she said to Henry. "Where's most of you gone?" Two crystalline tears appeared in the corner of each eye and two dwarves whipped out their pocket handkerchiefs for her.

"No, really," said Henry, "I'm all here. It's just that —" What? "It's just that I'm under a light curse so a lot of me's invisible."

"Partial invisibility," muttered the dwarf. "Danged if I've heard of that before."

"It's a strange old world," said Henry. "The thing is, one of you said he was going to send word to Rumpelstiltskin's mother to find out his second name."

"I did, Prince Henry," said another dwarf.

"Excellent. What is it?"

"I'm still waiting. You know how dwarves take a bit of time. Someone asks a question and a hundred years can go by before anyone remembers to answer."

"Damn," said Henry, "I need to know urgently – to help someone else who made the same bargain as me and is about to suffer horrendous consequences if we can't discover what that name is."

Horrendous consequences. That certainly meant something to the dwarves. As for Snow White, she burst into tears and was led away out of sight.

"The thought of those consequences," said yet

another dwarf, "together with your partial invisibility proved too much for that generous heart."

"Bless," said Henry.

"Amen to that," said several dwarves.

"Look," said Henry, "I don't mean to be pushy, but this is an emergency. Is there any way of speeding things up?"

"Can't rightly say," replied the first dwarf who had spoken and who apparently came from somewhere like Kansas, "but I reckon you could go to the mines yourself."

"Which mines would those be?"

"Where we were born and where Rumpelstiltskin's Ma still lives."

Henry remembered yet another place on the map. "I think I can go there."

"I reckon you can," said the dwarf, "but they're down the road a ways. You're looking at several days' journey."

"Don't worry," said Henry, "I have my methods," and he came out of the cottage and found the 'mines of the dwarves'. He clicked on it and found himself overlooking a great underground cavern, with passages at different levels disappearing into the dark, but otherwise lit by countless torches. There was a cacophony of banging and hammering, as the tiny distant figures of the dwarves were hard at work. In front of the camera, staring down over the cavern, was a fat dwarf with a gold chain suggesting he was an important office holder.

"Good day to you," said Henry.

The dwarf turned round with a lot of plump dignity. "Greetings, stranger," he said, "do you wish to purchase some armour – or at any rate a helmet, a breast plate and two shoulder plates?"

"Look," said Henry, "I can assure you —"

"Please," interrupted the dwarf, "great warriors come here in all shapes and sizes and in all sorts of conditions. We make no comment, we make no criticism, all we try to do is sort out the exact requirements of our clients."

"Thanks," said Henry. "May be later. For the moment I need to ask you about a dwarf."

"You've come to a good place then. There are lots of them here."

"Indeed," said Henry. "Now —"

"I am the mine supervisor. You are —?"

Henry wondered if he should lie, but decided to take the risk. "My name is Prince Henry."

"Difficult times Prince Henry," said the supervisor, without apparent animosity. "Now who are you searching for?"

"Well, I'm told by one of the dwarves who live with Snow White —"

"Isn't she a pearl?" said the supervisor.

"Yes," said Henry. "— that Rumpelstiltskin's mother lives here."

"No she doesn't"

"Oh. I was misinformed."

"I'm afraid so."

"I badly needed to speak to her."

"I'll get her then."

"You just said she doesn't live here."

"She doesn't. But she lives in a cave near the mine entrance."

Thirty minutes later a very bald old dwarf in a long

dress shuffled in front of the screen. She grinned up at Henry. Yes, Rumpelstiltskin had definitely inherited his looks from his mother.

"What a delightful frock," said Henry, who had been advised that she liked a bit of flattery.

"That's kind of you dear," she said. Her son had also inherited her melodious voice. "I do my best though my complexion's gone to pot. Tell me, have I got any hairs growing on my face?"

"Certainly not."

"I knew it! Shaving my beard off was a terrible mistake. It's never going to grow back again."

"I need to ask you —"

"I don't suppose the rest of *you* will either."

"I need to ask you a question about Rumpelstiltskin."

She pulled a face. "That odious little creep. Believe me, I tried."

"I'm sure you did," said Henry. "What's his second name please!"

"Second name!" she cackled. "He hasn't got a second name. One name's quite enough for a rotten turnip like him."

So both Henry and the Chancellor had been tricked, but at least the Chancellor could be protected from the consequences of his bargain. As for Henry, he felt very aggrieved. It was a void contract he had made with Rumpelstiltskin, yet he had been made to suffer because of it. He wanted some sort of recompense for that.

Henry sent the Chancellor an e-mail. The Chancellor phoned immediately and Henry quickly explained what he had discovered about the name, but nothing else.

"This is becoming absurd," said the Chancellor. "Why should I trust you?"

"Because I'm not a politician and because who else is there?"

"I'm not sure. This could all be an elaborate practical joke. Or a scheme by my enemies to bring me down." The Chancellor paused and reflected. "If only," he said.

Henry suggested they should go and confront Rumpelstiltskin straight away.

"I've no idea where he is at the moment," said the Chancellor. "We've a meeting arranged much later."

"Shortly before midnight I suppose?"

"Yes. It's in Covent Garden."

"Then we'll have to go there."

"But how safe will it be?"

"I can't say," replied Henry.

"If anyone sees me —" said the Chancellor anxiously. "Would you go for me?"

"No," said Henry.

"My reputation," said the Chancellor piteously. "He can't take my reputation."

What was behind all this, Henry wondered? Why was Rumpelstiltskin changing his legendary price? How did he get the power to demand it? And was he able to keep it for himself? Henry had a suspicion that others were making use of Rumpelstiltskin's special gifts. This was something he had to discuss with Wilfred, who owed him the fullest possible explanation, not little bits of information disclosed when convenient. The first question would be who exactly was Wilfred?

Henry phoned Wilfred. There was the usual recorded message.

"If you really must contact Wilfred's transport and delivery services, please explain why after the tone."

"Because," shouted Henry, "I want to throttle you."

"Very unlawyer-like language," observed Wilfred, choosing to speak on the phone. "Let us first get through tonight. There are things I need to do. Tomorrow, all being well, I'll fill you in on my background."

There was no moving him so Henry was forced to be patient. By nine-o-clock his patience ran out. It was almost an hour before he needed to leave, but he decided to head off for Covent Garden. He told his parents he was meeting some friends in the West End. His parents were startled. They had no idea he had any friends. They were also anxious, but he reassured them he was not disappearing again and would be back that night, though rather late.

The Covent Garden piazza was busy with people wandering about or sitting outside in the warm summer evening. It was not somewhere Henry had been before. He enjoyed the buzz. He found St Paul's church, where the Chancellor and Rumpelstiltskin were to meet shortly before midnight. It was a curious place for a rendezvous. Some street entertainers were performing in a large open space in front of the church. He was amused in a way he never had been before by this sort of comedy. He was becoming more like everyone else in their early twenties. Two months ago that would have horrified him. Now he was delighted. There was a board displaying further acts that were still to come. They were written in chalk, although a small poster was stuck next to the last act. He read it.

Let me conjure up your dreams

Rumpelstiltskin
show starts at 11 PM

Henry was astounded.

He hurried along to the hotel called Number One Aldwych where he was due to meet the Chancellor and Wilfred, and walked into the lobby.

"It's a miracle," remarked a voice from behind him, "that I didn't get a deep vein thrombosis on the journey."

"You were only on the tube," said Henry, turning round.

"A bus," said Wilfred.

"Whatever. A deep vein thrombosis seems very unlikely on a bus journey."

"Not with my cardio-vascular system," said Wilfred. "Is the Chancellor here yet?"

"No. Perhaps he won't come."

"I think he will. He needs to see for himself what happens."

A car pulled up outside. The Chancellor got out,

trying to look inconspicuous and thereby attracting a certain amount of attention. He entered the lobby, where people were far too rich and smart to be bothered about him. He gazed round vaguely until Henry and Wilfred approached. They found their way to a quiet corner of the bar.

"Are you a journalist?" the Chancellor asked Wilfred suspiciously.

"Do I look like a journalist?"

"Not entirely, no."

Wilfred was wearing a striped blazer and was carrying a boater so it was hard to say exactly what he looked like.

"Well I'm not," said Wilfred. "You might say I'm a researcher into the sort of events which have been causing you so much trouble."

"That could be a journalist," said the Chancellor. He glared at Henry. "You said you'd been doing research. Perhaps you're both journalists."

"We could be but we're not," said Wilfred irritably.

"I've got something to tell you," said Henry and alerted them to the imminent performance.

Wilfred shook his head gravely. "This is extremely serious."

"I don't want him conjuring up anyone's dreams but mine," said the Chancellor.

"We must go and see the show," Wilfred continued, ignoring him.

"You both think I've committed some terrible sin," said the Chancellor. He was pink round the eyes from fatigue. "You're viewing life in black and white. But life is full of compromises and balancing acts. Occasionally certain scruples have to be pushed aside to achieve something worthwhile. And I say again, how was I to guess the agreement was more than a joke?"

"Because the other thing life teaches us," said Wilfred, "is that it's rare for anyone to do us a favour, especially a huge one."

"I took a risk," said the Chancellor, "but in such a good cause. I thought of all the people I could help, the poor, the sick, the old — I sat brooding in my big office in the Treasury asking myself how I could achieve everything I came into politics for. Noone enjoys raising taxes. Rumpelstiltskin was the answer to my prayers."

"The main prayer being, 'Please let me be Prime Minister.'"

"There was an advantage to me, I admit, but why not? Our current Prime Minister is like an oily fish lost in a stormy sea. You should have seen him when I announced billions of extra spending to the cabinet. The others cheered. He just sat there with his mouth opening and closing, like a —"

"An oily fish?" Henry suggested.

Shortly before eleven they left the hotel and went to the open space where Rumpelstiltskin was to perform his conjuring tricks. There was a semi-circle of expectant people, many pleasantly drunk. The three of them stood at the back, having no wish to be seen by Rumpelstiltskin until they were ready to confront him.

A line of blue light crossed the piazza in front of the Church. Pounding rock music played. Coloured smoke swirled as a little cloaked figure appeared. Corny but effective. The audience applauded. The smoke cleared, the music changed and Rumpelstiltskin began his act. It was fairly impressive, as well it should have been, bearing in mind that he was undoubtedly using real magic for some of his tricks. Henry had no idea Rumpelstiltskin was so talented and, judging by the concern on Wilfred's face, neither had he. The Chancellor simply looked bemused.

Rumpelstiltskin knew how to work an audience with his mixture of glib tongue and charming voice. After a while he stopped producing gold from a sewing machine (the Chancellor shifted uneasily) and precious stones (assumed to be false by the audience) from the dust sucked up by a vacuum cleaner and turned to more traditional feats of stage magic. He picked up a magician's top hat and started to pull creatures out of it. There were the usual rabbits and doves, which might have been hidden somewhere. Then he started to produce them in a quantity which noone had ever seen a magician produce before – fifty rabbits, a hundred doves, all released into the piazza. The audience cheered or ducked, astounded by these triumphs of illusion. How could so many creatures come through that tiny hat! And in a street act. Finally he produced a roll of carpet which unfurled across the stage to reveal a beautiful and very startled young woman with curly chestnut hair. The audience went wild.

"This is very bad," muttered Wilfred to Henry, as the confused girl was led away. "He's getting them through from the world of legends. The barrier must be weaker than I thought."

Rumpelstiltskin dragged someone up on stage from the front row.

"Volunteer, I salute you," he said with his familiar

toothy leer. A stuck on moustache made his appearance
even weirder than normal, which was saying quite a lot.

"And I salute you," replied a flushed Scottish youth.
His friends in the audience shouted encouragement.

"Tonight I want to make a dream come true," cried
Rumpelstiltskin.

"O aye," said the youth beerily, "and how do you
intend to do that?"

Rumpelstiltskin stared into the young man's eyes,
which definitely made the volunteer uneasy. "I see a girl
friend and the need for a diamond ring!"

"It's a wee bit early for an engagement," said the
youth, to the cheers of his mates," but I don't mind
having one in stock so to speak!"

"A canny decision," congratulated Rumpelstiltskin.
"And you'll get one. But I need payment."

"I've nae money left," said the youth. "It's been a
great night!"

"I don't want coin of the realm," said Rumpelstiltskin.
"I've got a much more interesting bargain in mind.
What's your job?"

"I'm an investment manager."

"A good one?"

"The best."

"In that case, I want your reputation as a brilliant
investment manager."

"You could never take tha' away from me."

"Therefore," beamed Rumpelstiltskin, "you've
nothing to fear."

So the deal was done. Rumpelstiltskin conjured up a
diamond ring which naturally the young man assumed

to be worthless. He laughed as he signed the agreement. So did Rumpelstiltskin.

"My nineteenth satisfied client this week. It warms my heart. By the end of this week I expect to have doubled the number."

The audience cheered and Rumpelstiltskin found another volunteer.

"This is appalling," said Wilfred. "He's not even asking them to guess anything. He's taking something precious and they've no idea of the hideous consequences."

"We should stop him now," said Henry.

"Hell, it's such a public place," whispered the Chancellor

"I think we should wait until the stipulated time," said Wilfred, "or else you could be accused of breaking the agreement. He might claim payment as a sort of penalty."

They watched several more victims being gulled out of their reputations, before Rumpelstiltskin announced he was nearly at the end of his performance, but had one more thing to do. He walked towards them across the open space.

"Ah," he said, "there you are Chancellor."

The Chancellor cursed under his breath. "And my old friend Prince Henry, back from your trip. That's a surprise, but a nice one! — And Wilfred too. Three such distinguished people. You've made a — whatever I am! — extremely proud."

"Not my intention," said Wilfred.

"Ladies and gentlemen," said Rumpelstiltskin, "it's nearly midnight. And I've got a little transaction to complete with our very special guest, the Chancellor of the Exchequer!"

The audience laughed, not really sure whether this was part of the act, or for real, or what.

"Yes," continued Rumpelstiltskin, "I've got a question to ask him."

"Ask away," said the Chancellor with a ghastly grin, trying to pretend he was a thoroughly good sport, but failing impressively.

"What's my second name?"

"You don't have a second name," replied the Chancellor almost inaudibly.

"Eh?" said Rumpelstiltskin.

"You don't have a second name," repeated the Chancellor a bit louder.

"Oh," said Rumpelstiltskin, "don't I?"

"No," said Henry, "your mother told me you haven't"

"And mothers always know best don't they?"

"Often," said Henry, uneasy at this display of unconcern.

"Well," said Rumpelstiltskin, "she was right, she never gave me a second name."

The Chancellor breathed a sigh of relief.

"On the other hand," said Rumpelstiltskin, "that doesn't prevent me having a second name. I chose one for myself."

"Does that count?" asked the Chancellor like a protesting child.

"It counts," said Wilfred.

"So guess it," said Rumpelstiltskin.

The Chancellor looked despairingly at Henry and

Wilfred, who looked back, equally despairingly. "I don't know," he said, in a very sad voice.

"Really!" said Rumpelstiltskin.

"Really," said the Chancellor.

"Then I claim my payment," shouted Rumpelstiltskin. "It's midnight."

Was there supposed to be a thunder flash or lightning? There was neither. But things did happen. The line of blue across the piazza started to sizzle, lighting the front of the church in the same colour. There was some patchy applause from those who thought it was part of the act, but the applause quickly died. Rumpelstiltskin bowed and thanked the crowd which melted away. .

"I never believed you had it in you to cause so much harm," Wilfred said to Rumpelstiltskin

"Harm? What sort of harm? Do tell," said Rumpelstiltskin, playfully picking his ears. "Is it my fault people are so careless of their reputations!"

"You and Rupert," said Wilfred, "are damaging both worlds. He's blurring the sharp contrast between good and evil. You're bringing your corrupting magic into a world which can't deal with it."

"Em," began the Chancellor, "now you've claimed your price, does that mean you're not going to make any more gold for me?"

"For pity's sake," exclaimed Wilfred, "haven't you caused enough harm already?"

"But I need it, I need it, I've got so many plans!"

"O do shut up," said Wilfred. "It's a hot night, I've got a headache and your pleading is exactly what I don't require."

The Chancellor subsided.

"What I do require," continued Wilfred, staring hard at Rumpelstiltskin, "is for you to leave this world immediately."

"I dare say you do," beamed Rumpelstiltskin, "but I'm not going. I like it here. I'm a winner." He gave a little twirl and an elaborate stage bow.

"In that case I'll send you back."

"You can't send me back," jeered Rumpelstiltskin.

Wilfred reached into his pocket. Henry, now ready to accept anything as possible, was expecting him to produce a book of spells, a wand, a charm – or may be even a weapon. Hopefully not a weapon! In fact Wilfred produced a mobile phone.

" 'Who you gonna phone?' " asked Henry, " 'Ghostbusters!' " He very much wished he hadn't said that.

"Not the police," begged the Chancellor, who had lost all sense of dignity.

"I'm not phoning anyone," said Wilfred. "I'm sending a message to a partner in my delivery service." He smiled at Rumpelstiltskin. "You're right to some extent. I can't send you back on my own."

"The mirror," said Rumpelstiltskin, with a confident grin.

"Indeed," said Wilfred, "and my message has gone through."

"You're taking a big risk," sniggered Rumpelstiltskin, who was starting to fade.

"Hardly," said Henry. "You're disappearing."

"May be," cried Rumpelstiltskin.

He was dissolving into the blue glow and it seemed

as if Wilfred had been successful. Like all those years ago, Rumpelstiltskin's grin was the last thing to vanish.

"You've done it," said Henry. "Why didn't you try that when we got here?"

"Because," Wilfred answered, "I wanted Rumpelstiltskin to be beaten at his own game. Then I hoped he'd leave on his own, which would have been much, much better. But in case he didn't, I arranged a transfer at midnight, although I have to warn you —"

"Oh," moaned the Chancellor. "Look."

Rumpelstiltskin was becoming solid again. The grinning mouth returned first – "Hello again," it said – followed by the rest of him.

"Well," said Wilfred, "that's what I was going to warn you. It might not work."

"No," shouted the Chancellor, "I won't have it. He'll expose me."

He hurled himself forward and gripped Rumpelstiltskin by the neck. The two figures lurched into the blue light, the Chancellor pushing Rumpelstiltskin, who bit and nipped him back.

"Stop that," Wilfred cried.

"I should try to separate them," said Henry, startled at being so public spirited.

"No," – Wilfred grabbed his arm – "you must keep out of the blue glow."

The two wrestling figures began to fade away, and their grunts became fainter. Henry watched in amazement as the Chancellor of the Exchequer disappeared along with Rumpelstiltskin. Cabinet ministers did not usually evaporate, however much one hoped they might. A lot of other people in the piazza were equally surprised, especially those who had recognised the Chancellor. The performance area was now empty, but the sizzling line still crackled and spluttered. That could only mean something else was going to happen.

At first the image was so faint, Henry thought he was imagining it. Slowly though it began to solidify into the body of a woman. She was wearing a robe, dyed blue by the overpowering light, and a tall, twisted silver crown. Her face glowed with cruel confidence. It was the wicked Queen, and behind her other figures were also taking shape, palely recognisable as her guests on the day Rupert explained his master plan.

"We must leave at once," said Wilfred urgently. "Before they completely materialise. If they catch us here we haven't a chance."

"What about everyone else?" cried Henry, whose selflessness was reaching unbelievable heights.

"To help your world, we need to be free," answered Wilfred, moving remarkably quickly for a person with all his ailments.

"What do you mean 'help my world?'" asked Henry, running after him, but Wilfred was too out of breath to reply.

CHAPTER 17

Fuller explanations

TWO DAYS HAD gone by since the events in Covent Garden.

Henry had listened to the news expecting reports of amazing scenes in the Covent Garden area. Curiously, there was absolutely nothing about the new arrivals. What had happened to them? (The next few days were to make that very clear.) On the other hand there was a great deal about the Chancellor. There were eye witnesses who said they had seen him struggling with a magician at midnight, before both vanished from sight. This was obviously unbelievable. But where was the man?

On day one the Chancellor would have been extremely gratified at the media interest in his disappearance. There was endless discussion on air and in the press. There was some thought that he might have had a breakdown – or been murdered – but the most popular theory in the first 24 hours was that he had been kidnapped by international terrorists – and survival from that would have clinched things for him, as far as becoming Prime

Minister was concerned. On the other hand, why was nobody claiming they had him? Nor had any intelligence agency throughout the world offered even the inkling of a suggestion as to who the kidnappers might be.

The Chancellor would have been far less gratified at the media interest in the second 24 hours and thereafter. Slowly at first, but then with increasing enthusiasm, the journalists and media pundits began to attack his reputation. Had he done that much? Had he been that clever? As the days went by, the fate of the Chancellor was almost forgotten as his reputation was attacked and destroyed.

His absence had exposed some very troublesome facts. There was certainly more gold around than there should have been and economic experts found it difficult to offer a reason. On the other hand, if they had come up with something, would anyone have believed them? More to the point, although there was this extra gold, there was far too little to support all the extra Government spending promised by the Chancellor. The Government was finding it almost impossible to explain this away. Why had nobody brought a stop to the Chancellor's fantasies? It made the Government look either dishonest or incompetent – or both.

During the same period Henry received an e-mail from Wilfred. A long document was attached:

> *Dear Henry*
> *I owe you a much franker and more detailed explanation than you have had so far. Therefore let me set out some of my own history.*

The first point to make is that I come from the World of Legends. Does that surprise you? Perhaps you had deduced this already. I am a wizard, though not one most people know. Logically, however, I have to exist. Someone had to create the magic mirror. Therefore, as soon as the mirror came into being in the World of Legends, so did I.

I made the mirror to help people see into themselves and face up to the truth. In one unfortunate respect it does bear a resemblance to computers in your world. It tends to answer only what it is asked – not always very helpful! I have to accept this as a weakness in the original spell. On the other hand, it is quite keen to express an opinion, which tends to redress the balance.

I am not completely certain how the Queen obtained the mirror. Nobody reading her story usually cares much, so no satisfactory explanation exists. A combination of magic and murder seems likely. I have a vague recollection of others owning it before her, but I cannot bring to mind who they were. What I do know clearly is just how ancient the mirror is. That makes me ancient as well. Most dispiriting.

The great gift of the mirror is that it reflects the present. Because it is so old, it has learned how to reflect ever more widely, and how to interpret what it sees. It managed to see right up to the boundaries of the World of Legends. It then began to ask itself what lay beyond. It started to conjecture, but for some time had no basis to do more. Its opportunity came when a new legend developed.

You see, Henry, in order for events in your world to transfer as a legend into mine, there must be a necessary opening in the barrier between the worlds. On one such occasion the questing mind of the mirror noticed the transfer taking place and also identified the portal. It was via the ley lines which run simultaneously through your world and mine. The mirror therefore took the opportunity to cross the barrier the other way and discovered the existence of your world. It was so startled it very nearly shattered.

Initially it revealed nothing about its discovery, mostly because it was never asked an appropriate question. The Queen was largely concerned with her looks or her legendary enemies. Those are the matters she put to the mirror, which answered with its usual mixture of smoothness and sarcasm – not too much sarcasm in the case of the Queen in case she lost control and broke it. To this day I can't understand how the mirror developed its particular conversational style. Naturally, I accept responsibility for yet another regrettable error in my formation spells.

Although the mirror said nothing, I could tell something was up. After all, I was its creator. From time to time I was summoned by the Queen to make a few adjustments or give it the equivalent of an annual service. Left on my own with the mirror, I prised the truth out of it. I need hardly tell you I was extraordinarily excited.

I decided I would like to see the other world for myself. The mirror was able to tell me that a portal was open because a new legend was forming – that of Florence Nightingale as it happens. The mirror also told me where I could cross. In the World of Legends ley lines were operational in many places, but in particular near any powerful witch or sorcerer. You have seen the room where the mirror hangs. It was almost an open door.

I came through on December 1 1860. You may imagine my shock as I arrived in Victorian London. One day you might be interested to hear an account of those years in more detail. For the moment I report only the following. I have lived in my house since in 1870. I chose it in part because it was built on a ley line. Secondly I have developed a great love for your country.

Despite my initial excitement at being here, I feared I was going to be cut off completely from my real home. However, the mirror found a means to reach out to me. It is amusing that Rupert tried to make Rumpelstiltskin come through the large mirror at the top of my house. He was quite wrong about what that mirror could do – nothing can transfer through it – but quite correct in believing it had special powers.

It was used as a conduit to me by the magic mirror. This was how I kept in touch with the World of Legends.

I soon realised how limited my life had been there. I was little more than a jobbing wizard. I had certain tasks to perform and had gained a bit of knowledge, but there was no possibility of my developing any further. There was no need. Once I was in your world, Henry, I had the opportunity to study and ask questions. I learned about the relationship between the two worlds. I began to understand that my crossing the barrier was a very grave error on my part. By constant contact with me, the mirror had absorbed increasing amounts of information about your world. This naturally included information about how the characters in the World of Legends were not really independent. It never revealed this to the Queen, but the damage was done. Because the mirror has such a wide-spread magical reach, its knowledge leached into the World of Legends in the form of a general uneasiness. It led to a loss of confidence, which is why the heroes and villains have been failing more often. You have read this for yourself, Henry, on the web site.

As the heroes and villains failed, so the barrier weakened too. There have always been occasions when breaches occurred, but now it became susceptible to anyone with sufficient knowledge of how it worked. I decided my task was to become, in a way, a doorman. It meant I effectively banished myself from my own world. Helped by the mirror, I learned when anyone wished to cross and together we have tried to keep the two worlds apart. I have remained here ever since, never growing any older, although I was quite old enough already.

This was how I first heard about a new hero – a hero who might succeed in doing such deeds that the World of Legends would be put back on even keel. The legend was so strong it was trickling through even before the hero had done anything heroic. However, if the legend was beginning it meant the hero already active in some way or other. When Rupert and his family moved next door, I was overjoyed to meet a boy who had an absolute belief that my world existed. I thought at first he must be the hero. I never told him who I was, but I encouraged him in his interest. I was misled by his glib tongue. I told him too much. I even told him about Rumpelstiltskin and how they resembled each other. Even then the idea of a swap must have started forming. I never told him about the mirror. I certainly never told him how to cross over, but this he discovered for himself.

On that Halloween, Henry, when I was away, he managed to bring Rumpelstiltskin across. Of course the mirror was watching and managed to send him back again. I refused to have any more to do with Rupert after that Halloween, but by then he already knew too much. So did Rumpelstiltskin.

The rumours of the hero grew stronger and a name was mentioned. Working with the mirror I set up www.worldoflegends.com and www.parallelreality.universe to attract your attention, for I had learned how desiccated you were becoming and how unlikely to respond to a more direct approach. The mirror posted reports on episodes of special interest. We set you a challenge. I'm a stickler for tradition, I admit, and of course you solved the riddle – eventually! Unfortunately, I underestimated Rupert. He had hacked into my computer. He also solved the riddle.

Henry, I have watched you develop from a self-centred coward into, well, a less self-centred and no longer cowardly individual at any rate. You certainly have no worse a character than many others who became legends. We must now discover whether you will be a heroic success or a heroic failure.

Yours respectfully,

Wilfred

Henry had no wish to become either type of hero but he recognised the inevitable. Life in the immediate future was going to be far too interesting for his own good.

Chapter 18

"Jeepers creepers——"

THERE WERE STILL unanswered questions, but there were immediate practical issues to be resolved. Such as how to get the Queen and the other unwelcome visitors back where they belonged? Meanwhile they were likely to cause a great deal of trouble.

The night of arrival might have been quiet, but the incidents began quickly. The Chancellor soon slipped down the headlines and off the front page. The tabloids led with an unsavoury episode in Whitby. One might have expected the details to remain unpublished, certainly for a while. Regrettably, one of the police officers on hand blabbed to a local reporter. A young girl had woken in her bedroom in the middle of the night to find, allegedly, a continental gentleman in full evening dress bending over her. Apparently she had never screamed or anything (not easy to explain). She had then been bitten by him. This sounded like the ravings of an over-imaginative

teenager on drugs. On the other hand she had two gory
bite marks on her neck. She was also pale and anaemic,
requiring a blood transfusion of nearly two pints.

The following day there was another extraordinary
incident. It took place in London outside Buckingham
Palace. Two sentries were apparently turned to stone.
Except of course that could hardly have happened.
The Metropolitan Police Commissioner said in his
opinion this was a bizarre criminal act. The two guards
had been kidnapped and replaced by two statues. The
only surprising thing was that no one saw this unusual
version of the changing of the guard. There were others
however who offered a different view – religious mystics,
self-declared witches, even scientists. They all referred
to previous incidents of petrification, justifying them
from their respective vantage points. But who could
really believe anyone could turn to stone? What had to
be admitted, though, was the absolute resemblance the
statues had to the missing sentries. "Simply a case of
meticulous planning by an obsessive criminal," said the
Commissioner and this was the only logical explanation.

Other weird events were reported. Some sort of
monster had been seen several times on Dartmoor, but
when wasn't some sort of monster seen there? A dragon
had been reported flying over King Arthur's Seat in
Edinburgh. A coven of suburban witches, all highly
respectable people in real life, had met in a Birmingham
suburb, only to be joined by a new member who had
frightened six of them into giving up their hobby for
good. Someone claiming to be a wizard turned up in a
synagogue in North London, but was quickly accepted as
a valued new member and was given a flattering profile

in the Jewish Chronicle. There were several more reports of necks being bitten, each one progressively nearer to London, and of petrification. However, it was August, the silly season, and much of this was put down to newspapers desperate for good stories.

The most astonishing incident occurred in Harrods, although people's recollections were very hazy indeed. It was late night shopping on a hot summer evening. The store was full, largely with tourists, but of course foreigners were obviously less reliable witnesses than British witnesses. Even so, it was difficult to dismiss this incident out of hand. At about 6-o-clock several huge black vans had drawn up in Brompton Road. A beautiful woman had entered the store. She was wearing a crimson robe and a silver crown. (This had completely flummoxed the American shoppers). She had been accompanied by a large number of strong young men with vacant stares. Slowly she had drifted through the store, beginning with women's clothing then moving on to the furniture halls and carpets. Her companions began removing large numbers of items, dresses, chairs, lighting and so on. Nobody stopped them. Everyone, including the security guards, simply stood and stared, as if in a complete daze. By 7-o-clock she had left, and with her had gone nearly two million pounds worth of items. Most remarkable of all was that every one of those items was either black or a shade of red.

Mass hysteria, nerve gas, who was to say? Wilfred and Henry of course. And as Wilfred pointed out, this was only the beginning.

"Come round after dinner," said Wilfred over the

phone. "We need to plan what to try next. You'll have to do something brave."

"O really," said Henry without enthusiasm. "Like what for instance?"

"Kill a monster."

"Not really my style is it?"

"It's certainly not mine. And I'm far too frail. You must have noticed how ill I've been looking?"

"No," replied Henry who was not in a sympathetic mood.

"You've got used to the fact that I'm never well," said Wilfred. "You'll be old one day."

"Not necessarily," said Henry.

Henry had dinner with his parents. Afterwards he set off to visit Wilfred. He reached the crumbling Victorian house, of which he was becoming quite fond in a strange way. He rang the doorbell several times. There was no reply. Perhaps Wilfred really was ill. Perhaps he was dead, he was very old, but on the other hand old age was his general state of being and Henry was unsure whether Wilfred could die – unless of course, some violence were done to him. Wilfred had given Henry a key for emergencies. Deciding this was one, Henry let himself into the house.

As soon as he did, Henry decided the house was different. It was always a bit shabby and damp, but on the whole it was friendly. This evening it was cold and hostile. He called out Wilfred's name. No reply. He checked the sitting room and the kitchen, then, before intruding into other rooms he had never yet visited, went to the room on the top floor. The mirror on the big carved wardrobe was as dusty as ever. The laptop was on.

Its screensaver, Henry noted, consisted of a photograph of Britannia. Henry tapped on the mouse and the screensaver disappeared, revealing a page saying that www.parallelreality.universe was currently unavailable.

"Damn," said Henry aloud. "I wanted to speak to the mirror."

The mirror on the wardrobe started to shine as best it could in its dusty, tarnished condition.

"So speak to me," said a familiar voice.

"I'm pleased you're still connected to our world," said Henry. "What's happened to the website?"

"I'm in your world," replied the mirror. "She brought me through with her. I'm now trying to re-establish all my connections."

"What's happened to Wilfred?"

"Something bad I think."

"Then we need your help."

"You shouldn't have come here," said the mirror. "She knows about this house."

"Is there nothing you can say to me?"

"I wish you luck. And a good tailor. If you don't get the first you won't need the second."

"I was hoping —"

"Yes. Keep hoping. Now leave. If you can."

"If I can?"

"Prince Henry, if someone speaks to you, don't look at them."

"What's that supposed to mean?"

The mirror went cloudy, but not before Henry glimpsed in it the hazy image of a tall crown and a beautiful woman. The Queen.

Henry left the room and crossed the landing. Even

as he put his foot on the first stair he sensed another presence in the house. It might have been a common or garden burglar of course. If only it were. The sort of encounter he would have dreaded two months ago no longer bothered him. But it had to be something else.

"O bloody hell," he groaned inwardly. "Now what?"

The only thing to do was to keep going downstairs, heading resolutely for the front door. He reached the first floor without incident. He heard nothing, he saw nothing, yet he remained certain he was not alone. The mirror's warning troubled him. Not looking at an intruder would hardly save him from attack. It would only make him more vulnerable. Then he remembered an unexpected object he had noticed outside the house. Among the usual proliferation of weeds and overgrown bushes was a statue he had never seen before. It was a large dog with its mouth open in mid bark. With horror he now realised who the intruder must be. Medusa.

From a doorway behind him a soft woman's voice spoke to him.

"Brave warrior, I welcome you to my lair."

Henry nearly turned round. After all, it would be the first instinct of anyone to turn round when someone unexpectedly spoke to them from behind.

"It's not your lair," he replied. "It's Wilfred's home and you have no business being here."

"I do have business, brave warrior. It's with you." Her voice was unexpectedly warm, reassuring, almost seductive.

"I dare say it is. But I'm in a bit of a rush. May be later."

"O but I'm here now. And who knows how long I'll be staying in your world?"

"Interesting question as that is," said Henry, "I need to leave."

"It's hardly polite," said the soft voice, "to turn your back on a woman. Hardly the behaviour to be expected from a Prince."

"It may not be polite," said Henry, "but it's certainly prudent."

"What can they have told you about me? I do have a special gift, but it's mine to bestow when I choose."

"Gift," repeated Henry. "I don't think I'd quite describe it in those terms."

"No that's right," she said, sounding much harder. "It was given to me as a curse. It was meant to ensure I was always alone. If I cared for anyone I'd destroy them. But," and she sounded softer again, "I've learned how to control it. Now, brave warrior, you and I together can fight evil. Such a team. Unstoppable."

"Since when have you become good?"

"We've all had to modify our approach a little," she replied. "We have to move with the times."

You mean, thought Henry, in the World of Legends your power was weakening so not everybody turned to stone when you looked at them. But you won't turn down the chance of killing me. "That's very commendable."

"So why not look at me? I've always been considered a beauty. Just forget the hair."

She was getting nearer. "I would if I could Medusa. Unfortunately I'm a bit phobic about snakes."

He started to walk downstairs. He could hear her following him. He glanced into a mirror – what different roles mirrors seemed to have nowadays – hoping it was safe to look at her reflection. That's what the legend said. He caught sight briefly of her – beautiful once may be, now tortured, her hair a mass of writhing adders. How was he going to escape her?

"I'm fleet of foot, Prince Henry. I was a famous athlete once."

"Excellent," said Henry. "I thought that was Atalanta."

"I'm quicker than her. And I jump higher."

In other words Henry had no chance of escape. "Admirable. Perhaps tomorrow when my schedule isn't quite so hectic —"

"You can forget about schedules," said Medusa, suddenly landing in front of him.

Henry avoided her gaze by a split second. He turned and faced upstairs. "I realise I seem unnecessarily suspicious, but you do have rather a track record. I need a bit of time to get used to the newer, more caring you."

"It's the real me," she said, and jumped behind him again.

"I'm sure," said Henry, turning round. Only four more stairs to go, but such a long, long hall. And the front door was stiff.

"You are handsome, brave warrior," said the gorgon.

"Really!" said Henry in genuine surprise. Once again he very nearly turned to Medusa.

"Indeed you are. I already love you."

"Thanks very much. I'm sure I'll feel the same very soon. It's not that I don't believe in love at first sight. But I need to be sure it won't be turning to stone at first sight. That's not unreasonable is it?"

He managed to move down two more stairs.

"You don't trust me," she said, her voice hard once more. "You never will."

She leaped on him from behind. She grabbed his head, trying to make him look at her. Struggling desperately not to do this, Henry lost his footing and they both fell heavily to the bottom of the stairs. Medusa landed on top of him. The snakes wriggling from her head hissed as they tried to bite him. Venom or stone, one way or another this seemed to be it.

A great howl sounded from the landing above. It was a howl of defiance and a howl consisting of many voices. Medusa leaped to her feet and turned to see what it was. From his position on the carpet Henry watched a familiar group rush down the stairs. Thin figures, goat's heads, tangled hair, long slender limbs, gleaming white eyes – the phouka. Those at the front hurled themselves at Medusa. She slapped them away as best she could while they attacked her, doing their best to keep their eyes averted.

The front door opened. A shield and a sword were thrown in.

"Take them," shouted a second familiar voice, its owner safely outside the house. "Make use of the shield."

"I don't want to do this," Henry protested, recalling what the legend required him to do.

Henry might have faltered if one of the phouka had not made a serious error. The fairy cried out as a snake bit his arm. His eyes went to the wound, briefly, but fatally. When he looked up, Medusa was staring at him.

He turned to stone. A second phouka glared in anger. He too was turned to stone.

Henry inspected the shield. A mirror was stuck inside it. This evening Henry had to become Perseus.

"Leave her to me," he cried, addressing a wall in a grandiloquent manner that he instantly regretted. However, it worked. The phouka backed off.

"Brave warrior," said Medusa, "you sound annoyed!"

"The point is," he said, "you're cluttering up Wilfred's hall with unwanted statues." He held out the shield and glimpsed her reflection in the mirror. Her face was contorted. She was truly frightening yet he suddenly felt sad for her. She would always be friendless. But she would always be evil.

He advanced towards her. She laughed and jumped over him once more. Helped by the mirror, he managed to duck and swerve out of her reach.

"Wilfred!" she sneered. "You can forget about him."

In truth, Henry might never have managed to destroy her on his own. But one of the phouka leaped at her legs. She glowered at the top of his goat's cranium. It was only for two seconds, but in those two seconds Henry wielded the sword and cut off her head. Her eyes stared past Henry at someone by the entrance then her head fell to the floor. There was a loud thump from behind Henry. He spun round. A camcorder had crashed onto the front door mat. Standing next to it was the stone figure of the cameraman

"Damn," said Rupert peering cautiously round the door. "I hope the film's OK."

"What about the cameraman?" said Henry.

"That is a pity," said Rupert. "He was awfully good and I trusted him."

Henry shook his head in disgust. He turned back. Medusa's decapitated body was bleeding onto the stone floor. He found a large container and was sick.

"You'll have to toughen up," said Rupert, though not unkindly. "There'll be more of this sort of thing."

"When did you cross through?" asked Henry.

"Shortly after the Queen."

"What do you mean, there'll be more of this sort of thing?" Henry's voice was very trembly.

Rupert smiled knowingly

"A brave deed, your Highness," congratulated the leader of the phouka.

"You attacked Medusa with no protection," said Henry. "That's bravery. Two of your companions have lost their lives." He sat heavily on a chair.

"The right magic might restore them," said the leader. "But they won't resent it. Once we decided to serve you, self-sacrifice is part of our code."

"When did you decide to serve me?" asked Henry in surprise.

"After you challenged us as bulls, and refused to kill me. We discussed it. We decided you were becoming a worthy hero."

"That's – very kind of you."

"'Kind'," repeated the leader of the phouka with a hint of disapproval. "Forget 'kind'. We do what we consider honourable —"

"Of course. I wasn't implying —"

"— for a suitable price."

"Oh?"

"We *are* mercenaries Prince Henry. We need paying."

"I'm not particularly wealthy," said Henry.

"You will be. We can wait."

Rupert was now on his mobile phone. "It's an exclusive for you," he was saying. "But get here fast."

"Who were you talking to?" asked Henry.

"I decided this is so sensational," replied Rupert, like an actor confident of his Oscar for best supporting role, "I'd better go for the Sun."

"And that means —"

"They'll be here within an hour and the death of Medusa will be on their front page – and no doubt pages 2, 3 - no not 3 – 4 and 5 tomorrow morning."

"You want me arrested for murder?"

"Of a woman with snakes coming out of her head? Even the police might accept you had some cause for concern. But I don't want you about when the Sun lot turn up. It will complicate things for you when you need to be free. I've checked the camcorder. He got the attack. I'll get it edited and then we'll produce the video at the right time."

"Which is?"

"Soon."

"Where are we?" asked the leader of the phouka. "We were waiting in the forest, at the agreed rendezvous. How come we next found ourselves at the top of a house. We don't like houses."

"Ah well," said Rupert, "this was something arranged with Oberon and a missing third party, to make sure you were on hand to help Prince Henry."

"We should be treated with respect," growled the goat-headed fairy.

"Talking about being on hand," said Henry, angrily, "how come you were on hand to film me but not exactly on hand to fight off Medusa."

"Unfair," grinned Rupert. "I'm a Spinner, not a fighter. And the cavalry came didn't it?"

"And why do you now want to promote my legend?"

"O Henry, later, later. Go away, get a good night's sleep."

But first Henry wanted to complete his search for Wilfred. He found the old wizard in the kitchen, turned to stone with a frying pan in his hand.

"How safe am I?" enquired Henry. "What about the Queen? Am I being watched?"

"The honest answer," said Rupert, "is I don't know."

"We'll keep watch," volunteered several of the phouka.

"I do appreciate that," said Henry, "and don't take this the wrong way, but, em, hereabouts your appearance is likely to attract attention."

"We'll transform," said the leader of the phouka, who was called Seamus. "What do you want, bull, dog, horse, eagle?"

"Is human out of the question?" asked Henry.

He walked home accompanied by a troop of thin, slightly mysterious but definitely human companions, all wearing tunics and leggings, but, hey, there could have been any number of reasons for such quaint costumes. As they walked, Henry attempted to explain where they were. Once at his home, though, he decided that so many people loitering outside his house would only attract attention, so the phouka changed again.

CHAPTER 19

Heavy seepage

HENRY WOKE UP at three in the morning. He got up and looked out of the window. That was an awful lot of dogs! He went back to bed.

He couldn't get to sleep again. He had killed someone. She might not have been human, she might have been from another world, but he had ended her life. Whilst Henry would never claim to have higher moral values than the next man, killing did go against a fundamental set of beliefs. But what else could he have done? Phoned the police, contacted the army – and anyway he had no opportunity for that in the case of Medusa. It was kill or be killed. It was self defence.

He gave up trying to sleep at 7. He was too tense. He turned on the radio by his bed. There was a great deal going on which should not have been. There were more incidents involving the Queen and the witch. Three different eye witnesses had reported a dragon flying overhead. One of them was a farmer who complained that the dragon had flown off with his best milker. Somehow this little touch rendered his account amusing rather than credible. There was a very big story about a bizarre crime in Hampstead. In a vast neglected house a decapitated woman had been discovered. The Sun newspaper had managed to get round there before reporting the incident to the police. Their photograph plainly revealed the dead woman had snakes coming from her head. They were still living. Next to the body was a large handwritten note which read 'On no account look into the eyes of the deceased. The first Sun reporter – the second was more careful – and two policemen had regrettably failed to take heed of this warning. This did explain the incident outside Buckingham Palace but did not explain how such a thing could happen. Careful precautions were now being taken over the storage of the head. The owner of the house was an old man who was currently missing. Curiously there was a statue of him in the kitchen. (Poor old Wilfred. What was to be done about him?)

More disturbing to Henry were the references to some different legendary bad guys. A man with a bull's head was supposedly dragging girls along tunnels in the London underground. A casual reference to "Jack the lad" in a conversation about a clever salesman had attracted the attention of a giant who demanded to know where this person was. Dissatisfied with the answer, the giant did some serious damage. Another large individual with one eye in the centre of his forehead was also causing a substantial amount of harm. On the other hand three children swore they had gone for a ride on a magic carpet, and at the Britannia Inn, Portsmouth a woman dressed as

Britannia had been organising endless historical pageants. All in all it meant the barrier was severely weakened.

Were people travelling the other way? Henry knew that his Queen, Elizabeth II, was out of London and in Balmoral, but there was an intriguing item about how she had not attended the Highland Games and how a mystery virus seemed to be keeping her inside the castle, as nobody had seen her for the last three days. No doubt he was reading too much into this.

The sound of barking in the front garden attracted his attention. He looked out. The postman was cowering by the hedge. Five large dogs were snarling at him.

"It's OK," he shouted through his window. The dogs moved away. The postman edged nervously towards the front door. "Sorry," said Henry. "They won't be here tomorrow."

"They'd better not be," said the postman before rushing off.

Henry went downstairs, opened the front door and called them over. "We need to talk," he said – except not in full view of the street. "Well, later perhaps. Can't you be something smaller and sort of lurk somewhere? Discreetly. Please."

The sound of his father's angry voice came from the garden. A horticultural crisis had kept him at home. Most of the fruit on the raspberry canes and the loganberry bush had disappeared during the night, when the phouka must have returned to their normal shapes in order to feed themselves.

Rupert arrived during breakfast, bearing a copy of the Sun. Henry pushed him into the living room before his parents could see the newspaper.

"You look ever so dashing," said Rupert, holding out the paper.

Henry inspected the photograph of him holding the shield and sword. It was true, actually, he did look rather dashing. There was a complete absence of panic in his expression. Not now though.

"The police. They're going to track me down!"

"Probably," said Rupert. "It might be best if you contact them yourself, and arrange to go in at a time of our choosing. But definitely not yet. We've got things to do."

"OK," said Henry, munching a piece of toast, "what exactly are you up to?"

"I'm acting as your public relations guru," replied Rupert. "And for no fee. It's a very generous gesture. I am, after all, the best in the business."

"Maybe," said Henry. "How come you want me as a client?"

"Well, I've always watched out for you haven't I?"

"No."

"Certainly have. At any rate since the current events started. I saved you from the phouka on Hampstead Heath."

"I remember you inviting them to rip out my throat if I tried anything."

"Yes, but I knew you wouldn't. I also intervened on your behalf with Deathbreather."

"I wouldn't put it quite like that."

"And I helped to send you back to this world didn't I?"

"No doubt for your own reasons."

"That can't be denied," agreed Rupert. "But the

Queen would have killed you if you'd stayed. You weren't ready for her."

"Why should she want to kill me?"

"I do wish you were as bright as me," said Rupert without malice. "Don't get me wrong, Henry, you are bright, but not as bright as me."

"It's a cross I have to bear," said Henry. "Why would she want to kill me?"

"It's very simple," said Rupert. "Your reputation began in the World of Legends long before you actually did anything to deserve it. You must know that at least."

"Yes," said Henry. Why was Rupert always so infuriating?

"You started to emerge as someone who was likely to be one of the greatest heroes ever. But the fascinating fact was the prospective nature of your hero status. Everyone sensed your vulnerability. It gave the Queen, at a time when she was anxious about losing her powers, the wonderful possibility of nipping you in the bud."

"For example, by getting the phouka to kill me off."

"Folklore's mercenaries," said Rupert thoughtfully.

"Is that a yes?"

"Actually, that was a no. Their arrival on Midsummer's Eve was quite unplanned. As it happens, they were supposed to be waiting for me in the World of Legends – something I'd set up with Rumpelstiltskin when we decided to swap over. I thought it might be useful to have a little muscle in a strange new world. I made it a condition of our arrangement that he'd find some for me. He even spun some gold to pay for them!"

"What made them come through?"

"You of course. Like you made Gervase."

"Me?"

"Look," said Rupert, "even when all's going well, the barrier can often be crossed on Midsummer's eve and Halloween. That's why I chose Midsummer's Eve for the swap. But with you about, the barrier was especially weak. After all, you were expected on the other side."

"You mean it was almost an opening to let my legend through?"

"That's exactly right. Of course your legend's rather stalled recently. I'm going to kick start it again."

"No for love I'm sure. What's in it for you?"

Rupert seemed a little wistful for a moment. "I want recognition too, Henry, and I'm not going to get legendary status unless I do something in this world. It irks me having to achieve it as part of your team, but even a PR genius won't do it on his own."

"Does that mean you've lost interest in spinning for the villains?"

"Not entirely, but the challenge is gone."

"And does it mean you recognise the harm you've done to both worlds?"

"I didn't start that," said Rupert, "but I do want to protect the World of Legends. I don't think you've ever really understood how much I care about it. Now get dressed. You're about to have an exclusive interview. It's going to need very careful handling."

So would his parents, thought Henry. "What exclusive interview?"

"With the Daily Mail. A respectable tabloid. I ruled out the Sun, which would immediately prevent anyone believing you."

"I don't want to do an exclusive interview."

"That's beside the point," said Rupert. "You'd better prepare your parents."

Henry sat them down.

"This is rather difficult to explain," he began.

"You haven't got a girl pregnant?" asked his father.

"No I haven't got a girl pregnant."

"O hell," said his father, "you want to give up law and become a ballet dancer?"

"No of course I don't."

"It's not," said his mother anxiously, "trouble with the police?"

"Not yet."

"What have you done, for goodness' sake?"

"I've decapitated a gorgon."

Henry gave his parents one edited version of the truth and let them read another. He watched an impressive number of different reactions on his father's face – incredulity, anger, admiration, concern and, ultimately, confusion. His mother mainly looked shocked. What had happened to her son? Skilfully, Rupert managed to charm Henry's parents into a more relaxed frame of mind, but they all agreed this required further discussion later.

The reporter and a photographer arrived. Henry attempted to repeat what he had told his parents. However, Rupert gently managed to nudge the emphasis towards heroic monster hunter rather than a desperate act of self defence. It was done with almost no interruption, which would have irritated the reporter. It was mainly knowing smiles, raised eyebrows, shrugs. At the end the reporter asked Henry whether he had any other monsters in his sights. Henry was intending to reply with a definite "No", but Rupert forestalled him.

"It's all X Files territory isn't it and Henry is interested in any strange phenomenon. Believe me, we'll be in touch again!"

Once the reporter and photographer had left, Rupert said he had to go. Henry accompanied him to the gate.

"You're treating me with —" began Henry, pausing to find the correct word.

"Disdain?"

"Yes."

"Henry, how can you say that when I'm doing my best to turn you into a superhero?"

"Because I'm fitting in to whatever you want to do. It's just another game for you."

Rupert shook his head. "Of course I enjoy the game, but it's not just another one. And answer this honestly. Don't you view me with disdain?"

Henry acknowledged the truth of this. "Sometimes."

"For whatever reason, your well-being is my prime objective at the moment."

Henry accepted this. "Have you any idea what's going to happen? Because —" He decided to be honest. "Because this is a very frightened superhero."

Rupert grinned his Rumpelstiltskin-like grin. "I don't view you with disdain, Henry. I envy you."

This was a surprise. "Why?"

"Because you have a clear path."

"I do?"

"Yes," said Rupert. "Now I'm off to check the video. You'll like what we've done to it."

"When can I see it?"

"At one. On the BBC news."

"Oh," said Henry.

Rupert left.

Henry never did see the video. Not at one-o-clock anyway, though he did see it several days after it was broadcast. He thought it made fascinating viewing. It had been very well edited. Medusa looked unbelievably scary. He looked impressive. The phouka had somehow been removed completely. The reason he never saw it on this particular day was because Rupert phoned him and told him to come along to a TV studio where an interview had been arranged shortly after one. As he went through the front gate, a dozen or so bats flew after him out of the creeper growing up the front of the house. In the street the bats turned into human beings and a passing driver crashed into a tree.

They walked up to Hampstead Village to catch the tube. In Heath Street Henry began to be aware of one or two rather odd individuals wandering about in a state of either bewilderment or great curiosity. For example, there was someone who seemed to be dressed as an eighteenth century milkmaid. She was gawping at the window of a patisserie, but curtsied when she saw him. There was also a lumpy individual sitting on a bench. Lumpy was perhaps an understatement. Grey and rocky was more accurate. Troll like. Passers by went out of their way to avoid him and two police officers sitting in a stationary patrol car made no attempt to get out.

These characters were a bad sign, thought Henry. These were not major heroes or villains. These were merely the incidental characters of legend, drifting through the weakened barrier.

He reached a cafe and went inside for a quick cappuccino. Some of the phouka followed him in. The others hung around outside though Henry bought them all blueberry muffins. Their loyalty, albeit on suitable terms, was impressive. They must have found this a strange world, but kept their comments to themselves. They were ready to accompany Henry anywhere subject only to being fed. It was not – which was fortunate – appropriate to take them into a restaurant, as cooked food made them ill. However, bread or cakes did not seem to come into that category and the phouka had instantly developed a real passion for blueberry muffins. Henry rationed them to two each, as he doubted if their digestive systems would take more. Apart from that he bought lots of vegetables, fruit and raw fish.

They all set off on the tube for BBC television centre. The journey displayed the phouka at their best and worst. They took this extraordinary mode of travel completely in their stride. Phouka machismo prevented them from showing any fear or surprise, although the leader did ask what kind of creature was pulling the carriages. On the minus side, and there was no question of fault, they had a straightforward attitude to their bodily needs, many of which were on display during the journey. Henry and every other passenger in his carriage were unable to get certain pictures out of their memory for some time.

For the passengers, though, there were other aspects of the journey which they would never forget, subject only to hysterical amnesia or senility. The first was the sudden arrival of Gervase between Euston and Warren Street stations. He sort of ran out of nowhere into the carriage, where he stopped in amazement, panting for breath. A Spanish tourist crossed herself. A plump American fainted

"Gervase!" said Henry, completely astonished.

"Prince Henry!" cried Gervase, fizzing gently in a blue light. "Thank goodness. They're after me." He looked round. "They're not after me. Wow, where am I?"

"How did you get here?" asked Henry, realising at once that Gervase would have no idea.

"Where is here?" asked Gervase, beginning to take in the rumbling of the train, lots of startled expressions and also – "The phouka! We're in deep trouble. Unless you've got a sword on you this time."

"Don't worry about them," said Henry. "What frightened you?"

"I wasn't so much frightened," replied Gervase, "as running for my life."

At that moment there was a great crackle of blue light and a large group of creatures materialised in the carriage. They were outstandingly hideous, with green skin and large, pointed ears. The Spanish tourist fell to her knees, where she started to pray. Several other passengers followed her example. The plump American had started to come round but took the prudent course of passing out for a second time. Only two eleven year old boys, sitting open mouthed, got maximum value out of the total episode.

"Bit of a strange ol' place this, innit?" said one of the green creatures, showing some unpleasant, fang like, yellow teeth.

"Someone be tryin' a bit of magic on us, if you asks me," said another. "Won't do no good though. We got our quarry cornered."

"That's me," explained Gervase. "I'm the quarry."

"I'd guessed that," said Henry

"And who might you be?" enquired a third green creature, his long green fingers desperate to strangle someone.

"Prince Henry,"

"The discredited 'ero. Don't think you're going to cause us much trouble!"

"And you are?" asked Henry.

At this point on the journey Henry had separated himself from the phouka, who were grouped at one end of the carriage doing what came naturally. Henry had put himself at the other end, where the green arrivals were staring at him and Gervase, not having turned to inspect the rest of the carriage. They were unaware of the phouka coming up behind them.

"What they are," answered the leader of the phouka, "are scum."

The green creatures whirled round and inspected a dozen or so pale humans.

"And what you are," said the aspiring strangler, "is dead."

"Can we go a bit beyond 'scum'," said Henry, "as I'd like to know exactly who I'm dealing with?"

"Goblins," said Gervase. "I shouldn't have disturbed them."

"That's a wise remark," observed a goblin, "and the last you'll ever make."

At this point the train reached Warren Street Station. Passengers at the far end of the carriage rushed off the train, but quite a few were trapped in their seats, lacking sufficient confidence to ask the goblins and the phouka to move out of their way. Some new passengers stepped into the carriage, a mistake they regretted bitterly as the train moved off towards Goodge Street.

Henry was amazed at how calm he was, yet he was faced with a large group of vicious goblins. He had no idea what skills and abilities they might have. Of course, he did have some useful muscle with him, something the goblins had not yet discovered.

"I should go back where you came from," said Henry.

"And 'ow does you suggest we does that?" enquired a goblin, drooling as his eyes fell on the plump American tourist.

The blue light had faded away, so returning to the other world was no longer an option, if it ever had been.

"Well then sit down and keep quiet," said Henry. "You're upsetting the passengers."

"No they aren't," said one of the eleven year old boys. "We think they're cool."

"They'll never willingly give up a hunt," said Seamus. "It's their way."

"Their code, you mean?" wondered Henry.

"No your Highness," replied Seamus, affronted. "Creatures with green skin don't have codes."

As he spoke, he started to change, along with the other phouka, into their own shape, with goat's heads and white eyes.

"Wicked," gasped one of the boys, while the Spanish tourist screamed something about 'los diablos' before following the lead of the plump American and sinking into unconsciousness. Most of the other passengers cowered in their seats or pretended to read their newspapers. However, one keen Japanese tourist got out his camcorder.

"It's a skirmish," said Gervase with excitement. "At last I get to fight by your side Prince Henry."

"Good news indeed," said Henry, watching twenty or more goblins pull out knives and other sharp instruments. "Once again I seemed to have left home without my sword."

"O yes," said Gervase, "but I brought a spare knife with me."

"Excellent," said Henry.

At this point the train stopped at Goodge Street station. The opening doors and disembodied announcements caught the visitors' attention, so there was a pause in hostilities. The people who had got in at Warren Street rushed gratefully on to the platform, then watched a few more unfortunates take their place without attempting to prevent them. Well, people had eyes didn't they? The train continued.

"Here it is," said Gervase, proffering the knife.

"Thanks," said Henry, feeling deeply sick.

But Henry had no need to worry. By now the goblins had realised the nature of their opposition. An enemy who could turn into wolves, bulls and other creatures known to the goblins, if not yet to Henry, was best treated with respect unless outnumbered by substantial multiples.

"A moment if you please," said a goblin. "We're all, as you might say, creatures of the world."

"Yeah, but which world?" piped up one of the eleven year olds. Sixty four non-human eyes turned to him. He raised his hands in an appeasing gesture.

"Like I were saying," continued the goblin, "we don't want to 'ave no fight over a dim young lordling what trespassed into our forest."

"About that —" began Gervase.

"What I suggests is that you gives him over to us and we'll be on our way."

"No," said Seamus.

"OK then," said the goblin.

And the train journey might well have continued incident-free if one of the longer term passengers had not suddenly cracked. He chose this particular moment to pull the alarm chord. The train pulled to a juddering halt.

"Great," said Henry.

By chance they were all in the front carriage. The door to the driver's cab opened and the driver started to come through, intending to find out why the chord had been pulled. He moved into the carriage. He stopped. His mouth fell open. He mouthed several swear words. He returned to his cab and slammed the door behind him. Henry heard him begin to call in on his radio link, urgently trying to attract attention. Then he stopped. He cried out "O my —". There was the sound of smashing glass, an angry voice and a discouraging male scream. After that the driver was silent. There was a heavy pounding on the other side of the door. That also stopped. The door began to open once more.

Instead of the driver, a large muscular individual appeared, naked except for a loin cloth and a pair of elaborate Greek style sandals. He was mostly human, except for his vast bull's head bearing gigantic curved horns.

Henry turned to the leader of the phouka. "That's not one of you is it? Messing about?"

"I wish," answered Seamus. "It's the minotaur."

"O dear," sighed Henry, turning back. "I suppose you've just gored the driver?"

"I don't know anything about drivers," rumbled the minotaur. "But yes, I gored that fool. He wouldn't answer my questions."

"Which were?"

"What's happened to my labyrinth and why hasn't anyone left me a maiden where I can find her?"

"For pity's sake," shouted Henry, suddenly losing his temper. "Just get off the train will you."

"I like to know the names of those I kill," said the minotaur

"I'm Prince Henry."

"O right. The discredited hero!"

"Change the bloody record."

The minotaur lowered his head, ready to charge. The goblins moved out of the way. This wasn't their fight. The phouka began to metamorphose into something more useful than mere human beings. They were still in mid-transformation when the minotaur started to run up the carriage. Once again, as when he faced the phouka, time stretched for Henry. He leaned over and picked up a skateboard belonging to one of the eleven year old boys. He flung it at the minotaur's head. Knocked unconscious, the minotaur fell to the floor, breaking a horn as he did so.

"Oo er," said a goblin, "'e's not gonna like that."

CHAPTER 20

The legend takes flight

As RUPERT EXPLAINED to Henry, the incident on the underground train was most untidy (i.e. Rupert had not orchestrated it.) What particularly annoyed him was the acquisition of the Japanese tourist plus his camcorder by a TV station without Rupert having any editorial control. However, he rescued the situation by presenting himself as Henry's sole agent and offering an exclusive interview. Events prevented the interview but at least the video was shaped to Rupert's satisfaction.

It was quite a few hours before Henry and Rupert even managed to meet up again. There was a tremendous melee once the tube train finally reached Tottenham Court Road tube station. The phouka managed to keep out of it because they had made themselves human again. Despite witnesses who swore they had turned into something else, it was much simpler and more obvious to concentrate on those creatures who were definitely not your average human being. How could anyone account for the angry, sore-headed minotaur, struggling up and down the platform with a fair number of London Transport police grappling with him? And what about all those ugly green men? A rumour which quickly grew and never quite died away was that they were from outer space, especially when one of them claimed to come from a different world. Of course, their broad West Country accent was a little difficult to explain.

There were other theories. The boys thought the green creatures were demons. The Spanish tourist spoke about devils – all those horned heads! – and angels – she had spotted Gervase's wing, now hidden under his long sleeve. The American tourist, a 'Lord of the Rings' devotee, announced definitively that the green creatures were orcs. She might even have been right

Several passengers were full of praise for Henry, who had so valiantly brought down the minotaur with a skateboard. One of them had seen Henry's picture in the Sun that morning. Henry was worried this information might be shared with the police. They would be eager to take him along to New Scotland Yard to assist the CID with their enquiries into the incidents at Wilfred's house. Henry was a law abiding citizen. Therefore he obviously wished to help the police. On the other hand, his was rather an awkward story to tell. Even restricting it to his last visit to the house meant he would have to explain why he had killed a young woman with a sword. True, the police were aware this woman had an unusual deformity and a lethal gaze, but how willing would they be to see her as a major force for evil, best destroyed? Even if they eventually decided Henry was acting in self defence, their questions would keep Henry tied up for hours. There was too much going on for that. Henry needed to be free.

Fortunately, the police were occupied with non-human misbehaviour. Once they had the minotaur vaguely subdued, he began roaring loudly. The goblins were also causing a lot of trouble, running through the station, looking for a way back to the world they knew. Police and underground staff ran after them. Passengers were startled at these ugly green creatures, and were scared stiff when the goblins decided to stand and fight. They were right to be scared. Two were strangled and others were badly gouged. Although Henry had been asked to wait quietly until the police could ask him more questions, it was easy for him, Gervase and the phouka to slip quietly out of the station.

The first thing Henry had to do at street level was reassure Gervase. Even the phouka were pretty phased by Oxford Street, yet at least they had had the experience of a London suburb. Gervase on the other hand was truly astonished. He did his best not to show it, but he was shaking with alarm. Henry led his party quickly through to Soho Square, where they could sit down on grass and see some trees.

"This is not your world," Henry said to Gervase, "and I'm sorry that you're here. I think I might be responsible for it."

"Your Highness," said Gervase, "my place is at your side, whatever world you're in. I'm happy to have found you again."

Henry felt guilty. "What were you doing just before you came here?" Gervase looked too young to be doing anything except studying for his A levels.

"Well, looking for you really. I know you sent us away, and after we got home my brothers told me I shouldn't stay in your service. But recently we started hearing all sorts of good things about you. All the bad stuff got less and less and my brothers changed their minds. They concluded it would honour the family name if I were serving you again. I decided to search for you."

"But where?"

"I remembered you wanted to find Rumpelstiltskin's mother. I thought I'd start off by going to the mines and see if they had any idea where you were. Unfortunately, I got lost on the way and bumped into those goblins. O dear." Gervase was suddenly dejected.

"What's the matter?"

"You must have such a low opinion of me, running from them like that."

"At odds of twenty to one," said the leader of the phouka, "running was definitely your best bet."

Gervase perked up.

"Of course," Seamus continued, "now you plan your revenge or your name will be dishonoured for ever. You must kill each one of those goblins. In single combat."

Gervase gulped. "You bet," he said.

"How's Elise?" asked Henry, turning pink, which irritated him.

"Rather moony," replied Gervase. "If you ask me, Prince Henry, she's got a bit of a thing about you."

At this point Henry phoned Rupert, to inform him about the incident on the train. Rupert said only that everyone should stay in town and lose themselves in one of the parks. He would meet them there as soon as he could. Meanwhile he would have to track down the Japanese tourist, his video, the TV station etc etc.

It was nearly quarter to four when Rupert phoned. They were relaxing in the shade of some huge trees in Green Park. The phouka were dozing. Professional fighters, they took their rest when they could. Gervase was eating an ice cream cornet and was much calmer. Henry had done his best to explain what was happening without going into the mysteries of how Gervase had come into existence. Gervase listened politely if vaguely. Basically he was content. This was an adventure, he was with his Prince, he liked ice cream – all was right in his life. Henry was on edge. Occasionally he spotted another legendary individual, major or minor, wandering or flying by. The ordinary members of the public would give them some odd looks, but on the whole seemed to take these phenomena in their stride. On the other hand, the 'Evening Standard', which Henry was attempting to read, led with the arrest of the minotaur and the goblins. It was breathless with excited speculation about their identity.

"Henry," said Rupert, "a lot's been going on. For one thing, the Prime Minister's missing."

"Really!"

"He was on a walking holiday in Scotland. He was travelling on a ley line and disappeared."

"Is that bad news or good news?"

"It hasn't been decided!"

An enormous insect, some thirty centimetres long, floated past.

"Greetings, Prince Henry," it said.

Henry stared. It was a fairy. "Do you know where you are?" he asked.

"No," replied the fairy, drifting away, "but Oberon's about somewhere. He seems to have an idea."

"Did you hear that?" asked Henry.

"Yes," said Rupert. "You're attracting all these arrivals from the other world. They're coming through elsewhere, but mainly it's near you."

"Because of my legend growing and the weak barrier?"

"That's exactly right – Henry, the Queen's in Buckingham Palace."

"That's where she's supposed to be."

"You mean our Queen and no she's not. She's supposed to be in Balmoral – where in fact she isn't. This is the wicked Queen. She's taken up residence."

"That's impossible," said Henry. "People would notice."

"You've seen what she can do. The palace staff are in a trance."

"But it's August. The tourists are allowed in."

"May be she doesn't use the state rooms until after they've left. Or else they don't see her. I'm not sure. What I am sure of is that we're reaching the grand finale. The Queen's in the palace and the palace is on a major ley line. I hate to think who she's bringing through."

"Who told you about the Queen?"

"It's on the site. The mirror's connected again. And Henry, there's something else. She's got Elise."

Henry went cold. "How do I get in?"

"Wait till I get to you," said Rupert. "I'm only a few minutes away."

"With a TV crew and several tabloid reporters I bet. Grand finale! Rupert, this isn't a game."

"No it isn't. Don't do anything rash. You need me."

"You should have been here then," said Henry and turned off his phone. He looked at Gervase. "I'm sorry, but remember that evil Queen —"

"I remember lots of evil Queens," said Gervase.

"Snow White's mother. She's captured Elise."

Gervase's mouth, covered in ice cream like a little boy, fell open.

"I'm going to see the Queen," said Henry. "On my own."

"No, your Highness," objected Seamus. "You need your posse. We'll come with you."

"And I must," Gervase insisted. "I'm your squire and it's my sister."

It was such a perfect August afternoon, hot but not humid. The park was full of tourists and noisy children. No sign of evil, yet it was there, less than half a mile away. All Henry had to do was work out how to enter Buckingham Palace.

"Of course," he cried, "we can buy a ticket."

"Prince Henry," said a voice in his right ear, "still callow and youthful, though granted, less so."

Henry accepted the accuracy of this statement, yet was about to object on principle, when he realised the speaker was Oberon, hovering by his right ear.

"King Oberon," he said, bending his head, "it's a privilege to see you again."

Oberon stared at Henry with his intense emerald eyes. "If you hadn't really meant that, I'd have left you to make a very foolish mistake."

"Which would have been —?"

"To go into that palace without me. What makes you imagine you can take on an enchantress of her ability?"

Henry thought, which was something he might sensibly have done a few moments ago. "I see your point, but I've survived so far."

"And that would be entirely by your own efforts?" enquired Oberon, landing on a bench.

"I wouldn't claim that," said Henry. "I'm grateful for everything —"

"Forget any idea you might be developing about me helping you defeat her. My role is purely as a minder, may be even as a facilitator. I'm here to see things done right and fairly. After that, it's up to the participants."

"You're a sort of referee?" That didn't sound quite grand enough. "An umpire?"

"Exactly. If I go any further I get drawn in and lose my neutral status."

"An umpire over what?"

"You've read enough stories. There are rules. The Queen should be setting you a challenge. If you succeed, then you've defeated her. But if you simply march into see her, the way you were going to, she would destroy you there and then. Very cruelly."

"A challenge mightn't be a great deal better for me," said Henry.

"True."

"But at least," said Seamus, with a respectful bow towards Oberon, "you would die with honour."

"Such a comfort," murmured Henry.

Gervase gave him a sympathetic look. The practical implications of heroism were beginning to sink in.

"Rules," repeated Henry.

"Certainly," said Oberon. "Or may be you'd prefer to call them expectations, but it comes to the same thing. They have to be respected. You're a lawyer. You can appreciate that."

"I can," said Henry. "Who makes the rules, King Oberon?"

"Your world does."

Rupert and a camera crew came jogging towards them.

"A fine sight," said Henry. "The spinner in a spin."

"No," said Rupert, "only in a hurry." He bowed to Oberon. The two man camera crew swore in amazement.

"Rude mechanicals —!" observed Oberon dryly. He turned to Rupert. "You'll all be at risk. This is a different world and the arrivals are confused. The rules might get broken."

"Understood," said Rupert, "but Henry and I have to go through with this. As for the mechanicals, it's the scoop of a life time. Do you think a quick interview —?" Henry glared at him. "Later then."

The party ran off across the park. It was an interesting group – Henry, Rupert, a bemused camera crew, a young man with a visible swan's wing, twelve thin, white faced mercenaries, and a glittering eighteen inch humanoid flying above them – which attracted a certain amount of attention. They reached the public entrance at fourteen minutes past four.

"I want to buy some tickets," said Henry.

"It's too late," said an attendant. "The last tour starts at quarter past four."

"There's another minute to go," said Henry.

"May be," said the attendant, "but all the tickets have been sold in advance. And noone told me anything about a camera crew."

"Unbelievable," said Oberon.

"Bloody hell," exclaimed the attendant. "What's that?"

"Haven't you got any returns or uncollected tickets?" asked Henry.

"It's highly unlikely," said the attendant. He searched lightly, only to find an envelope with a name on it – "Henry Prince." Inside was a bundle of tickets.

"That's me," said Henry, producing a wallet with a student pass, which had his name and photograph.

"Please leave that toy here." The attendant indicated Oberon.

"Forgive me," said Oberon. He stared at the attendant whose head became that of a donkey. "There's a limit to how much mortal idiocy I can take."

They all attached themselves to the last group of visitors trekking through the state rooms of the palace. Oberon decided to make himself inconspicuous by flying up to ceiling level.

They reached the Throne Room, dominated, as the guide book might say, by a pair of winged figures of Victory holding garlands above two thrones. While they stood there, the figures started to change into leering demons. Every bit of gold turned to ebony and the huge room became an amalgam of red and black. The rest of the group plainly noticed nothing strange as they went on their way, leaving Henry and his companions behind, forgotten, unseen. Two attendants were supposedly guarding the room, but they were completely out of it. The doors closed behind the tourists. Another set of doors opened. A procession entered.

At the front were either goblins, or close relations, wearing dark ornamental armour. They were followed by liveried footmen, with glazed expressions and dreamy movements. After them came some of those Henry had glimpsed on the website, and others like them. Witches, warlocks, monstrous beings – jabbering, dribbling, squealing, shrieking. The Queen was last. In crimson silk and her tall twisted silver crown, she took her place on one of the thrones. Many creatures bowed. The TV crew did their best to film and record the whole scene. They were astounded. On the other hand they were professionals. They had no idea what was going on, but they intended to capture every weird second.

"King Oberon," said the Queen, as beautiful and misleading as a perfume bottle containing acid, "how unexpected!"

"O well," said Oberon, "I was in the neighbourhood." He withdrew to one side. All those present moved respectfully out of his way.

"And Prince Henry," said the Queen. "How expected!"

"I'm honoured," said Henry, approaching the throne. "I've seen you in the mirror room on occasions and —" He stopped. He might already have revealed too much.

The Queen frowned slightly. "Have you indeed. I hadn't realised magic was one of your skills."

"There you go," said Henry, "one needs a few tricks up one's sleeve."

"So true," agreed the Queen. "The nastier the better.

But in our world it's difficult to keep that sort of thing secret. We usually know all the important facts about everyone significant. Give me a name, I'll give you their main strengths and weaknesses."

"Dear me," said Henry, "that doesn't make life too interesting."

"I don't want interesting," said the Queen. "I want certainty." She considered him dispassionately. "No, I don't think you're a magician."

"I agree one hundred per cent," called out a witch. "No magic vibes there."

"Not too many princely vibes either," said the Queen. "This should be a ceremonial meeting. I've rolled out the red carpet." She looked down. The carpet was black. It quickly turned red. "I arranged a procession. You might have made an effort."

"To do what?"

"Dress like a prince."

"This is designer stuff," said Henry, touchy. Since his recent interest in clothes he was a bit sensitive about any criticism. "I paid a lot for all this, more than I should have done. Perhaps Moschino isn't to everyone's taste —"

"What's Moschino?"

Henry was aware that he was going off course. He was about to address the main issue when Rupert came forward.

"Your Majesty is absolutely correct," he said. "Image is important. Image makes a statement about a person. It's part of their reputation."

"That's why Prince Henry's is so shaky," said the Queen.

"No," replied Henry, "my reputation is growing stronger. Yours is shaky. Isn't that why you left your – our world?"

"Your Majesty," said Rupert with a confident smile, "I am here to promote your reputation."

"Then why have you changed sides?" asked the Queen. Henry felt like putting the same question. Its full significance, especially for Rupert's future, caused the noise to subside.

"What I've been doing," said Rupert, apparently unperturbed, "is working to ensure that what's about to happen becomes a major legend."

"That doesn't answer the question," said the Queen.

"With respect," said Rupert, "it does. My aim is to strengthen your world. I help strengthen your world by strengthening your power. I strengthen your power by enhancing your reputation. And I do that by making sure that your struggle with Prince Henry receives maximum exposure."

"He means," explained Oberon, "whatever side he is on is irrelevant."

"I wouldn't have put it quite like that," Rupert protested mildly.

"Anyway," said Oberon," the point is, he's correct."

"Your Majesty," said Rupert, "I'd like to film an interview with you and Prince Henry. To set up the struggle."

The Queen glanced at her supporters. "In that case, we'll go somewhere else. It's a freak show in here."

Oberon flew across and hovered by her crown. "They're such second raters aren't they!"

"May be," said the Queen. "But look how many there

are. And others are coming, including some big names."
She got to her feet and walked down the steps from the
throne.

"I'm bringing my friends with us," said Henry.

"Those creatures!" The Queen was scornful. "I don't
think so. They're not fit friends for a hero. Perhaps that
tells me something about you."

Henry considered this. "It does actually — If they
stay behind, what's going to happen to them?"

The Queen gave a bored sigh. "They'll be killed.
Eaten. Whatever."

"Wrong moment," ruled Oberon.

"O please," said the Queen. She waved her hand.
Gervase and the phouka disappeared. "Happy now?"

Henry was startled. "Where are they?"

"No idea," she replied. Oberon gave her a look. "O,
all right, somewhere in the palace."

"And where's Elise?"

"She's in the garden," said the Queen, "on a lovely
sunny evening. What more do you want?"

"I'm leaving now," said Oberon, "but please remember
this. Prince Henry is under my protection until your
challenge. When I will officiate." He flew away.

"I just know I'll find a way to squash him," said the
Queen. "Personally."

"What challenge?" asked Henry.

"All in good time," she replied.

Henry, Rupert and the camera crew followed her
through the door by which she had entered. They felt
smothered. The Queen's favourite incense was choking
humanity out of a place where it was never that strong at
the best of times.

They walked through a series of rooms, all drenched in black and red, until they reached one which closely resembled the Queen's special chamber in her own palace. On a wall was the familiar mirror, its glass cloudy, but clearing the moment they approached it.

"Ooh," said the mirror, "what do I see here? Bad judgement I would say."

"If you mean sartorial," said the Queen, "I agree."

"No," said the mirror," we're a bit beyond the insignificant aren't we!"

"What do you mean then?"

"This meeting," replied the mirror. "Not a good idea."

"For whom —"

"After all," said the mirror, "I know what you're planning."

"And —?"

"Nothing else," said the mirror. "I don't foretell the future."

"Spare me that again," said the Queen. "Perhaps I should have left you behind. This world contains those who are more than willing to weigh up the risks and predict a result."

"Like me," said Rupert brightly.

"I was thinking of management consultants," said the Queen.

"Good choice," said Rupert. "Unless you want an accurate prediction."

"Is Elise safe?" Henry asked the mirror anxiously.

"Hardly," answered the mirror, "but she's alive." It went cloudy.

The Queen sat down in a chair. As it happened, a

window was behind her and a vase of crimson roses next to her. To the camera man looking through his lens this was uncannily similar to Elizabeth II's position for her Christmas message.

Rupert approached. "Your Majesty, if you permit I will ask Prince Henry to sit nearby." The Queen shrugged. "Then we can record your conversation and you can tell people whatever you want. I may ask the odd question."

To make sure you get on screen, noted Henry silently as he also sat down. He wanted to see Elise.

"This evening," began Rupert, "we have a remarkable opportunity to witness a conversation between two legendary individuals —"

"One legendary individual," interrupted the Queen. "Don't count on Prince Henry being more than a burp."

"Two remarkable individuals," Rupert continued smoothly, "who are meeting before what might be —"

"The Queen who lived here," said the Queen to Henry, "she understood about being a symbol?"

"Yes," said Henry, "but in her case that's all it was, a symbol but no power."

"She deserved to be ousted. I am a symbol and I have great power. You told me my reputation was shaky."

"Well it is."

"Was may be, but not now, not here. I've boosted it."

"I don't follow," said Henry, although he had a horrible feeling he might.

"Rumpelstiltskin," said the Queen. "All those reputations he's acquired. They were for me."

"But," – Henry was puzzled – "what do you want

with being a clever Chancellor of the Exchequer? Or an investment manager?"

"What are you talking about?"

"Well, those are two of the people Rumpelstiltskin tricked out of their reputations."

"Hardly tricked," said the Queen. "Anyway, it didn't matter what the reputation was for. That was irrelevant. It was the power of the reputation I wanted." She stared at him. "Yours was coming in pretty handy." She smiled and her smile had all the warmth of a twenty five watt bulb. "I still have some of it."

"What will you do with all this power?"

"First," she said triumphantly, "I'm going to sponge up that dollop of over sweet syrup called Snow White."

Henry wanted to agree. He felt deeply ashamed. "And next?"

"I'll make sure I remain the fairest of them all."

"By magic?"

"Of course by magic. Helped along by maiming and slaughter. That's way quicker sometimes." She picked up a copy of Vogue from the side table. "And may be taking advantage of this season's beauty tips." She leafed through the magazine. "Except they don't do my colours."

"Try looking up a few goth sites on the web," said Henry. "They should give you some ideas." The Queen gave him a puzzled stare.

"And after that," said Henry, "I suppose you'll take over the country."

"I'm a brilliant sorceress. I live in the royal palace. What's to take over?"

Henry realised he had been thinking of her in ordinary human terms. He had to recognise she was a character from a fairy tale, whose mind was set on the goals of her own story. That was not to say she had no other desires, and the longer she stayed in his world, the more she would learn about it – its differences, its difficulties, its enormous opportunities. For the moment her vision was a very narrow one. Even so, she seemed to be doing rather well on it.

"Your Majesty, what do you make of this world?" Rupert asked her.

"Confused. Too many shades of grey. I like things to be in black and red."

The Queen stood up and crossed over to two French windows. She opened them. To their amazement, Henry, Rupert and the camera crew followed her out on to the balcony at the front of Buckingham Palace.

"This is excellent," said Rupert.

"You want us to be seen here," observed the Queen. "Only when I'm willing to let it happen."

It was already, it should not have been, sunset. Henry glanced at his watch. How had over three hours passed? Down below, the usual tourists were milling about outside the railings, taking photographs, peering at the sentry, waiting for the changing of the guard which had happened hours ago. They might have been even more interested in the changing of the Queen.

Such a great view down the Mall to the distant Admiralty Arch. Yet something was odd. The wide avenue should have been full of traffic, but there was none. Instead, a group of people was ambling along the centre of the road, approaching the palace. At first they were difficult to distinguish. When they reached the end of the Mall they became all too clear. There were some human beings, or they resembled human beings at any rate, dressed in various styles of costume from across the ages and across the globe. There were also less obvious humans, squabbling and yelping with laughter. There were various misshapen creatures who had captured the imagination of Hieronymous Bosch. The group were joined by others who came out of side roads or St James's Park - a giant, a cyclops, gargoyles flying from the tree tops.

Some ordinary passers by cheered and clapped at first, thinking this was a special parade. The more alert recognised all was not right. They stood and stared in astonishment. Sensible individuals hurried away. The Queen raised her hand in salutation. She was noticed by every one and every thing.

"Why are they all coming here?" asked Henry.

"It's a conference," answered the Queen. "We're in a different world and we need to lay down some turf rules."

"I would like to see Elise," said Henry, who had a terrible feeling that he was about to see her, and pretty much everything else, for the last time.

"I've told you," said the Queen, "she's in the garden."

"How do I get there?"

The Queen looked at him impatiently. "You're supposed to be a hero. Go on a quest!" She turned back to the new arrivals, now about to come through the gate. Henry left the balcony. If he could reach Elise quickly, perhaps they could escape by going to the end of the huge garden and finding a door into Grosvenor Place.

Except it would be locked. First things first. He had to find Elise.

"Wait," said Rupert. "We need to be with you, but we're not finished here."

"Tough," shouted Henry and rushed off.

He managed to work his way round to the back of the palace, though had some difficulty in getting down to a place which gave him access to the garden. At least no one tried to stop him. He passed an old woman who must have been a witch, but she was busy putting a curse on a photograph of the Duke of Edinburgh. The few servants about were too dazed to pay him any attention. He ran along corridors, into rooms, down stairs. When he finally got outside he was hot and sweaty – and scared, not for himself, for Elise. Time had sped on once more. It was now twilight, with the sky a deep shade of blue. A huge full moon was gearing itself towards maximum silver effect.

He raced round the huge garden calling her name. He heard her answering him, but had no idea where she was. Then he spotted her. She was standing by a tree. As he got nearer he realised she was actually chained to it.

"Elise," he cried, "What's going on?"

She smiled at him. "If you've now achieved your heroic peak," she said, "that would be nice."

"I'm getting there," said Henry, "but I can't guarantee it's a peak worth shouting about. She did this to you?"

"Yes."

"Why?"

"I'm a gift, Prince Henry. Well actually I'm a meal."

Henry shivered. "For whom? For what?"

"For an ally. That's all she said."

Henry went up close to her. She was scared. Who wouldn't be in a situation like this? He examined the chain uselessly, but there was no way he could unlock it.

"I don't know what to do," he said helplessly, "except offer myself instead."

"O no," said Elise," that's a waste of a good hero. Anyway, she won't let me go."

"I don't know what to do," Henry repeated. "But I'll work out something," he added lamely.

"Excellent," said Elise, "because we're going to need it."

The full moon was shining very brightly indeed. Floodlights were also turned on. It was extremely easy see the creatures who were coming through the garden towards them. It was a whole new group and all of them fed at night. There were ghouls, creeping in a phosphorescent glow. Werewolves prowled across the lawn, barely able to keep themselves under control. Zombies lurched along side them. Vampires, fangs on display, pulled along two stumbling footmen as if they were bringing food to a midnight feast. But then they were.

"There's not enough of me to go round," said Elise with a beautiful sad smile.

"I'll challenge them," said Henry. "It might gain us an extra vital three seconds!"

"I love you," said Elise.

"That's brilliant!" said Henry, suddenly feeling incredibly strong. "Does everybody mind telling me exactly what they think they're doing?"

"Supper," replied Count Dracula. "But first an aperitif." He grabbed one of the humans with him and bit into his neck. "Aach!" He spat out a gobbet of blood. "All the goodness has been sucked out of this one."

"Let's start her," howled a werewolf, in a feeding frenzy.

"No!" It was the Queen's voice. She was standing on the terrace. Rupert and the camera crew were next to her. "That girl is not for any of you."

"We're hungry," protested the creatures of the night. "We're thirsty."

"I repeat 'no'," said the Queen. "Do what you want with Prince Henry. But that girl is for a special guest."

This was a bad moment for Henry. "One day," he said to Elise, "I'll have a sword when I need one."

He would struggle, but mentally he prepared himself for the first bite.

A series of alarm bells made everyone turn round, and round again. The garden was being invaded. Climbing down over the walls was a motley collection of the good guys. Henry recognised the classical heroes with Atalanta racing in front. There were also Beowulf, Gilgamesh and others Henry had not seen before. With them were the swan lords - but not Gervase - and the phouka - but not, in so far as Henry could tell them apart, Seamus. A chariot was rumbling across the lawn, drawn by two horses and bearing Britannia. And together with these major league figures came lots of humans, elves, dwarves, unicorns – the unknown heroic foot soldiers.

Out of the palace roared the villains from the throne room and the horde who had marched up the Mall. Some surrounded the Queen, while the rest ran towards Henry and the advancing heroes. The camera crew went on filming, while Rupert shouted a commentary aimed at sealing his own legend.

The skirmishes had begun when Henry found Seamus and Gervase standing next to him. Gervase held out a sword.

"From Oberon."

"Fleshbiter?" asked Henry.

"You bet," grinned Gervase, who also had a sword of his own.

Henry took his special sword. This was hardly the moment to study it, but it was obviously ornate and very scary. It certainly scared him. He had no idea how to use it, but he would wield the sword to protect Elise. Yet when Henry looked, she was no longer there. Her chains had fallen to the ground. He swung about desperately, hoping to spot her. She was nowhere to be seen.

"Your sister's gone," cried Henry. How deeply he regretted speaking. Gervase was standing proudly next to him, flashing his blade like a schoolboy in front of a mirror. At Henry's words, he turned, dropping his sword arm. He probably had no chance in any case, but at least he would have tried to save himself. He would have had a soldier's death. Instead he fell, unaware of his attacker, his heart torn out by a monster with claws and black empty eyes.

Henry swung his sword and for the second time in less than a day decapitated an enemy. On this occasion he didn't feel sick, but very angry and deeply distressed

"He was brave," said Seamus. "We will honour his memory."

"That hardly helps," said Henry.

The camera crew arrived and the camera man tried to film the dead body. Henry pushed him away.

"Show him some respect," he growled at Rupert, who nodded.

For a moment the battle eased. Everyone stared up into the sky. A great winged creature was circling downwards. It could have been any dragon. It had to be Deathbreather.

"This is your challenge," said Rupert. "Take Elise off him and you can win today. But of course, that's impossible."

"And you knew, didn't you," Henry accused him.

"I guessed – once I heard Elise had been captured."

"You could have —"

"— told you. I could have, yes."

The battle had started again, when a huge voice boomed. It echoed throughout the garden as if amplified and would have reached beyond the walls to the gathering bystanders. "Prince Henry will face Deathbreather. The fighting must cease." The voice was distorted, but it was recognisable. It belonged to Oberon. The combatants obeyed.

"Still alive, Prince Henry?" called the Queen across the garden.

"Yes – and kicking."

"Never mind."

"I thought you'd set this challenge up specially," said Henry.

"Sure, but I wasn't going to complain if you died in battle. Which you would have done."

Which he would have done. Still, a duel with a dragon was a pretty reliable alternative.

He had to find Elise.

"Jump on," said a voice. Aladdin was sitting on his carpet currently floating a metre above the ground. "I know where she is."

"Is it safe for you?" whispered Henry. "Isn't it supposed to be just me and him?"

"I'm not going with you, don't you worry!" said Aladdin. "She's on the island in the lake"

Aladdin slipped off. Henry clambered unheroically onto the carpet, gripping its edges while it rose into the air. Some creature tried to drag him back, but was pulled away. He headed towards the lake at one end of the garden. Hundreds of legendary beings watched.

Henry could see her. He looked up. Deathbreather was gliding into land. The dragon looked down. He opened his mouth and roared. A flame headed towards the carpet, now crossing the lake. Startled, Henry lost his grip and fell off. When he rose spluttering to the surface, orange sparks were fizzing in the lake like a dying firework.

Henry scrambled onto the island. There was Elise. There was Deathbreather. And here he was, dripping, hardly in a position of strength, yet somehow still clutching Fleshbiter.

"What a pity," said Deathbreather to Henry, "all that water is going to affect your flavour. I don't like steam cuisine."

"Here's a suggestion," said Henry. "Don't eat me."

"Sensible," agreed Deathbreather. "I'll burn you to death."

"But of course you'll eat me?" Elise said wryly.

"Absolutely," said Deathbreather. "I haven't devoured

a maiden for ages. In fact I haven't tasted human flesh since I entered the agreement proposed by the Spinner. Believe me, I bitterly regret it."

"It was in your own interests wasn't it?" Henry reminded the dragon. "After all you were losing belief in yourself. What makes you so sure you're going to win now?"

Deathbreather stretched his body, shining like pewter in the moonlight. Several specimen trees were knocked over, something which would cause great anguish to the Prince of Wales. "I might admit to the odd senior moment and occasional loss of confidence. But that was in the other world. In this one I feel quite reinvigorated."

"Make the most of it," said Henry.

Elise looked across at him proudly.

"Eugh, the look of love," sneered Deathbreather.

Henry was impressed at his own speed. He had leaped to one side and rolled back into the lake before the jet of flame had incinerated a substantial amount of royal vegetation. As he pulled himself out again, Henry saw the dragon grasp Elise and rise into the air with great flashes of his wings. The downblasts were so fierce that Henry was knocked to the ground. Was that how his heroic journey ended, on his backside?

"I'll eat her in the open," shouted Deathbreather. "Where I can be seen. There's one lesson from the Spinner I do accept. If you've got a good news story, give it maximum exposure!"

Henry leaped to his feet, almost crying with frustration. From the garden came the sound of cheers and catcalls.

Deathbreather landed on the palace roof. "I accept

your gift," he called to the Queen. "And I'm prepared to reach a three year joint sovereignty agreement with you."

"That wasn't on offer," replied the Queen. "I discussed a trade agreement, a non-aggression pact and a military alliance. May be open borders. I never mentioned joint sovereignty."

How quickly they were adapting to the ways of Henry's world. And once they had adapted completely – A flying horse came across the lake towards him. It resembled the pegasus Henry had seen in the World of Legends, but lacked its homogeneity. The wings were those of an eagle. It landed next to Henry.

"Mount," it said.

"Seamus?"

"Yes. Don't waste time. I don't know how long I can hold this. Parts of two creatures at once. I've never tried it before."

"You want me to attack Deathbreather!"

"Can there be any doubt about that?"

"No," replied Henry, "of course not."

"We have virtually no chance of destroying him."

"Hardly the point," said Henry.

So the point was for them to die honourably, in the case of Seamus without any reward, which was certainly above and beyond for a mercenary. The good news was that a blast from Deathbreather would be quicker and less painful than a wound in battle. The bad news – there was his death of course, and also Elise's death. Therefore there could be no good news and bad news. There could be only success.

Seamus leaped into the air and soared towards the

roof of the palace. There was a cacophony of anguished howls and a quantity of gargoyles flew up after them.

"Hell. I thought noone was supposed to intervene," gasped Henry, clinging on.

"What do you think I'm doing?"

"Facilitating?" Too nice a distinction for gargoyles!

There was another disturbance from below as eleven giant eagles took off after the gargoyles.

"My boys," said Seamus.

His boys set about the gargoyles. Henry sensed there would be casualties on both sides but he was too preoccupied to watch. He was approaching Deathbreather.

"Ah," said Deathbreather, "thank you for coming to me. It saves me returning to you. I think you'll find I'm third time lucky."

"I doubt it," said Henry, urging Seamus not to get too near, although he had no idea how far the dragon could throw his flame.

"Best to release me before it's too late," said Elise gamely. She was clutched firmly in Deathbreather's talons.

"I don't think so," said the dragon.

A droning sound was suddenly noticeable overhead. Deathbreather seemed unaware of it or perhaps he was too deaf to hear. Henry glanced up very quickly. It was some old plane. No, it was not some old plane. It was a Second World War Spitfire and it was passing over the garden. This might be his chance.

"Up there," he shouted. "A creature more powerful than you."

The dragon must have caught the sound, for he did

look up and was mystified. He discharged a burst of flame, but the plane took avoiding action. While Deathbreather was watching the plane, Henry urged Seamus towards the roof. Henry had one chance. He aimed his sword and they skidded on to the roof in front of the dragon. Fleshbiter indeed, forged by dwarves, the sword sunk into the dragon's chest. Deathbreather let out a great roar of anger. He loosened his grip on Elise to strike out at Henry. He missed. But Elise toppled forward and fell over the edge.

Henry felt sick as Seamus took off once more. He looked down, expecting to see Elise smashed on the terrace. She was not. She was floating away, borne by a mass of little winged figures. Henry sobbed with relief.

"I'm breaking up," said Seamus.

"What?"

"I can't hold myself together much longer. I've got to revert."

"Of course," muttered Henry.

"Also —"

"You're bleeding!"

"His talon caught me."

"Seamus!"

The Spitfire passed over again. The pilot leaned out of the window and beckoned. He was heading back towards the Mall.

"He wants me to follow."

"I'll follow," said Seamus.

"But —"

"I'll follow."

He did and swung after the plane, though avoiding getting too near Deathbreather, who remained on the roof, also bleeding, and very badly. Down below in the garden there was pandemonium. Goodness only knew how many were going to survive this struggle. And the Queen, what would she be doing? What would any of the witches, wizards, necromancers be doing if it came to it? Henry had to make it stop.

The plane landed in the Mall, much to the astonishment of the police who were beginning to assemble there. Through Admiralty Arch great tanks were rumbling and it was fortunate the armed forces were not fully in place.

Seamus collapsed next to the Spitfire. Lying there, he began to take his real shape. Henry could hardly be certain the leader of the phouka was even breathing, but had no time to check. He had to abandon Seamus. Henry understood what was now required, though how could he make it work? It required yet another untaught skill. He ran over to the plane and climbed in. Even as he did he could hear the sound of helicopters. They had hardly any time.

The Spitfire turned round and took off again towards the palace.

"Glad to see you're in one piece," said the pilot. "All those missing limbs stitched on again?"

"Yes," said Henry. It was simpler.

They passed over the palace roof, but Deathbreather was not going to be a sitting target. He was in the air and rushing towards them. He could have no idea what the Spitfire was, yet he recognised an enemy. It was one particularly vulnerable to fire. His first blast singed a wing, but no other damage was done.

"Man the gun sir," ordered the pilot.

"But how —?"

"Simple," replied the pilot and gave Henry some rapid instructions while turning the plane at a sickening angle. The smell of petrol hardly helped.

The dragon came at them again and his flame hit the engine causing – Henry just knew it had to be – a great plume of black smoke.

"One chance," shouted the pilot.

One chance. Wasn't it always? Henry aimed, he pressed, he looked – and Deathbreather was hit. The old dragon tried one more gust of fire, but it did no damage to the plane. On the other hand it did an awful lot of damage to Buckingham Palace as Deathbreather crashed into it and died somewhere in a ruined state room.

The pilot had no alternative. He landed in the palace garden, mowing down too many creatures good and bad as he did. Henry almost wept to see it. They came to rest back by the lake, hurled themselves out and ran. The plane exploded behind them, doing further harm to grounds which would need a lot of restoration before any more garden parties were held.

Finding Elise was the only thought in Henry's mind at that point. She had been rescued. Where was she? He could see the Queen, standing on the terrace. She seemed to be laughing, hardly a reaction he had expected. But perhaps she won either way. She would be pleased at the dragon's death. She knew the story of these events would feature her as a prime mover. She would come after Henry again.

Henry kept running through a scene bathed in blue light. People remembered different things about that night depending where they were, but everyone remembered the blue light on the palace and other parts of London too – in fact other parts of the whole United Kingdom. Henry hated that light. It meant he had succeeded but it was there too quickly. All remaining alive in the palace garden started to fade into it. He called out "Elise" but noone could tell him where she was and soon, even if they had, he would not have been able to hear them.

He saw Rupert, standing by his camera crew, still filming the scene. Rupert had an ecstatic look on his face until in front of him his double started to appear, the only creature coming through the other way. Rupert was startled, then annoyed and Henry watched as he began to grapple with Rumpelstiltskin, who cannot have fitted into Rupert's plans. For a moment they were both firmly in this world, then the force of the return took the two struggling bodies back into the World of Legends. Without caring, Henry watched them grow fainter, seem to merge then disappear. They were the last. The blue glow vanished.

Henry was left in the garden with a living camera crew and too many dead bodies, including the corpse of Gervase. He guessed Seamus was lying dead in the Mall. His adventure had ended. He had lost friends. He had lost Elise. He had no idea if he could ever see her again. And o yes, not that it mattered, he was a hero.

The end of Episode 1

Lightning Source UK Ltd.
Milton Keynes UK
29 October 2009

145541UK00001B/1/P

9 781440 163203